"I have a question ⟨

Sophie's eyes widened slightly. "Oh, really?"

"All night I kept wondering how you'd taste." Blake didn't stop to ask for permission. He intended to take full advantage of those lips.

He leaned forward and cupped her chin, refusing to even think about how stupid this was. He'd probably guarantee himself another sleepless night, but at the moment he really didn't care.

He took her mouth. Just took. No asking, no excuses, no apologies. And as he'd suspected—as he'd feared—she tasted like heaven.

Sophie pulled away from him slowly, her lips wet and swollen from his kisses. "Well?" she asked, looking richly pleased with herself. "Did you get the answer to your question?"

It took him a moment to remember what he'd asked. "You taste like...more."

She chuckled, deep in her throat, the satisfied sound of a woman comfortable in her own sexual power.

"Maybe you'll get another taste sometime."

One thing Blake knew for certain. There'd be no maybe about it. He was finished with tasting. He was ready for the seven-course meal.

Dear Reader,

Breathless was born while I was driving home from a writing conference with my friend Katherine Cook. I told her I had this idea about a woman with no sense of direction (we may have already taken seven or eight wrong turns by this point). Since I've been plagued with no sense of direction all my life, I loved the idea of sticking some unsuspecting heroine with the same curse.

So many generous people helped with the research of this book. First I have to thank Detective Scott Driemel of the Vancouver Police Department. Blake is a better man and a more realistic character because of Scott, who unstintingly shared his time and expertise with me.

Fellow writer and music major Isabel Sharpe helped with the opera research, my own banker, Anne Crooks, helped me launder money—in fiction only! Judy McAnerin, Gayle Webb and another Nancy Warren also gave invaluable banking help, Betty Allan was my medical expert and Lee McKenzie McAnally knows guns. Susan Lyons knows grammar. I kept a lot of people busy, and I thank each and every one of them.

For a change of pace, watch for my Temptation/Duets trilogy coming in February and April 2003. You can find me on the Web at www.nancywarren.net.

Happy reading,

Nancy

P.S. Don't forget to check out www.tryblaze.com!

Books by Nancy Warren

HARLEQUIN BLAZE
19—LIVE A LITTLE!
47—WHISPER

HARLEQUIN DUETS
78—SHOTGUN NANNY

HARLEQUIN TEMPTATION
838—FLASHBACK

BREATHLESS

Nancy Warren

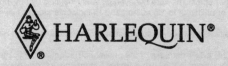

HARLEQUIN®

TORONTO • NEW YORK • LONDON
AMSTERDAM • PARIS • SYDNEY • HAMBURG
STOCKHOLM • ATHENS • TOKYO • MILAN • MADRID
PRAGUE • WARSAW • BUDAPEST • AUCKLAND

For my editor, Jennifer Tam,
who is a pleasure to work with and who embarked on her
own Happily Ever After this year.
With thanks and best wishes.

ISBN 0-373-79061-9

BREATHLESS

Copyright © 2002 by Nancy Warren.

This edition published by arrangement with Harlequin Books S.A.

® and TM are trademarks of the publisher. Trademarks indicated with
® are registered in the United States Patent and Trademark Office, the
Canadian Trade Marks Office and in other countries.

Visit us at www.eHarlequin.com

Printed in U.S.A.

1

SOPHIE MORTON WAS LOST.

That wasn't news. It happened all the time. Trouble was, she'd managed to lose herself in the worst part of Vancouver.

She'd been so certain she knew the way back to her bank's head office, but now she wondered if she'd taken a left when she should have turned right. Or was that a right that should have been a left?

If she weren't driving, she'd be tempted to bang her head against the steering wheel. She was cursed with no sense of direction. None whatsoever. She could never figure out why, with a high IQ and perfect vision, she was perpetually lost.

Maps didn't help. Strangers on the street who shouted directions like ''go north at the next corner then south after the third light'' didn't help in the least. Where the hell was north when you were totally and hopelessly lost?

Then there were those clowns with their ''hang a roscoe, then a louie, then another roscoe, you can't miss it.'' Hah.

Breathe, she ordered herself as her heart rate picked up speed. She flicked a glance out the side windows hoping for a benign-looking pedestrian or a mail carrier or cop. But on Vancouver's grimy and crime-ridden East Side, even the weak October sunshine seemed to be staying away.

A drunk snoozed in a doorway, an old woman in a

woolen hat dragged a rusty shopping cart full of her possessions, a pock-faced scarecrow of indeterminate gender
rooted through a trash can. A group of teenage addicts
were shooting up in the shadowed doorway of a pawn
shop, the barred windows giving them the look of ragged
prisoners in an overcrowded cell.

Sophie flipped the locks on her car and turned her attention back to the road, her hands tightening on the wheel.
She heard a wheeze and knew it came from her own chest,
where her heart felt as if it was expanding into her throat.

No. Not now. She willed herself to calm down. It was
bad enough getting lost, but the helplessness and frustration that resulted sometimes triggered a panic attack. Sweat
prickled her forehead, but she couldn't release her two-
fisted death grip on the steering wheel to mop her brow.

*Nothing to worry about. It's the middle of the afternoon.
Ten minutes ago you were in a residential shopping plaza
at a bank branch for an on-site management meeting.*

Breathe.

Perspiration damp and sticky between her breasts, she
tried to calm herself by listening to the opera music playing on her car's CD player.

Focusing on the CD wasn't helping. She had to get out
of this depressing place. The next intersection was bound
to lead somewhere. She'd turn... Oh, Lord, the intersection
was almost on her, the light green. Right or left?

Her heart hammered painfully; there wasn't enough air
in her lungs and yet she couldn't seem to suck in fresh air
fast enough. Something was in the way, pressing.

She was in the right lane. That must be a sign. She'd
turn right.

Gulping like a drowning victim, she forced her stiff fingers to turn the wheel to the right...into a small, mean
street that would be flattered to be termed an alley. Any

fool could see it wasn't going to take her anywhere she wanted to go.

At least there was no other traffic.

Dizzy and gasping, she pulled the car to the broken curb, shaking so badly she knew she'd have to breathe into the paper bag she always carried with her.

Breathe, damn it, breathe. She reached toward the glove compartment, knowing the crumpled paper bag was in there.

As she turned, the back view of a man, striding along the sidewalk a few feet ahead of her, caught her attention and held it. After the sad bundles of humanity she'd passed, it was a relief to see a well-built man. Maybe that's why she couldn't drag her eyes away.

This was good. Finding something to focus on was an excellent calming technique. Athletic and toned, his back view pushed all her female buttons. He wore a red baseball cap and long wavy-brown hair fell to his shoulders. A navy windbreaker couldn't hide the muscular shoulders, but it was the way his well-worn jeans molded to his hips and thighs that riveted her attention. He moved with speed and purpose and the way all his muscles worked together in harmony was poetry to the eye. Sophie's therapist would be delighted if she could see how well her client was using that focus technique.

She was so busy ogling the guy's rear that Sophie didn't spot the woman a few feet ahead of him until the man was almost on top of her. She was Asian, small-boned and in a terrible hurry, a clunky shopping bag bouncing against her thigh as she moved.

Sophie's eyes widened with horror as she watched the hunk grab the woman's arm and shove her up against the soot-smeared side of an old brick building. Beside them was an iron railing, the kind that meant a short flight of cement stairs led to a basement entrance.

The man was tall, and he loomed over the helpless woman, saying something, his face right in the woman's. Sophie rapidly revised her initial opinion from hunk. *Macho, thug bully.*

Through her car window, Sophie watched the woman struggle, saw her mouth opening; probably she was yelling for help.

Sophie's gaze darted up and down the alley, but it was deserted. There was no one there to help. No one but her.

It made her sick to watch a big muscle guy intimidate a woman. Whether he was trying to mug his struggling victim or worse, she had no idea, but she was horrified she'd been ogling the backside of a criminal.

Suddenly her lungs opened wide and she sucked huge gulps of air as anger overpowered her panic. 9-1-1. She'd call 9-1-1. Her fingers scrabbled frantically for the leather bag in the back seat that contained her cell phone.

Then she saw the gun in his hand.

"Oh, my God, no!" she yelled. But of course, no one heard her from inside her car.

She grabbed for the door handle.

No time for 9-1-1—that woman could be dead before she made the call.

She didn't stop to think, but opened her door, rounded the hood of her car, and dashed the few steps that separated her from the attacker and his victim. She lunged, throwing her body at him in a running tackle that would make her brothers proud.

She came at him from an angle so her head butted his side, knocking him over. She wrapped her arms round him just as her big brothers had taught her when they were kids.

For a crazy moment she and the gunman were airborne. There was a tumble and churning of limbs as though they were pieces of clothing in a dryer. She heard his grunt of surprise, a low, vicious curse, then the crunch and smack of a body hitting cement.

She cried out with pain as her hand scraped the rough, rocklike surface at the bottom of the stairs. Then she landed and the breath was knocked out of her with an *oof*.

A moment passed in utter stillness. Her face was planted against a warm, muscular chest that heaved once in a shuddering gasp, the only sign of life.

She lay sprawled across the gunman like a spent lover. When she inhaled, she smelled soap, sweat and man.

For a dazed second she felt an urge to snuggle into his solid warmth and rest for a moment, then reality reasserted itself. She was lying on top of a dangerous criminal.

Her eyes popped open. He wasn't merely dangerous. He was deadly. *The gun.* She hadn't heard it go off, so the woman must be safe, thank God. But danger still prickled at the back of her neck. She had to get that gun.

They'd landed on a cement pad the size of an apartment balcony in front of a dented metal door. She glanced over her shoulder and up the half-dozen cement stairs. The Asian woman stared down at them, her mouth open.

Sophie sighed, thankful the victim was unharmed. Together, they'd call 9-1-1 and one more abuser of women would be off the street. She'd have a few bruises and a badly scraped hand, but it would be worth it.

"Help me," Sophie called to the woman, her voice shaky but holding. "Help me get his gun."

The woman's eyes widened, and she shook her head as though to clear it. Then, without a word, she turned and ran. Maybe she didn't understand English. Probably she was going for help. All Sophie had to do was get the gun and restrain the thug until help arrived. She could do that.

Dragging herself to her hands and knees wasn't easy. As she tried to move, a cool draft where no draft should be informed her that her skirt had flipped up over her hips. Shifting her weight, she tried to wriggle the skirt back in place, causing her crotch to press intimately against something warm. Something warm that stirred as the man beneath her groaned.

Oh, Lord, she was pressed crotch to crotch with a gun-toting attacker of helpless women. The more frantically she tried to wiggle off him, the more the bulge beneath her…well, bulged.

"What the…?" he muttered indistinctly, and she realized that if he'd been knocked senseless, he was now beginning to recover.

She reared up to her hands and knees, until she crouched over him on all fours, and found herself staring down into a face that made her quiver with fear.

Stone-hard, the jaw squarer than a clenched fist, thin lips pressed together, a nose that thrust forward with belligerence, two deep grooves in lightly stubbled cheeks. Altogether it was a tough-looking package. But it was the eyes that grabbed her attention and wouldn't let go.

They were green, but not the green of grass or emeralds or anything friendly. They were a green as cloudy and cold as the North Sea. She shivered and forced her gaze away, up over dark brown hair that spilled round him, looking as though it hadn't seen a comb in a while.

His arms had fallen wide when he'd hit the ground, no gun in either open palm. Vaguely she remembered hearing the clatter of metal on cement. She looked ahead. There was his cap, where it had been tossed off his head, and there, in the corner of the retaining wall, was the gun.

Just seeing it gave her the creeps. She didn't want to touch it. But if she didn't, he might.

She reached for it, knowing the stretching movement would pretty much dangle her breasts in front of his eyes, but she couldn't waste time untangling herself and risk him getting to the weapon first.

Once she got hold of it she'd feel a lot safer. If he tried anything fresh she could shoot him. Well, she could threaten to. Unfortunately the only thing she knew about guns was what she'd seen on television.

He shook his head, as though his brains were scattered, which they probably were. Unlike her, no one had broken his fall. He'd struck bare cement.

Ignoring him, she stretched, reaching until she felt her ribs would snap apart and still her fingers stopped a few inches from the butt of the gun. She felt the warmth of his breath against her nipple as she strained forward. Her sexual antenna quivered, knowing without having to glance down that he was staring at her chest. With a horrible pang of embarrassment she felt the tingling in her nipple, the instinctive response to a man's warm breath just there and she knew damn well that response was visible.

She knew he was a bad man, but her body didn't seem to care. Their entwined position reminded her how much she missed having a man in her life. How much she missed sex. Since she'd broken up with David four months earlier, she hadn't been intimate and her body was letting her know it wasn't happy about the situation. If she was responding sexually to street scum, she'd better get back to the dating scene and find herself a real man.

Well, if ogling her breasts kept him occupied long enough for her to reach his gun, she supposed it was worth it. With a final push, she shoved off her knees.

Just at the moment her fingers touched cold, gray metal,

warm air huffed against her chest in a muffled curse, so close she could have sworn she felt the brush of his lips against her nipple. Then, with a grunt, he grabbed her around the waist and hauled her back down his muscular length.

But she hadn't grown up with three older brothers for nothing.

Even as he wrestled her down his body, she angled a knee between his legs and jerked it up, swift and sharp.

His strangled cry was her call to action. She shoved and rolled herself off and away from him. Scuttling on hands and knees until she grabbed the gun, she ignored the breeze that reminded her her skirt was still flipped up over her hips.

While he was fully occupied holding his crotch and swearing atrociously, she rose shakily to her feet then dashed around his body up the first couple of steps, the weapon heavy and sinister in her hands.

She heard the roar of an engine, and breathed a huge sigh of relief. The woman must have found help. Their ordeal was almost over. From his position on the ground, green eyes stared at her in pain, anger and something else. When she caught the direction of his gaze she threw him a withering glance and pulled her skirt hastily in place.

Trust a man never to miss an opportunity to stare up a woman's skirt, she thought, as she pushed her free hand through her hair, before climbing the rest of the steps.

She was just in time to watch her own car squealing away from the curb, the other woman at the wheel.

Her jaw dropped and she ran forward, waving her arms madly. "Wait!" she yelled. "What are you—" The rest of her cry was drowned by the screeching of tires, and her car, which she still owed two years of payments on, made a sharp U-turn, careened past Sophie and sped round the corner.

Great. Just great. She fervently hoped it was blind panic that had caused the woman to hijack her car, and that she'd bring it back along with the cops.

Now that the adrenaline rush was wearing off, she realized she was alone, defenseless but for a gun she didn't know how to use, with a guy who attacked women in broad daylight. Her whole body ached, her clothes were a mess, she'd lost a shoe and her hand was bleeding.

She'd had better days.

On the plus side, duking it out with a potential mugger or murderer seemed to have cured her panic attack. Go figure.

Slowly, she returned to the top of the stairs. The attacker had hauled himself up and was sitting with his back against the wall of the building. He hadn't tried to rise, so he must believe she knew how to use the gun. She curled her hand more firmly round the rubber grip, the finger grooves unnaturally wide for her hand, and tried to point the thing at him without letting him see her index finger was nowhere near the trigger.

He tipped his head and stared at her with stormy eyes, but didn't say a word. He didn't look so hot: pale, his forehead sheened with sweat, his lips thinned as though biting back a curse. She wondered why he bothered. He'd been free enough with his curses a minute ago.

The silence lengthened to the point of discomfort. She had no idea what the protocol was in a situation like this. All she knew was what she'd seen on TV and at the movies.

"Don't move," she ordered.

He continued to stare at her, and if anything his eyes grew colder.

Another long silence passed.

They couldn't sit here all day staring at each other while the gun seemed to gain weight in her not-quite-steady hands. Action was clearly required. "I'm calling the police," she informed him firmly.

He didn't argue, merely raised one eyebrow a fraction. Then she remembered. "Oh. My cell phone's in my car."

"Use mine." His voice matched his eyes. Cold, angry, clipped. He started to reach inside his jacket.

"Freeze!" she yelled, waving the gun a bit in case he'd forgotten she was holding it. Did he really think she was that stupid? He probably had a whole arsenal inside his windbreaker. The very idea had goose bumps running up and down her spine.

She'd reach in his pocket herself. How hard could it be? Keep the gun out of the guy's reach, keep her eyes on his so he didn't try anything funny and see for herself what was in his jacket.

"Put your hands up where I can see them," she ordered. Her voice was getting stronger by the second, she was pleased to note.

She could have sworn he rolled his eyes, but she just glared at him until he complied. She lost a bit of dignity stumbling down the stairs in one medium-heeled cream leather pump and one stockinged foot.

He muttered under his breath as she reached into his jacket and she could have sworn he said, "Hurry up."

It wasn't that easy to search him while keeping her gaze glued to his. Her peripheral vision wasn't all that clear, plus the expression in his eyes rattled her. Staring into a man's eyes for any length of time was usually an intimate, romantic gesture—a trading of smoldering messages. Staring into her prisoner's eyes was like staring into a fathomless frozen sea.

She shivered as she slipped her hand inside his jacket. In contrast to his gaze, his body was startlingly warm. Her hand brushed his chest, rigid with muscle, the heart thudding against her searching fingers.

For a second heat flashed behind the green ice of his eyes and she felt an instinctive quiver in her belly. His gaze moved lazily, insolently to her breasts, once more shoved into his line of vision as she bent forward to search him, and her response was almost as bad as when she'd felt his breath on her earlier. She usually kept her Marilyn Monroe breasts tucked away behind jackets and loose sweaters for work, but she'd left her jacket in the car.

"Like the view?" she snapped, inordinately annoyed at her own response. She must be insane to find such a man attractive.

"Spectacular," he said, his gaze roving the contours of her chest with as much deliberate slowness as though he were using his tongue. She'd intended to admonish him. She should have known better. A man who wasn't afraid to attack a woman wouldn't care about being caught staring at a convenient pair of breasts.

Her hand moved more rapidly, all business, feeling the outline of a pectoral muscle, a soft roughness that must be his chest hair and the small bump of his nipple.

"Jacket pocket, not shirt pocket," he said through gritted teeth.

She felt hot and uncomfortable and wished someone would come to help her. "Sorry," she whispered, her lips dry.

She fumbled a bit, batting at the jacket lining, then found it. Not another weapon, but a cell phone tucked into an inside pocket, precisely as he'd said.

Relieved to be able to get back to a safer distance from his deeply disturbing presence, she scuttled back to the stairs, found her shoe and slipped it on.

"Who are you calling?" he asked as she flipped open the phone.

"9-1-1."

"Get patched through to police. Tell them you've got Blake Barker."

Her eyes widened. Wow. He must be one of America's Most Wanted if the police knew him by name. Her dashed ego was restored. What was a scraped hand and missing car when she may have single-handedly caught a desperate criminal?

He must have read her thoughts, for his eyes narrowed. "*Detective* Blake Barker."

She almost dropped the phone along with her jaw. "Detective?"

Something that might have been amusement flashed across his face as he took in her obvious horror. "I'm a cop."

He must be yanking her chain. "But—but you pulled a gun on that poor woman."

"I was *arresting* that poor woman." He grimaced and she watched a drop of sweat roll down his temple. "And you better tell them to send an ambulance."

Her heart thudded painfully. "An ambulance?"

He glared at her once more. "You broke my damn leg."

2

ONLY NOW DID Sophie notice that one of the man's legs was twisted at an odd angle. "Oh, my. I'm—"

"Just make the call."

Her fingers trembled as she punched in the numbers. Ignoring his instructions, she asked for an ambulance as soon as the 9-1-1 dispatcher answered.

"What is the nature of the accident or injury?" a calm female voice asked her.

"He has a broken leg."

She gnawed her lip, staring down at the injured man leaning back against the wall. Now that she was no longer pointing a gun at him, his eyes drooped, only to jerk open again as though he were fighting sleep. "I think he has a concussion, too," she said, her stomach so heavy she felt as if she'd swallowed one of the cement stairs.

"What is your location, ma'am?"

"Location..." She glanced wildly around her, but of course there was no street sign. In this mean alley there wasn't so much as an address painted on any of the grim buildings. She could be absolutely anywhere. "Just a moment," she said to the operator.

"Excuse me," she said to her captive. It looked as though he'd dropped off to sleep, but she knew he shouldn't sleep if he had concussion, so she called louder. "Excuse me. Mr...Detective Barker."

His eyes opened slowly. "You still here?"

"Where are we?"

"I don't know about you. But I'm in hell."

"The…um…ambulance needs a location."

In a few terse words, he gave her the location and the closest main streets. She passed them on and then, giving him the benefit of the doubt, said, "The injured man claims he's a police officer. He says his name is Detective Blake Barker." She finished the call then settled down to wait.

It would be easy enough to find out for certain whether he was telling the truth. If he was a cop, he'd carry ID, but the very idea of putting her hands in his pockets again was more than she could manage. She'd find out soon enough.

She bit her lip, wondering if she'd be the one who ended up arrested. She was about to ask him when she noticed his eyes drifting shut again. "Hey, you mustn't fall asleep. You could get brain damage."

He opened his eyes with an apparent effort, looking her up and down. "Unless you're planning to finish the job and shoot me, put that thing away."

"Sorry," she said and placed the gun on the step beside her, the barrel facing away from both of them. She wasn't stupid, though. She only had his word for it that he was a cop. She wasn't letting that gun out of her immediate reach.

But, whoever he was, cop or robber, she had to keep him talking, to stop him from falling asleep. She remembered when Hank, her oldest brother, had that concussion after the big football game. The doctor had told her parents to wake him up throughout the night and ask him questions. His birthday, what day it was. That kind of thing.

Blowing out a breath, she leaned her elbows on her knees and hoped the ambulance wouldn't take long.

"Detective Barker. When is your birthday?"

He didn't even bother opening his eyes. "You planning to buy me a present?"

"Yes. A book on manners."

His mouth crooked up in a tired smile. "May fifteenth. Nineteen-seventy."

She did the mental math and discovered he was four years older than she. Not that that meant anything, of course. He wasn't an interesting possibility she'd just met at a party. Oh, how she wished he was, that they'd met under almost any other circumstances. "You're a Taurus. Why am I not surprised? You know what the symbol for Taurus is? Detective Barker?"

This time he opened one eye and pushed his hair behind his ears. "You're a real pain in the ass, you know that?"

She nodded. "That's what my brothers always say. I should warn you, I never give up, either, once I put my mind to something. Of course, that's a good quality in a career-driven woman, but it can be very annoying socially. Do you know what the symbol for Taurus is?"

"The bull," he muttered. He must have got the message that she'd keep pestering him until he answered her questions. Maybe he even realized it was for his own good.

"That's right. Even on our short acquaintance, I'm inclined to think it suits you. Bulls are stubborn and, well, bullheaded, aren't they?"

Either he was ignoring her or he'd fallen asleep again. She'd shake his shoulder but she was afraid he might do her injury, so she stuck with her bright conversation. "Do you have a favorite color, Detective?"

"Pink."

She chuckled. If he was making jokes, even sardonic ones, his brain couldn't be all that damaged.

"Do you know what day it is?"

"I have a headache. Would you just shut up?"

Well, it wasn't the correct answer, but so long as he kept talking she didn't suppose it mattered much what he said.

"Did you always want to be a police officer?"

"Right now I want to be a murderer."

She put her hand on the gun beside her. She couldn't keep this up much longer. She was getting chilled sitting on not-very-clean cement stairs without her jacket. The sun was out, but it was a pale reminder that fall would soon give way to winter.

If she couldn't keep him talking, she could at least keep him awake by talking herself. She took a deep breath and started babbling, keeping a careful eye on her prisoner/patient. "My brother Carl always wanted to be a police officer when he was a kid. Well, that or a garbage man. He loved watching those guys jump on and off moving trucks." She chuckled at the memory. "He ended up as a stockbroker."

No response.

"Do you have brothers or sisters, Detective?" It was hard to imagine him with brothers or sisters or parents for that matter. Her first guess would be that he hatched from demon spawn.

His eyes opened, but only so he could glare at her.

So she told him about all her brothers. She'd launched into the story of how her parents met when she finally heard the blessed sound of a siren.

She picked up the gun and ran up the stairs to signal. Her heart lifted with relief when she saw the ambulance turn into their alley—then sank when she noticed the police cruiser following it. She had an awful feeling she'd soon find herself handcuffed and tossed in the back of the cruiser for assaulting a police officer.

BLAKE OPENED HIS EYES when he heard the siren, wondering what had taken them so long. He forced himself to focus on the woman who was hovering over him again. It wasn't easy. She wavered before his vision like an unwelcome mirage.

His leg hurt like a bitch, his head pounded and he couldn't see straight. On top of that, there was a throbbing between his legs reminding him that Blondie may have prematurely ended his sex life. But worse than that, she'd helped Li's girlfriend escape. The diminutive woman had at least six kilos of heroine in her shopping bag which she was delivering for her boyfriend. Blake had planned to arrest her and convince her to work with them. He'd seen the bruises on her face and the skittish look in her eyes, and he was hopeful that if they offered her protection she'd help them catch the elusive Mr. Li.

But, thanks to Blondie here, not only had she escaped, but she now knew he wasn't an ambitious dealer working his way up the ranks, but a cop.

His cover was blown.

His gut churned, adding one more unpleasant sensation to his overloaded system.

"Please, it's really important you stay awake." She glanced over her shoulder then turned back to him. "Help's almost here."

"Go away." If she'd just shut up, maybe he could get his jumbled thoughts straight. Take a little nap. He leaned his head against the wall, letting the pale October sunshine wash his face. Just a little nap and he'd...

"Detective, please." She was shaking him again. Damn woman wouldn't leave him alone. "Tell me...tell me about the woman."

"None of your business," he said.

"It is my business," she said, indignation in her tone and sparkling in her eyes. Gorgeous eyes, he noted. A

clear, unwavering blue, set in an angelic face. And yet
there was something about the full-lipped mouth that
hinted at devilry. An intriguing combination. Blond hair
curled at her shoulders. Too bad her brain matched her
hair color. "That woman stole my car," she said.

"My heart bleeds. Go jump on her and break some
bones."

White teeth gnawed her lower lip. "The ambulance is
here." She paused and an expression of acute anxiety
crossed her face. "And the police."

He merely grunted. Behind and above her he could
make out the steady beat of the lights. They'd cut the si-
rens, at least, but he hated lying here in a heap knowing
the ambulance was for him. He hated it almost as much
as he hated the failure he could taste like blood on his
tongue. No, damn it, that *was* blood he tasted. On top of
all his other injuries, he'd bitten his tongue when the hellcat attacked him.

Before the paramedics got to him, one of his handlers,
Detective John Holborn, vaulted down the steps, weapon
drawn. "What the—"

The hellcat gave a squeak of alarm as John grabbed the
gun they'd both forgotten she was holding and shoved her
against the wall, slapping her hands above her head.

She gazed at John as if he'd sneezed and forgotten to
say excuse me.

In spite of his misery Blake wanted to laugh. "You're
supposed to say, 'Get your hands up where I can see
them,'" he informed John in a loud TV cop way.

She glared at him over John's shoulder, pinkening under
his mocking stare. "It's what they say on TV."

He chuckled, amazed he was capable of it. Bloody am-
ateurs. "Let her go, John. She was…" Her gaze snagged

on his and he saw the embarrassment, pride and a touch of fear. She must know attacking police officers was not going to earn her a public service medal. He shook his head, knowing she must have done his brain a serious injury since he was going to let her off. "She was trying to help."

"How hard did you hit your head?" John asked him, frowning, his weapon still trained on the woman. "She had a gun."

"My Beretta. She was…" It was tough to think through the throbbing in his head, leg, groin and most other parts of his body. "She was keeping watch. Wai Fung Li's girlfriend's in the neighborhood. She just stole this woman's car. Get the details, maybe we can apprehend her."

John hesitated then nodded brusquely, holstering his own weapon.

Eyes wide and nervous, she slowly lowered her arms. He might be damaged, broken and concussed, but he was still able to appreciate the sight of her stretched out against the wall. Her elegant blouse was missing a crucial button, which he hadn't bothered to tell her about. Now that the silky fabric gaped, he got a glimpse of full creamy breasts cupped by a lacy white bra. Nice long waist, he noted, a swell of hip and then the skirt which hid her thighs, but not the shapely calves and ankles.

He and John exchanged a glance, but they'd been partners long enough to communicate on less. *Nice rack,* they agreed.

There was a smear of blood on her blouse and he wondered what other part of him she'd injured, then he noticed her hand was scraped raw. "Get somebody to look at her hand."

Before John could protest, another figure jogged down to join the party. Vaguely Blake recognized the uniformed

paramedic. A young guy still new at what he was doing
and enthusiastic about it. Just his luck. The medic
crouched at Blake's side, ran gloved hands over his head
then shone a flashlight in his eye.

He flinched. "I broke my leg, you idiot. Not my eye."

"Is it a very bad concussion?" the woman asked over
his head, as if he was a little kid or someone who didn't
speak the language.

"Hard to tell," the paramedic answered her. The hands
kept moving over him, down his side, behind his back. No
doubt they were checking for more damage, but it made
him feel foolish, especially with those clear blue eyes
watching every move.

When the paramedic's hands moved up his inner thigh,
he'd had enough. He clamped a hand on the guy's wrist.
"One more inch and you're a dead man."

"Just doing my job." The medic shot a glance at John
and said, "Cops are always the worst."

"Tell him the family jewels came through just fine," he
told John, since no one seemed to want to speak to him
directly.

It wasn't entirely true. His balls still throbbed thanks to
Miss Citizen Crusader. His gaze settled on hers. "Well,
mostly fine," he amended, and she blushed scarlet.

John had his cell phone out. "We'll see if we can track
down your car, ma'am. Give me the make and model number."

She and John stepped to the side while the perky paramedic chatted to him in his best stretcher-side manner.
"Can't give you any good drugs, Detective. They'll have
those at the hospital. We'll just stabilize you and put you
in an aluminum splint. Have you out of here in no time."

"Color?" John asked Blondie.

"Blue."

Blake wondered foggily if her car color matched her eyes.

After John had relayed the information, including location and time of the theft, he pocketed his phone and turned back to Blake. "So, Li's girlfriend did this to you?" His face creased in puzzlement. "You should have called for backup."

"Not exactly."

The paramedic had finished his initial inspection and jogged back up the stairs only to reappear with a temporary splint. In the background was a second attendant and a stretcher. Soon they'd be carting him around like a papoose.

Once more his gaze meshed with a blue one. As blue and innocent as a summer sky. "I tripped and fell," he said. "The girlfriend resisted arrest, stole this woman's vehicle and got away."

John hadn't been born yesterday. He frowned his disbelief then turned to stare at the woman blushing and wringing her hands—the picture of guilt. Finally, his gaze skewered Blake once more. "You tripped and fell."

"That's what I said." He glared up at John, having to squint against the sun. Normally, since he was the taller of the two, he looked down a couple of inches when he was speaking to his handler. He didn't like the view from flat on his back. Didn't like it at all.

"Look, Blake—"

"Are you putting that splint on me or taking it to the prom?" he snapped at the attendant who was hovering, hugging the temporary cast against his chest.

"We'll have you fixed up in no time," the paramedic said in that falsely jovial tone Blake associated with nurses and playschool teachers.

He glared at John for a second, making a slight motion

with his chin toward the woman. He wanted John to bugger off and take Blondie with him, before the paramedic started stuffing his broken leg into the splint and the swearing began.

Goodbye, Blondie. She looked like an angel from heaven, but it would be obvious to a man much more stupid than Blake that she was nothing but trouble. Sexy, but trouble.

John's narrowed gaze said he had some explaining to do, which he knew.

"Shouldn't we…" She turned back to gaze at Blake, worry creasing her forehead.

"He's in good hands," John said firmly, and urged her forward.

She took one step, turned back and mouthed, "I'm sorry," before continuing up the cement steps.

His vision might not be twenty-twenty at the moment, but he could still enjoy the sway of her hips, the long legs and slim ankles. The view was even better since she was walking away from him. Out of his life forever.

From the neat business clothes she wore, he assumed she was some kind of office worker. Of course, they weren't neat now. Apart from one crucial missing button, the lady had a hell of a run in her stockings.

Then the paramedics worked his broken leg into the cast and he forgot all about her bewitching body and concentrated on keeping his curses too low for her to hear.

3

WHAT KIND OF FLOWERS could possibly say, *I'm sorry I broke your leg and let a criminal get away?*

Sophie scanned bouquets and bunches in the hospital's ground-floor florist shop and gnawed her lip in indecision. She couldn't forget the second message: *Thanks for not turning me in.*

The roses were beautiful, but heady with the scent of romance. Definitely not roses. A single orchid in a Japanese-style setting of tranquil simplicity appealed to her, but orchids were high maintenance. Detective Barker hadn't struck her as an orchid-fussing type.

Tiger lilies were too obvious, a potted plant too homey—this wasn't a housewarming present.

She scanned the shop once more, thinking perhaps she'd overlooked the perfect gift.

She hadn't, of course. There was no gift, no plant, no flower arrangement that could gloss over the fact that Detective Barker was in the hospital because she'd put him there.

Oh, the hell with it. Tired of her own indecision, she hauled out her brand-new temporary credit card—the one she'd picked up this afternoon along with a temporary driver's license and a rental car—and pointed to a big bunch of blooms. The chrysanthemums and dahlias were as bright and colorful as a Rose Bowl parade. The florist arranged them in a clear glass vase together with a metallic balloon that said Get Well Soon.

Perky as hell.

She *was* sorry, and maybe these bright happy flowers would lighten his mood and his pain.

She winced as she recalled her own stupidity. *Look before you leap, Sophie.* How often had her mother read her that homily as she bandaged knees, iced black eyes and wrapped sprains. But Sophie the child had grown sick of being the little one, and a girl. The one teased and picked on until her temper flared and she flew at her older brothers.

Besides, the black eyes and split lips Mom had iced hadn't all been hers. She'd learned from her big bros, and had given as good as she got.

On one memorable occasion she'd caused her second oldest brother, Matt, to have to go to emergency for stitches. That, she recalled with satisfaction, was the day her brothers started to respect her. They were all strapping great men now, two with their own families. But there wasn't one who didn't step carefully when Sophie was in a temper.

Still, in all the years of spectacular family clashes, not once had any of the siblings ended up as badly injured as Detective Blake Barker.

If she *had* accidentally broken one of her brothers' legs she'd be devastated for she loved every last bullying one of them. She'd do everything she could to make sure they were comfortable.

Thinking about her rough-and-tumble brothers helped calm her nerves. She'd take the flowers and pretend it was one of her brothers laid up in hospital. She'd apologize without groveling. There was a way of being sorry that still left a person their pride.

She continued her self-administered pep talk as she took the elevator up to his floor. She took a deep breath and headed for the nurses' station, inhaling the hospital smell of disinfectant and sickness. She recalled the detective's disgusted expression when the paramedic had started working on him. How he must hate being here. She clutched the vase tighter. "May I see Blake Barker please?" she asked the nurse behind the counter.

The woman checked the clock. "Sure. Visiting hours end in thirty minutes. His room is the last on the left."

"Thank you." She headed down the hall.

The nurse's voice stopped her. "Ma'am? I said left."

She turned around and walked the other way. "Of course you did." Left, right, north, south—she pretty much always got them wrong.

When she arrived at his room, the door was ajar. She peeped in, heart thumping uncomfortably, hoping there'd be a crowd of officers or friends and family with the detective and that she could leave her flowers and bolt. But Detective Barker was alone. The scowl on his face must have scared everyone away.

The picture before her had her smiling in spite of unease. Detective Barker *did* remind her of one of her brothers laid up and in a foul mood. He was propped up in a white hospital bed and obviously wished himself elsewhere. It was a semiprivate room, she noted, but the second bed was empty. No doubt he'd terrified the other patient into discharging himself.

He wore a short-sleeved green hospital gown which showed off impressive biceps. One leg was tucked beneath a yellow blanket, the other propped on top. Where the gown ended she had a glimpse of tan, muscular thigh with a sprinkling of dark hair, the knob of a knee and then a heavy white cast that stretched from just below his knee to his toes and had her biting her lip again.

Her gaze jerked back to his face. He did not look like a happy man. His hair was still unkempt, she saw, but he'd pulled it back in an elastic band so she got the full benefit of a mighty scowl.

Biceps bunched as he turned a page of the magazine he was reading and she caught a glimpse of the cover. *Ladies' Home Journal.* He flicked another page, looking bored, irritable and uncomfortable.

She took a step backward. No way she was going in there. She'd pretend she'd found him asleep and leave the flowers with the nurse.

Even as she stepped backward his head rose, like an animal scenting prey. As he spotted her, his stormy green eyes darkened.

"Hello," she said softly from the doorway, fighting the urge to turn tail and run.

He did not appear overjoyed by her visit. Only the fact that he had a cast hampering his movement gave her the courage to enter his room.

She held out the flowers like the peace offering they were and, since he didn't reach for them, she crossed the room and placed them next to a box of tissues on a narrow table that sat under the window.

He flicked a glance at the flowers and didn't bother to thank her.

She fussed with them, buying time, turning the bouquet until the best side showed, wondering how many minutes she ought to stay for politeness' sake.

"I don't even know your name," he said at last. His voice sounded gruffer than she remembered.

And wouldn't it be nice to keep it that way. She turned and stepped over to the bed. "It's Sophie. Sophie Morton." She was so flustered, she extended her hand for him to shake.

He glanced at her and a shaft of reluctant amusement lit his eyes, bringing them to sexy, powerful life. His hand was as big and strong as the rest of him and surrounded her fingers as he squeezed. It was so warm she wondered if he had a fever.

"Nice to meet you," she said, compounding her inanity.

"Likewise, I'm sure," he murmured and damn if the thread of amusement didn't do something seriously chaotic to her libido.

She pulled her hand back and glanced around, wishing she'd had the stupid flowers delivered. He didn't want to see her any more than she wanted to see him. What was the matter with her?

Guilt, that's what. Her gaze was drawn to the white cast. "Is it very bad?" she asked in a small voice.

"It'll heal." As she recalled from earlier today, he was a man of few words.

"And your head?"

"They're making me stay overnight for observation." He shrugged. "It's a hard head. It'll be fine."

She nodded, completely able to believe he was hard-headed.

"Would you like to sit down?" He indicated the chair beside his bed.

"No, really, I should be—" She gasped as his hand clamped down on her wrist.

"I'd like some company. I'm sick of women's magazines and fishing journals. We could have a nice talk." The words themselves were pleasant enough, she supposed; it was the steel beneath them that made her heart jump into her throat.

"I can't think what we have to talk about." She tried to struggle free, but his hand shackled her wrist.

"Let's start by what the hell you were doing when you knocked me down the stairs and broke my leg."

Tugging was useless and undignified so she gave it up. "I've already apologized. I *am* sorry. I thought you were attacking that woman."

He stared at her as though she were crazy. "I had a gun."

"I know. That's why I tackled you. I was only going to call 9-1-1 from my cell phone in the car, but then I saw the gun. How did I know you weren't going to kill her?"

If anything, the pressure on her wrist increased. She wouldn't be surprised if he left burn blisters. "I could have killed *you*."

"You weren't looking my way."

His mouth crooked up on one side. "That's a mistake that cost me."

Guilt assailed her. "If there's anything I can do… I got a pretty good look at that woman. If I see her again I'll—"

"You stay away from her." His hand squeezed tighter and she winced. His eyes were coldly furious once more. "She and her friends kill first then ask questions." He shook her arm up and down as though he'd forgotten he was holding it. "You see her and you run, you hear me?" His fingers were hot and implacable as they squeezed her flesh. Any tighter and she'd be the next one in a cast.

Sophie nodded. She felt herself trembling. Even though it was warm in the room, she felt cold.

As quickly as his anger had come, it faded, replaced by an awareness that was very male and very unnerving.

The fingers that had all but branded her a moment before

now traced a lazy circle on the sensitive skin of her inner wrist. "Who are you?" he finally asked.

"I told you. Sophie Morton." This was not happening. She was not feeling attracted to him. That was not desire climbing her arm like a rash. She'd treat her attraction like a panic attack. It was just as irrational and inconvenient. All she had to do was deny it and it would go away.

"Is your head bothering you again? I should call the nurse." She searched for a call button. Nurse, doctor, janitor, she didn't care. Anyone who'd rescue her from being alone with this frighteningly sexy man would be most welcome.

He shook his head with impatience. "I mean, where do you come from? What do you do? Why were you in that alley today? Didn't look like your regular beat."

The call button was on his other side, but she'd throw herself out the hospital window before she'd lean across his body. She remembered only too clearly how it had felt to be pressed intimately against him, chest to thigh. She cleared her throat. "I'm in human resources. I was at a meeting this morning and I took a wrong turn on the way back to the head office. I got lost."

"Did you ever." He let her go at last and eased his head back against the pillows as though it were throbbing.

She put her hands behind her back so he wouldn't see her rubbing her sore wrist. "I have no sense of direction. It's a curse. That woman. Is she a very bad criminal?"

"I don't know much about her. Her boyfriend's one of the worst. He's the head of an Asian gang that's trying to build a base here. They deal drugs, run gambling rings, smuggle illegal human cargo, dabble in murder and intimidation." He ran a hand through his hair. "We hoped to use her to get the boyfriend."

She dropped her gaze to the gleaming tile floor feeling

as guilty as if she were the vicious criminal. "Why did you lie to Detective Holborn? You didn't tell him I broke your leg."

There was a short pause as though he wasn't sure why, either. In the hallway a doctor was being paged, the tinny sound of an amplified voice echoing against the pale green walls and polished floor. "You tried to help. You were…brave but misguided. I figure you lost your car, that's punishment enough."

Her car. Her very own half-paid-for car. "I should check and see if they've found it yet."

He snorted with humorless laughter. "Your car's gone. It was probably in a chop shop within an hour."

"Oh." She tried not to picture her poor seminew car being broken up and sold for parts. It was her own fault for being foolish and impulsive. When would she ever learn? "Well," she said, glancing at her watch, "visiting hours are almost over. I'd better go."

His gaze held hers for a moment and she felt momentarily breathless. It was the kind of look a man gives a woman he wants. Her pulse jolted under the raw heat in his expression. If they'd met at a party or club, would they have been attracted to each other?

She was pretty sure she knew the answer. At least on her side.

"Yeah," he said gruffly. "I guess you'd better."

"I'm…um…I'm sorry." Sorry for his broken bones, his botched arrest and very sorry they wouldn't have a chance to explore the strong pull between them.

"I'll live."

"Well, I… Do you have a card so I can call you if I see that woman again?"

His brows rose and he glanced down at his hospital

gown. Any fool could tell he was naked beneath. "Not on me."

"No, of course not." Her gaze settled in his lap where the gown had rucked itself round a very respectable bulge. She recalled the moment when she'd tried to move off of him in the alley and found her crotch pressed against him. Even at rest his male equipment had felt impressive.

"Did you lose something?" He'd followed the line of her gaze and once again that thread of humor laced his tone, only now it held a husky note.

"I'm not sure," she said slowly, letting her gaze travel very deliberately up his body to his mouth, "but I think maybe I did." Mmm, he was sexy, and if he could play games, so could she. "Maybe we both did."

She could tell her frankness had surprised him, but he didn't deny her statement. What was the point? She knew he was thinking the same thing she was.

So caught up was she in reading the X-rated messages in his eyes that she didn't notice his arms creep round her waist until she tried to back out of the room. Her eyes widened in surprise.

"You hurt me bad," he said huskily. "The least you can do is kiss it better."

She leaned forward slowly, wanting quite fiercely to kiss him, knowing from the way her blood was already heating that she wouldn't be able to stop there.

"Which part of you hurts most?" she asked.

"I hurt all over."

"I was afraid of that." She let a hand rest on his wide chest as she leaned into him, feeling the thump of his heart beneath her palm. It wasn't fair that this man both frightened and excited her at the same time.

Her body was aching all over, as well, with need. It was embarrassing to feel this way about a virtual stranger, but she never had been able to control her libido once it decided to take charge of her body.

His lips were near. She loved their shape and firmness, and based on every other part of him she'd touched, they'd be warm. Her own lips parted in anticipation and she watched as his did the same.

He lifted a hand and tucked a curl behind her ear, brushing the sensitive skin near her lobe so she shivered.

"What if someone comes in?" She couldn't keep the amusement out of her voice. Battered and concussed he was about the sexiest man she'd ever seen. She couldn't imagine what he must be like with all his wits and limbs functioning.

His lips curved. "Maybe we'll get thrown out and I'll be able to leave the hospital."

He didn't know about her embarrassing sexual quirk. "Believe me, someone would come. And you'd end up with a worse headache."

His hand moved to the back of her head, thrust deep in her curls and he pulled her slowly forward. "I'll risk it," he said.

Look before you leap, Sophie. She'd ignored that excellent advice once too often today. This time, she decided to be smart. But it cost her.

She pressed her lips to his forehead. "Get well soon," she said softly, and pulled away before she could change her mind.

4

SOPHIE GROANED AS SHE literally dragged herself into work at Investment Bank of Vancouver the next morning. One knee was so badly bruised she couldn't bend it and had to haul it behind her as she struggled up the three stone steps outside the building.

She'd popped a couple of pain relievers to help fight both the pain in her leg and the pain in her scraped, bandaged hand, but still her whole body felt bruised and battered.

And on the mental side things weren't looking all that cheery, either. There was the major load of guilt she was packing. As she dragged the stiff leg behind her, she wondered how Detective Barker would make out with his much stiffer and far more unwieldy broken left leg. Then there was the personal loss. There was still no sign of her car and after Detective Barker's comments she had to assume it wasn't even a whole car anymore.

She also had the nuisance factor of the theft to contend with. Even though she'd already had her locks changed, cancelled her credit cards and changed her bank accounts, she had to do something about other documents such as her birth certificate.

She realized with a scowl that the thief would even get her free cup of coffee since she'd just filled her frequent drinker card from her favorite café across the street. The café where she'd be at this very moment grabbing her first java of the day if her knee wasn't so sore. It wouldn't be long before she'd filled another frequent coffee card, but it was the principle of the thing that irked her.

As she entered the side entrance of the bank and crossed to the elevator, she continued her mental inventory of all the not very important but convenient cards in her wallet. There was her library card, video membership, the card with birth dates of all her family along with their sizes and favorite colors.

Forcing a pleasant smile to her face, even though she wanted to kick something, she emerged from the elevator to the fourth-floor administration offices and made her way to her own. If she concentrated, she could walk without limping. Much.

She picked up a blank notepad and stuffed it into a vinyl portfolio case she'd been given at a banking conference. Then she flipped on her computer and printed out her notes for today's management meeting.

She stopped in at the coffee room to fill her mug before heading to the boardroom. Her bad mood worsened when she sipped the toxic sludge, wishing she'd dragged herself across the road after all.

Ellsworth Timson, senior account manager in Private Banking, was the only other early bird. He raised his gray-blond head and stared at her as she limped into the room with a carefree smile pasted on her face like too much lipstick.

"Sophie! What happened?" She'd decided simply to say her car had been stolen and she'd tripped over a curb while chasing the thief. No need to go into details of how she'd single-handedly botched an important police investigation and wounded an officer in the process.

But Ellsworth was a friend and at the moment they had the room to themselves. She couldn't lie to him. She told him the truth, stopping short of describing Detective Barker's injuries. She'd noticed how much Barker had hated being helpless and injured, and an odd sort of protectiveness stopped her from describing that part of her misadventures.

"Here, let me help you sit down." Ellsworth fussed over her as she told the story, pulling up an extra chair for her to rest her bruised leg on, asking her three times if she'd be more comfortable at home.

"No," she assured him three times. She wouldn't. The bank chairman and the president were headed for a conference in New York the next day, and she felt she ought to be here today since it would be the last operations meeting for two weeks.

"At least let me run across the street and get you your coffee." He must have noticed her grimace as she sipped the office brew.

She shook her head, smiling at his thoughtfulness. "This stuff tastes like they sucked it straight out of the tar sands, but it's loaded with caffeine. It'll do."

"Are the police considering any...?" He made a vague motion with his pen.

"Charges?" She shuddered and dropped her head in her hands, wincing as the bandage shifted against her scrape. "No. I certainly deserve it, but I suppose they think since I had my car stolen I've been punished." She reached out and touched his sleeve. "Don't spread the story around, okay? It's too embarrassing."

He patted her sore knee. "Of course not. You seem a little pale. I could have someone drive you home."

"No. Really." She tried not to snap, he was only trying to be helpful. "I'm fine."

Although, for all the good she was to anyone in the meeting, she might as well have gone home. She couldn't concentrate when her mind was still cataloging the contents of her briefcase, bag, glove compartment. Argh! Her workout gear was in her gym bag—in the trunk. One more item to replace.

Ruby Ferringer, the queen bee of Private Banking, wanted hiring authority over the department she managed. It was an old scab, but she picked at it almost every week. Sophie was never certain whether it was because she was so much younger than Ruby that she resented her or whether Ruby would make life difficult for anyone who hired for her department. Today's complaint was that certain assistant account managers were taking too long to complete routine paperwork.

"If I hired my own people, I'd make certain they were efficient," she argued. She used to harp about Ellsworth coming to the management meetings, but, since he was the top producer in the department and a friend of the bank chairman, Henry Forsyth, Ruby had finally given up and started picking on Sophie instead.

Henry was too much of a gentleman to tell Ruby to shut up, which, Sophie imagined, every other person around the table was itching to do. Instead, he leaned back in his gentleman-banker pose, and took them all on a trip down memory lane to his younger days, before the age of computers.

While he reminisced, Sophie went back to her catalog of missing stuff. She fretted about work-related documents that had been in her car. She tried to recall all the information in her day planner and the few files she'd been carrying. It wasn't supersensitive information, but she hated knowing it was in the hands of a gang of criminals.

She'd tried to do a good deed and instead caused a heap of trouble—not only for herself. That was the part she hated most. It seemed small punishment to suffer the inconvenience of a rental car, a sore knee and having to replace a slew of documents when Detective Barker had suffered broken bones, as well as the loss of a suspect.

Knowing the fault was completely hers hurt. It hurt badly.

She managed to stumble through her own brief report before Mr. Forsyth turned to Ellsworth. "And how's your week been? Won any more awards? Broken any more records?"

He teased, but there wasn't a person at the table who didn't know how proud he was of the prestige Ellsworth brought to the bank. He had an uncanny sense with investments and had made his clients and the bank huge amounts of money in his long career. With less than five years till he retired, there was a flurry among the younger account managers to recreate his magic. In fact, it had been a quiet week for his department, with markets uncertain and no big new clients to boast.

"Come on, I'll walk you to your office," Ellsworth said a little while later, and she realized the meeting was over.

"Thanks." She shut her portfolio before he could see she hadn't made a single note. Hadn't heard more than a word in ten, come to that.

After she lowered her foot from the extra chair, he moved it aside so she could rise more easily. She thanked him and they walked out together. Well, he walked. She shuffled like an old woman.

"I was thinking about how brave you were yesterday. You should get some kind of medal."

She snorted, not with amusement but with self-derision. "I don't think so. I botched an arrest and the suspect escaped in my car."

"Yes, but you were trying to be a good citizen." He shrugged and sent her an avuncular smile. "Did you get a good look at the woman? Maybe you'll see her again one day and be able to recognize her.''

She nodded, realizing the woman's countenance was etched in her memory. "I'd recognize her again, and this time I'd make sure the police caught up with her.''

She supposed he'd known her long enough to recognize mulish determination, for he took her arm. "Those gangs are bad news. If you ever see that woman again, run.''

They'd reached her office now, and he paused by her door as she glanced at him in surprise. "You sound like the police detective. That's what he said.''

"You make sure you take his advice, hmm? Were there any other witnesses?''

"Nobody that I saw.'' She shook her head. "It's too bad you had that other meeting to go to yesterday or I would have followed you and saved myself a bunch of trouble.''

He touched her hand where the light bandage covered the oozing scrape. "From now on, we'll have all meetings involving you take place at head office. All right? If you need a few days at home to recover, you know your staff can cover.''

"I'll be fine.''

He nodded. "If there's anything you need…'' Then he turned down the corridor that led to his own office.

She dragged one of her visitor chairs over to her desk to prop her sore leg on, and hoped she wouldn't have to go anywhere today. She checked her in-house e-mail. That done, she reached absently for her briefcase to pull out her day planner. Her eyelids drooped in frustration. Her day planner was in her briefcase in her car, which, according to Detective Sunshine was at this very moment being sold off in tiny bits.

Would they do the same with her briefcase? She'd have to check eBay for brass locks and briefcase sides.

Her assistant, Gwen, stuck her nose in the door. "What are you giggling about?"

"It's incipient hysteria. My day planner was stolen along with everything else. Do you have any idea what I'm supposed to do today?"

Gwen grinned and returned to her desk to pull up her own superefficient computerized version of Sophie's schedule. Sophie hauled herself out of her chair and leaned against her doorjamb while Gwen scanned her appointments. "I'll do you a printout, but the only thing I can see for today is a meeting on the third floor."

She grimaced, thinking there was a good reason the meeting had slipped her mind. "The queen bee?"

"Ruby, yeah. Meeting's in her office." She gestured to Sophie's leg. "Want me to ask her to come here instead?"

Ruby was known as the queen bee of Private Banking for several reasons. She'd been here at head office longer than anyone else except the chairman and had been one of the first female account managers. In an industry where personnel were moved around to gain experience, she'd refused every transfer and, through a combination of factors, mostly stubbornness, had ended up with her own empire in a twisting labyrinth of offices, appropriately called The Hive.

The only thing Ruby didn't completely control was the hiring for her department, and for that slight Sophie paid dearly. "No. She'll be easier to deal with on her turf. What's the problem now?" she asked Gwen, wondering if she should take Ellsworth's advice and take a couple of days off.

Coward.

Gwen skimmed the notes she'd made regarding the

meeting. "She's not happy with her new assistant account manager, Phil Britten."

Sophie's eyes bugged. "I thought she'd love Phil. He's a teetotaler like she is and a health nut. He doesn't even eat meat."

"Really?" Gwen's eyes widened. "But he's so buff for a vegetarian."

She nodded, remembering his résumé and some of the get-to-know-you chats they'd had during his interviews. "He's an amateur weightlifter."

"Oh, that explains it. Well, Ruby's got some concerns about his performance she wants to discuss in private."

"My ass. He probably forgot to raise his hand and ask permission before going to the bathroom." She sighed and rubbed her temple where a headache was starting to form. Since her knee had taken to throbbing in counterpoint to her scraped hand, she figured she'd get her money's worth from a painkiller.

She hobbled back to her desk, popped one in her mouth for her aches and pains, swallowing it with cold coffee and popped a second one in preparation for seeing Ruby. "What time's the meeting?"

"Eleven."

She checked her watch. Just after ten.

"I think I'll go see Phil first. He's done something. Once I know what crime he's committed it will be easier to smooth the queen bee's feathers—wings—whatever."

"Good luck."

Sophie set off with the same portfolio she'd taken to the management meeting, moving slowly on her stiff knee. She took the elevator down to the third floor when normally she would have jogged down the stairs, then stepped through the door that led to Private Banking. She'd been on this floor dozens of times, but she dreaded every one.

The place was a maze of devious design guaranteed to confuse anyone, never mind a chronically lost person.

Ruby's office was the only landmark that was easy to reach, since it was at the center of things. All corridors led, eventually, to her. Naturally.

Phil, as both a new hire and not a very important assistant, was on the outskirts. Was his cubicle to her left? She tried to recall from her earlier visit—the one she paid every new head office employee a few days after they started. Yep, definitely left. She turned and walked down the hallway passing cubicles and offices, waving to people she knew. She still hadn't seen Phil, so she popped her head into a random cubicle and asked the way.

"Keep going down this corridor. Take a left at the water cooler and a right at the women's washroom."

"Great, thanks." She carried on. There was the water cooler. Excellent. She kept going, hoping she'd see the women's washroom soon, after all the coffee she'd drunk this morning.

A few minutes later she was even more confused. She had no idea where she was, but she'd obviously stumbled into a disused portion of office space. A relic of the predownsizing days, she imagined. She made a note. Maybe she could use this area for training, if she could ever find it again.

Just as she was thinking about retracing her steps, she heard Phil talking. Hmm. Maybe her sense of direction was faulty, but some kind of intuition seemed to have taken her right to him.

Unable to believe her good luck, she listened more closely. It was definitely Phil. He had an odd voice. Both gravelly and higher pitched than she would have expected for such a muscular man. He spoke rapidly and softly, which had her guessing it was a personal phone call.

Probably he'd found a quiet area so as not to be over-heard through the thin cubicle partitions. Good, she could talk to him more frankly here where there was some privacy.

Following the sound of his voice, she turned yet again. It was almost spooky back here, away from the buzz of phones and the persistent background hum of computers. Her feet were soundless on the well-tracked carpet. Even the air-conditioning seemed to hold its breath.

For some reason, she felt like holding her own breath. Then she came close enough to distinguish Phil's words. He must be on the phone with a client. He was talking about money transfer and some big numbers. But Phil's next comment made her pause.

"I think one million dollars is a fair price for my silence," he said in a tone that suggested he was in the middle of an argument.

She stood, rooted, her mouth gaping. *Silence?* About what?

"I'm not some two-bit blackmailer who's going to bleed you dry. Let's call it a performance bonus. A one-time payout guarantees I'll develop a bad memory."

Oh, it must be some kind of joke. He'd probably seen her coming and cooked this up to make fun of her.

Phil laughed softly, sounding as normal as a guy swapping jokes on a golf course, and she let herself smile as relief washed over her. She stepped forward.

"I'll give you a million guarantees. If you can't trust your banker, who can you trust?"

Her stomach sank once more and her footsteps faltered to a stop.

There was a short pause, then a sound like fingernails tapping a hard surface. She shivered.

"No. I need it sooner than that... Sure, I know it's tied

up. In offshore accounts, I bet?'' The tapping increased in tempo. ''I don't blame you. North American banks aren't as safe as they used to be, are they?''

There was only one office with its door closed up ahead. He must be in there, but with open ceilings and no one else in the area, she could hear him with chilling clarity.

''No. I can't wait. You've got until tomorrow at midnight. Plenty of time to wire money to an account number I'll give you.''

Nausea churned in her stomach. Offshore accounts. Wiring money. *Bank fraud?*

Blackmail?

''No. Tomorrow night. Or I'll have to report the terrible news of the white-collar crime I uncovered in my own bank.''

Oh, no. Not someone in the bank.

''You'll go to jail.''

The tapping increased. ''I'll get you the number today. You get me the money by tomorrow night. I'll check my bank balance at midnight our time. The money needs to be there or I'll have no choice but to report you.''

As the shock started to wear off she realized she couldn't stand in the middle of the hallway where Phil would stumble over her. Holding her breath, she crept into the closest doorway, still half waiting for the shouts of ''Surprise!'' the laughter and teasing: ''You should have seen your face...''

If he walked this way, he'd see her through the half window. So she grit her teeth and forced her bruised leg to bend as she sank, painfully, to her knees.

Phil's conversation was barely distinguishable now as she crouched in the abandoned office feeling as ridiculous as a child still playing hide-and-seek after all the other children have gone on to a new game.

Only this was no game.

She had a problem. Two humongous human resources problems, actually. One of whom was Phil. The professional part of her cringed that she'd made the final decision to hire a man who'd turned out to be a blackmailer. The second problem was the unidentified person on the other end of the call. Who was it? And what had they done that they could be blackmailed over?

She rose carefully to a crouch, checking the older-style telephone on the desk, but no lights were blinking. She pushed a line and lifted the receiver, but there was no tone. If the phones in this area had been disconnected, there was no way for her to overhear both ends of the conversation. Phil must be on a cell phone.

She ducked back down and waited, her head bowed, gaze fixed on the blue-green industrial carpeting until Phil concluded his call. Then silence. She imagined him emerging stealthily, checking the corridor right and left, then sauntering casually back to his office.

Or waiting, keeping watch, in case he'd been overheard. A shiver scuttled down her spine and she glanced at her watch then made herself wait, despite how uncomfortable she was, for five full minutes. The longest five minutes of her life.

She took her time getting up, lifting her head and peeking out the window into the corridor. Empty. Slowly she rose. Determined not to act suspicious, she simply walked out of the doorway. She gazed left, breathed a sigh of relief when she saw nothing but deserted hallway ahead of her, then reversed and turned right, back the way she'd come, or so she hoped.

The abandoned office area seemed endless. Every doorway loomed, a sinister darkness waiting to swallow her. Her heart was pounding so hard her blouse was bouncing.

All the airways leading into her lungs were squeezing shut. She could feel them clamping down as dizziness assailed her.

No, she cried silently. *Not now.* She had paper bags stashed everywhere, but not in the temporary portfolio which was all she had with her.

She gasped, her racing heart feeling like a jet engine at takeoff. But if there was ever a time that a panic attack made sense, she had to admit it was now. She'd overheard a bank employee blackmail another bank employee for a million dollars. Now she was stuck in a deserted maze of twisting hallways and empty offices knowing the blackmailer was nearby.

Panic seemed an entirely appropriate response.

5

STOP IT. BREATHE. She repeated the mantra her therapist had given her. *It's a panic attack. Acknowledge it. It will pass.* She tried to find a spot to focus on, but she was too busy trying to get back to the hum of activity, the safety of the crowded workplace.

The sanctuary of her office.

Right now, she couldn't face a meeting with Ruby, concerning Phil of all people. Whatever Ruby was accusing him of, Sophie was certain it wasn't criminal activity. No way she could listen to a litany of complaints about how he filled out forms incorrectly when she was holding this awful knowledge inside her chest. Literally choking on it.

No. She had to think, to figure out what to do.

She'd reached the populated part of the third floor by pure blind luck, and there, like a magic throughway back to reality, was the door that led to the elevators. She bypassed it for the stairs. Once in the stairwell, she sat down on the first step and put her head between her knees.

She'd catch her breath then go to the in-house auditors and report what she'd overheard.

"Are you all right?" Gwen's eyes widened as Sophie staggered into view.

She shook her head, feeling weak and ill. "I'm a little under the weather. More shaken up by yesterday than I realized. Can you reschedule Ruby? Apologize." Sophie paused to drag in a breath. "Tell her anything you like."

"Sure." Gwen frowned with concern. "Did you get lost down there again?"

Sophie nodded. Had she ever.

"Why don't I call you a cab?"

"I only need to sit a minute."

Feeling completely foolish, she dug a brown paper bag out of a desk drawer and stuck it over her nose and mouth. In and out she breathed, focusing her gaze on the framed picture on her wall, a scene from *Der Rosenkavalier,* one of her favorite operas, where another Sophie falls in love amid much pomp and waltzing in Strauss's Vienna. She stared at that other Sophie, with her powdered hair and huge silver-blue skirt, thinking her problems were a lot simpler.

When Gwen pressed a glass of water in her hand she didn't resist. She hoped her assistant didn't notice the tidal waves on the surface of the water, caused by her shaking.

She dreaded riding the elevator to report her overheard conversation to the internal auditors—the bank's version of Internal Affairs—knowing she could be ending Phil's career. He could even end up in jail.

She closed her eyes and leaned back in her chair, rubbing a damp hand over her heart, wishing she could find some benign interpretation to Phil's conversation. Wishing she could delay turning the information over to the auditors. However, Phil had demanded the money by midnight tomorrow, so there was no time to delay.

Mechanically, she straightened her desk, and closed down her computer. Anxiety was making her feel rotten, but it wouldn't kill her. Once she'd completed her unpleasant errand she could go home and eat a lot of chocolate.

She entered an elevator, fortunately empty, and pushed the button for the seventh floor, which was completely taken up by the auditors. Nausea churned and it wasn't caused only by panic, but by distress at what she had to do.

As the doors opened onto the seventh floor, she took a deep breath, knowing she was about to destroy one career, probably two.

Her breath whooshed out in a gasp.

Phil Britten stepped toward the elevator, and with him was Henry Forsyth, the bank chairman. It was obvious they'd been chatting when the doors opened. What was the chairman of the bank doing chumming with an assistant account manager? And what were they both doing on the auditing floor?

Even as she stood there with a dumb smile pasted on her face, her brain raced. What if the person on the other end of Phil's phone call was one of the *auditors?* Or, equally possible, what if it was the bank chairman himself? If she went to the auditors now, she could merely end up warning the guilty party. He'd take care to cover his tracks, he'd alert Phil and...

And if it was Mr. Forsyth whom Phil had been talking to on the phone, they were the last couple she wanted witnessing her visit to the seventh floor. What reason could she possibly have for being here?

Henry Forsyth held the elevator door, politely standing back to let her out before the men stepped in. His brows were raised in mild surprise. She glanced from one to the other. Had a suspicious glance passed between them?

Suddenly she felt like a spy in enemy territory. She had no idea whom to trust, and had to treat everyone as a potential traitor. She made herself laugh, and step back in manufactured confusion. "I must have pushed the wrong button. I wanted the sixth floor." If pressed, she could come up with a reason for visiting the stock analysts on six much more easily than she could think of a reason to visit the auditors. It wasn't a department that had anything to do with her. She didn't hire them, or manage personnel issues. They were a closed shop, designed that way to prevent corruption.

She waited until they'd all shared a small laugh. For once, she was grateful that her habit of getting lost was legendary, and punched the six button.

There wasn't time for small talk, so they all stuck pleasant expressions on their faces and watched the seven fade as the elevator slid smoothly down one floor. Still, she managed to cast a searching glance at each of them under her lashes. Phil was doing isometric exercises beneath his jacket. She could see the bulge and release of his biceps.

Mr. Forsyth remained still, his pleasant smile never wavering. But what thoughts hid behind that smile? she wondered. She was just as curious to know what they'd be saying to each other if she weren't standing between them.

Secret conversations, blackmail, criminal cover-ups: they all seemed so unbelievable. Still, she left the elevator with a businesslike stride and headed straight to the department manager's office where she whiled away ten minutes discussing the Christmas holiday rotation. It was lame, but she figured it was better than marching into the women's bathroom for a few minutes and then sneaking away. At least now, if anyone checked up on her, they'd find out she'd conducted business on the sixth.

A wave of anger swept through her. Why should she be sneaking around, having pretend meetings, acting as though *she* were guilty of something? She wasn't guilty of anything except being a wimp. If the auditors and the bank chairman were both suspect, she only had one option. She returned to her office and called a cab, glad now she'd taken one in this morning because of her sore knee. She was already a basket case. Driving to an unfamiliar loca-

tion on top of her second panic attack in as many days
would about do her in.

With time running out and no idea exactly what nefar-
ious activities were being conducted at the bank, she had
to put protocol aside and concentrate on doing her best to
safeguard the interests of the investors. The sensible and
logical course of action was to go to the police.

Then she gulped, almost staggering as her heart damn
near pounded itself through her rib cage like a convict
breaking out of prison. Oh, Lord. The last time she'd got
involved with the police it hadn't worked out so well.

She left the building and stood outside waiting for her
cab, wishing she could run home and put her brand-new
lock and dead bolt to good use. She didn't want to go to
the police. She couldn't blurt this horrible news to some
front-desk sergeant, but even worse, she couldn't blurt it
to the one and only police officer she knew. The one she
never wanted to cross paths with again.

No, wait. As a yellow cab drew up in front of her, she
realized she knew two cops.

With relief, she realized she wouldn't have to see Detective Barker since he'd spent the night in hospital. She
could talk to the other detective: John something. He'd
seemed like a nice man. He'd clearly not believed Barker's
story regarding her role in the disastrous events of yesterday, but hadn't pressed her for details. She liked that kind
of restraint and had immediately liked him.

He was a kinder, gentler detective and he'd given her a
business card with his number on it. He'd waited for the
ambulance driver to disinfect and bandage her hand then
had driven her home himself.

"Head toward Cambie Street," she told the cabdriver,
sliding into the back and pulling out her brand-new cell
phone and Detective Holborn's card.

She was delighted when he picked up the phone himself on the first ring. She identified herself and if he was surprised to hear from her, he hid it well. "Something happened that I'd like to discuss with you," she said, not wanting the cabdriver to know her business.

Detective Holborn must have been accustomed to cryptic conversations for he didn't ask her a single question, merely gave her an address and asked her to meet him there in ten minutes.

TEN MINUTES LATER she stood outside the address Detective Holborn had given her. It wasn't a police station, but an apartment in a nondescript residential neighborhood. Suddenly she wished the cab ride had taken a lot longer. Like a couple of years.

She didn't want to cause trouble for the bank. Didn't want to be this close to the police after the fiasco of yesterday. Detective Barker might have fessed up and for all she knew there was an APB out for her arrest.

Stop it, she chided herself and forced her reluctant feet through the door.

"Look before you leap, Sophie," she reminded herself bitterly as she knocked on the door of apartment 303. She felt someone scrutinizing her through the peephole and then the door opened and Detective Holborn was there.

"Come in," he said to her, as though she'd arrived for a coffee party.

Inside it was an ordinary apartment, with a living room minimally furnished, a coffeepot on the go. Doors that she assumed led to a bedroom and bathroom were shut.

"Don't you work at the police station?" she asked the detective.

"This is a safe house," he said. She wondered why he

wanted to meet her here instead of at the precinct, but didn't like to ask.

She glanced around again, but her surroundings were no more glamorous despite the exciting term. She thought of a safe house as a place with a private army and high walls. This was a perfectly normal apartment, although there was a notable absence of personal items and a desk sat in the corner with a computer quietly humming.

"Sit down," said the detective.

She sat on a brown velour couch and refused his offer of coffee. She was jittery enough.

"How's your hand?" he asked politely, not seeming the slightest bit surprised to see her. If he was dying of curiosity, he hid it well. But then she imagined a detective couldn't go around with all his emotions showing on his face.

She glanced down at the bandage. "Fine, thanks."

He smiled at her in an encouraging way.

There was a short pause. "How is Detective Barker today?" she asked out of politeness. She wouldn't want anything terrible to have happened to him overnight, but if there were a special therapy he'd have to take in a different part of the country, well, that would suit her just fine.

John didn't answer right away. He settled back into an oatmeal-colored easy chair. "He doesn't take well to being incapacitated."

"They should have kept him in the hospital for anger management therapy," she said before she considered.

Even as she gasped, he'd thrown back his head on a shout of laughter. "Barker will definitely want to hear that."

"Hear what?" came a belligerent and most unwelcome voice.

Sophie jerked her head toward the doorway only to have

her worst suspicion confirmed. Detective Blake Barker leaned on crutches, wearing gray sweats that only just fit over the leg cast, a navy pullover and a scowl. He'd managed to wash his hair at least, it hung in dark waves to his shoulders.

His partner recovered from the shock first. "What the hell are you doing here? You're supposed to be in bed."

"I'm fine." Barker snapped. "What's she doing here?" He glared at her until she bristled. She was sorry. She'd apologized, visited him in hospital with a bouquet of flowers. What more did he want from her? Had her refusal to have sex with him in his hospital bed brought on all this aggression?

"We haven't got to that yet," his partner said calmly. "Here, let me help you."

Blake shook him off, still staring at Sophie as if she was a wild animal that might spring at any moment. "You just keep her on that side of the room and I might survive in one piece."

Indignation had her firming her lips. If she'd known he'd be here, dragging his foul temper with him like a barely restrained Doberman, she wouldn't have come. Besides, maybe she was being rash. There must be another avenue she could pursue. "I think I'd better go," she said, rising.

Those stormy gray-green eyes never faltered. "Sit."

There was something in the eyes that made her do just that.

The temperature in the room seemed to rise several degrees and the atmosphere could only be termed hostile. "Why do I think my day's about to go downhill?" John pondered with a sigh.

Sophie and Blake both ignored him, gazes fixed on each

other while Blake angled himself awkwardly into his chair, then let the crutches clatter to the floor.

"What are you doing here?" he asked her.

She bit her lip in uncertainty, then, knowing she wouldn't get past him until she'd told him, blurted, "I may have witnessed a crime."

She didn't know what she expected from her breathless revelation—certainly not a snort. "Don't tell me, you saw a little old lady jaywalking so you shot her?"

"No." Okay, so maybe she deserved his derision. She'd noticed the careful way he eased himself into a chair—he was probably in pain.

"Let's see. A kid littered so you broke both his arms?"

John had risen to pour himself a coffee, but she heard a hastily suppressed chuckle.

She crossed her own arms under her chest. If he knew anything about body language, he might think about shutting up already. "No."

"Hmm." He was enjoying himself, she could tell, but being the butt of these stupid jokes was starting to tick her off. "A dog tried humping your leg so you..."

Enough was enough. She opened her eyes wide and finished the sentence for him. "Cut off his balls?" she replied sweetly.

Another muffled snort could be heard from John's direction.

Heat arced between her and Detective Grumpy. He knew it and it only made him madder. If he thought she was thrilled by the unwanted sexual pull he was entirely mistaken.

Silence reigned and the word *balls* seemed to echo in the sudden stillness.

"Why are you here?" he asked her more calmly.

"I'm the human resources manager at the Investment

Bank of Vancouver." Barker's impassive face went rigid for a second and she saw him flick a glance at the other detective.

"What?" she asked, on seeing his reaction. "Are you a customer? I can assure you your money is safe."

"I'm sure it is." There was no doubt she had both men's full attention.

She stalled there, not sure how to continue. "What I wish to tell you is confidential. If the media got hold of it, I could lose my job."

She glanced up and Barker was still staring at her, but the mocking hostility had faded from his face.

"John and I aren't in the habit of running to reporters with confidential information, Ms. Morton."

She wished she hadn't come. Her brow furrowed. "I overheard one of our employees, a man I hired myself— not that that matters...his references were excellent. I never would have believed... Anyway...I overheard him blackmailing someone for a million dollars."

"A million bucks? That's a lot of money." John glanced from her to Blake.

Barker didn't say a word. He kept staring at her, forcing her to continue. "He said he knew what this person was up to and he wanted the money to keep quiet."

"What exactly did he say?"

She closed her eyes and did her best to recall every word of the one-sided conversation. As she repeated Phil's words, she was surprised at how she could hear them echoing in her mind, still feel the confusion and growing dread as though she were once again crouched in an empty office unwillingly eavesdropping.

"What's the name of the employee you overheard?" Barker searched the coffee table and John rose and retrieved a notebook from the top drawer of the desk and handed it to him along with a pen.

She hesitated, but what was the point of coming to the police if she wouldn't tell them who the blackmailer was?

"His name is Phil Britten. He's an assistant account manager in our Private Banking Division. I... In cases such as this, I'm supposed to go to the bank's auditors, but Phil was there when I got to their department, with the bank chairman. Since I don't know who he was talking to, it occurred to me it could be one of the auditors or even the chairman himself. That's why I had to come here. If Phil's expecting the money by tomorrow night, we don't have much time. Maybe you could talk to him, find out the name of the person he's blackmailing and why."

They glanced at each other and she felt the unspoken communication that passed between them.

John tapped his fingers absently against his coffee mug. "We'll need a list of all bank personnel and their positions, a list of bank clients—with the Private Banking clients highlighted—"

"I can't do that. You're asking for proprietary information. Look. All I want you to do is talk to Phil. He's young, smart, ambitious. I'm sure he'll see that he's better off cooperating with the police to root out whatever's happening at the bank than going to jail for blackmail. Can't you offer him a deal?"

Barker shifted his injured leg so the cast bumped noisily against the floor. "Why does every yahoo who watches *Law & Order* suddenly think they know more about policing than the real cops?"

She rose, feeling as though her day had been about forty-seven hours long, and it wasn't even one o'clock. "I've obviously wasted your time. Goodbye, detectives."

She almost ran from the room and paused at the front door, fumbling to get it open.

She felt a strong hand close about her arm and glanced back, with no surprise, to find Detective Barker manhandling her.

"Would you please let go of my arm?" She gave him a level look, designed to remind him what harm she was capable of inflicting, trying to ignore the heat and strength coming from him.

He removed his hand but said, "I'll walk you out."

By this time John had appeared with crutches. "Take yourself on home," he told Blake. "I'll handle this." He opened the front door, checked the hallway, nodded, then motioned them out. "We'll be in touch, Ms. Morton."

Barker grabbed the crutches with a nod, then hobbled alongside her, making her feel, once again, guilty. "How's your head?" she asked.

"Fine."

"And the leg?"

"Fine."

Mentally, she rolled her eyes. Why did she even bother trying to be pleasant? She abandoned small talk for the same taciturn silence as her companion.

Even the crutches were silent on the carpeted hallway.

Her nerves ratcheted up a notch or two. He wasn't glued to her side to be polite.

"You did the right thing, coming to us," he told her. "If you give us the information we need, we can put a stop to whatever's going on at your bank."

But how much confidential information could she pass on to the police without compromising her own ethical responsibilities to her employer?

As they neared the exit, she turned to him, certain she'd be more clearheaded without him around. "You need to rest. Why don't you leave the Investment Bank investigation to your partner. Just forget I was here."

His eyes crinkled at the corners and she was reminded again how disconcertingly attractive he could be when he wasn't scowling at her. "You are completely unforgettable."

Her eyes narrowed. From any other man that would be a compliment, but, coming from Barker, she wasn't so sure.

"Where are you parked?" he asked.

"I'm not. I came by cab." And thank goodness for that. At least now she wouldn't have to face the prospect of him walking her to her car.

"I'll drive you home."

She stopped dead and her mouth dropped open. "Thank you for the offer, but I'm fine with a cab."

He faced her, once again with that disconcerting gleam in his eye. "It wasn't an offer. Consider it an order."

Huffily, she crossed her arms. "One. I'm not getting into a car driven by a man with a broken leg. Two. I don't take orders from you."

He sighed noisily. "Are you ever, for one second of the day, not difficult?"

"Don't make me break your other leg."

He looked almost relaxed, slouched over his crutches. "One. My left leg is the broken one. I can drive fine. Two. I can take you home or arrest you. Your call."

"Arrest me?" Her voice rose and she felt her mouth drop open. "What for?"

"You just threatened a police officer with violence. And yesterday you assaulted one."

"But...but you said you wouldn't tell anyone about that."

"And I won't. I only want to drive you home."

She narrowed her gaze at him. "There must be some law against what you're doing."

He shrugged, his wavy hair shifting with the movement. "I'm the one with the badge."

"I don't—" It was pointless to keep talking; he was back in motion. She paused for a moment, wondering if she should simply return to the main entrance and call a cab, or, even better, grab his crutches and make a run for it. Some instinct told her it would be easier in the long run to let the detective drive her home.

BLAKE GLANCED AT HIS passenger. He imagined victims being dragged through the streets of Paris to the guillotine had looked happier.

His own face was doubtless no picture of radiance, either. How much could he tell her? That was the problem. How much did he even know for certain?

No. Figuring out how far he could trust her wasn't his biggest problem. His biggest problem was figuring out if his innocent-looking attacker was part of the money laundering operation running out of her firm.

For all her sweet-as-honey appearance, he couldn't be certain she wasn't involved. She'd neatly botched Li's girlfriend's arrest yesterday. She could be throwing suspicion away from herself by coming in like Suzie Q. Citizen to tell them about some bogus blackmailer.

Except why would she want to draw police attention to the bank? Unless the perps knew they were under suspicion and she was merely trying to find out what, if anything, the authorities knew.

He rubbed his temple absently, wishing he could see inside her thoughts. John would be checking her out right now, he knew. His gut, which he usually trusted, told him she was on the level.

"Headache?" she asked softly.

"Yeah."

"You should spend a few days in bed."

If she was in it with him, he could probably be persuaded. "Where do you live?" he asked. They were motoring along in his dusty SUV. She'd spent the first few minutes with her unwavering attention fixed on his driving. Since she'd stopped staring, he had to assume he'd proven he could drive an automatic without the use of his left leg. What a genius.

She gave him her address, then lapsed into silence. He let it lengthen, pegging her for the kind of woman who'd fill it sooner or later, whether with cheerful chitchat about the weather or more information on what was going on inside her bank. He was hoping for the latter.

Out of the corner of his eye, he saw her fidget. Yep, he'd guessed right. Chatter was building up inside her. She reached forward to his stack of CDs and started flipping. He saw her eyes widen as she went rapidly through them all then once again, more slowly this time, stopping to study one or two closely. He waited for the usual smart-ass comment about his choice in music.

"Is this *your* music?" She sounded half stunned.

"Yep."

"But these are opera recordings."

"That's right. Play something if you like." He stashed a grin and waited.

She sighed with all the enthusiasm of a woman approaching orgasm. "Could I play Verdi's *Don Carlo?* I can't believe you have the live recording with Carlo Bergonzi and Renata Tebaldi. It's almost impossible to find."

Now it was his turn to stare. Sure, she fit the operaphile profile better than he did, but not by much. He gulped. "You putting me on?"

She shook her head and blinked as though her eyes had deceived her and the CDs were really all heavy metal bands. She slipped a disc out of its case and slid it into the machine, and soon Verdi filled the car.

"Detective," she said, the stunned expression receding only slightly, "you may have some redeeming characteristics after all." She sighed and settled back, in apparent bliss, to listen.

He discovered that her love of opera turned him on. Oh, hell, *she* turned him on, this babe with the linebacker's tackle. He'd dreamed of her last night—when he'd been allowed to sleep. Whatever drugs they'd given him had conjured lurid fantasies of Sophie Morton and him in every exotic and erotic pose his concussed brain could create.

Turned out he was more creative when concussed and drugged than he'd ever been in his life. For instance, he'd never thought about the sexual possibilities inherent in a hospital bed before. In his dreams he'd draped Sophie all over the damn thing and raised and lowered it to the perfect height for a variety of activities.

Maybe that was why he'd wanted to be alone with her for a few minutes today. He needed to dispel the urge he had every time he saw her to take her mouth with his and then climb on top of her.

He smiled to himself. Must be some kind of death wish.

"Is something funny?" she asked tartly.

He glanced over and there was her mouth, all glossy and pink. "I dreamed about you last night."

He left it at that, wondering how she'd reply, or if she would.

Only a second or two passed before she asked softly, "What did you dream?"

"After the way you left me, what do you think?" She

must have seen his almost painful state of arousal in that flimsy hospital gown.

She bit her pretty pink lip and shot him a glance of half mischief and half guilt. "Strangling me?"

He chuckled. "I only think those thoughts when I'm awake. In my dream you didn't go home and leave me…frustrated."

"I didn't?" she replied in a soft, turned-on kind of voice.

He shook his head, letting the images come back to him. "You and I did things in that hospital bed that have never been done before."

She gave a gurgle of amusement. "What about your leg?"

"Everything was in working order." In his dream, he was Viagra on legs.

"Were we…" she petered out on a blush, but he knew exactly what she was wondering.

"We were spectacular." He answered her unspoken question not without a certain amount of pride. Dreams could be good for the ego.

"You should still be in bed dreaming, and I should have caught a cab," she said tartly, but he wasn't fooled. He heard the wanting. It echoed his own.

He changed to the left lane, preparing to drive her to False Creek where she lived. "I want to talk to you about this blackmail plot."

"I'm not sure I can—"

"Unofficially. I haven't known you a long time, but in my short acquaintance I've noticed you have a…well, I think it's fair to say you have an impulsive personality."

She nodded, her big blue eyes guilty, as though he'd discovered a terrible secret. How could she appear so innocent and give him such erotic dreams? Amazing.

"Be careful. Maybe it's nothing, maybe it's something, but for now don't tell anyone what you overheard."

She turned to stare out the passenger window, but he didn't think she was checking out the silver BMW in the next lane. The next instant she turned back. "You suspect something. At the bank."

Was she teasing him? Baiting him? Or just smart? "What makes you say that?"

"You looked funny when I mentioned Investment Bank of Vancouver, and you glanced at your partner. Also," her brow furrowed and he had a feeling she was working this out as she went, "you didn't ask the obvious questions, the general stuff about our firm. I got the feeling you already knew the answers."

Oh, man. He really didn't need this. "I think you should keep your suspicions to yourself and keep a low profile at work."

"I'm right, aren't I? You do suspect something."

Did they suspect something? Oh, yeah. For two years he'd been working on different files, always on the Black Dragons, gathering information, cultivating informants. The last three months he'd been undercover on the streets, working his way into position as a dealer to trust. And yesterday three months of careful work had gone to hell.

He was the only cop who'd seen Li in person. At least he had that.

But even if his part of the investigation had suffered a terminal setback, there were other cops, other files. One of which was the money-laundering investigation. The guys in commercial crime and fraud had dug up a whole lot of links between the Black Dragons and the Investment Bank of Vancouver.

He pulled up in front of her building and cut the engine. His head would be only too happy to ache if he gave it half a chance and his eyes were gritty from lack of sleep and the aftereffect of painkillers. He rubbed them with the palms of his hands to buy him some time, as well as to try and clear his foggy thoughts.

"Did you get any sleep in the hospital?" Her soft, sexy voice was full of concern.

"Not really." He'd been poked and checked and mauled when awake and when he was asleep he'd been having acrobatic sex with Sophie. Her nearness tantalized him with wanting to turn those fantasies into pulse-pounding reality.

"Did the noise keep you awake? Hospitals are very un-relaxing."

Oh, the hell with it. What more could she do to him? "Something was bothering me all night. A question." He turned to her slowly, unsnapping his seat belt as he did so. "Only you can answer it."

Her eyes widened slightly as he unsnapped her seat belt and turned his body to face her.

"All night I kept wondering how you'd taste." He didn't stop to ask for permission, or even gauge her re-action, beyond the widened eyes and parted lips of shocked disbelief.

He intended to take full advantage of those lips.

He leaned forward and cupped her chin, refusing to even think about how stupid this was. Her nearness, her scent, the sight of that damn mouth was driving him crazy. He'd probably guarantee himself another sleepless night kissing her like this, but at the moment he really didn't care.

He took her mouth. Just took. No asking, no excuses, no apology. He slipped his lips over hers for a long, thor-ough taste.

As he'd suspected—as he'd feared—she tasted like heaven.

Her lips were warm and resilient, pulling him into madness.

What he'd imagined she'd do when he kissed her he had no idea, but still she surprised him. She stiffened and he waited for her to shove him away and then slap his face. But she didn't do either of those things.

She sighed, right into his mouth, and everything went soft. Her lips relaxed and parted beneath his, inviting him deeper, the tension in her muscles eased and she melted into his arms.

He wasn't a man to turn down an invitation like that. Deepening the kiss, he teased her with his tongue, trailing it along her bottom lip before venturing inside where she was warm and sweet. She tasted of cool mint toothpaste. That was the first taste his desire-sharpened senses noted, but like a wine connoisseur, he concentrated, letting his mouth experience all the complexity of flavors. Under the mint was the deeper, richer taste of bitter coffee, and under that, the most complex and desired flavor of all: woman, hot and wanting.

All his animal impulses roared to the forefront of his mind. He pushed a hand into her hair, letting the soft silk bunch and play between his fingers. He let the hand that still cupped her chin travel. As lazy as his tongue in her mouth it trailed down her throat where a pulse beat frantically, skimmed her sweater and found buttons.

He liked buttons. Much better than feeling up a woman under a T-shirt—that always reminded him of high school. Not that necking in cars in broad daylight was exactly adult. Still, he considered briefly, he could always blame his behavior on the concussion.

He skimmed over the buttons, toying with them, with her and with himself as her breathing thickened. Softly, he let his hand drift to the fullness of her centerfold breasts, where her hardened nipples were nearly as prominent as the buttons. As he touched her, he felt the tug on his scalp as her hands pulled at his hair, and she moaned, her voice blending with the opera.

Dimly, he wondered why he'd ever lost the habit of necking with girls in cars. It was outside but nicely enclosed to keep out bugs and rain. Intimate and yet the possibility of discovery was always present. Anyone could be watching them. Even though they were only kissing, the exhibitionist in him responded—as well as the atavistic male desire to show off his hunting trophy.

And he'd bagged himself a hot one. King of the hunters, top of the jungle hierarchy, that's how he felt with Sophie in his arms.

Somewhere, a horn honked, loud enough to penetrate the lust-filled atmosphere and to bring cold reason to one of them at least.

Sophie pulled away from his mouth slowly, her lips wet and swollen from his kisses, her eyes heavy and passion-drunk. She'd gone from innocent angel to sensual earth goddess in just a few minutes and, though he instinctively covered his *cojones,* she didn't seem angry.

She looked richly pleased with herself. "Well?" she asked, pushing her disordered hair behind her ears.

"Well what?" If she'd asked him something, he couldn't for the life of him recall what. He hoped it was some version of "would you like to come up and see my etchings?"

"Did you get the answer to your question?"

His question? He must have looked as dim-witted as he felt for she laughed softly.

"What do I taste like?"

He licked his lips, as though trying to recall her taste when in reality it was forever imprinted on his memory.

Her breathing hitched as she watched the gesture.

He leaned closer. "You taste like...more."

She chuckled, deep in her throat, the satisfied sound of a woman comfortable in her own sexual power, and reached for the door handle.

"Maybe you'll get another taste some time."

He watched her all the way into her building and he could have sworn there was an extra twitch in her tail just to drive him even wilder. His left leg wasn't the only thing she'd rendered stiff and aching.

One thing he knew for certain. There'd be no maybe about it. He and his sexy angel had some serious hanky-panky in their future.

And he was done with tasting. He was ready for the seven-course meal.

6

SOPHIE HAD BARELY swallowed her first sip of French roast when her phone buzzed. Something about the tone of the buzz suggested there was bad news on the other end. She slugged a big hit of caffeine as she picked up the receiver. "Sophie Morton."

"Sophie? It's Ruby."

Yep, she thought. Her intuition was bang on. Forcing her voice to remain pleasant, she replied, "Good morning, Ruby."

"If you hadn't cancelled our meeting yesterday I could have told you how unreliable Phil Britten is becoming. Comes and goes whenever he pleases, spends far too long on simple paperwork, and he's pushy. I'm not saying ambition's a bad thing, but…"

Sophie mentally calculated when Ruby might retire. She was second only to Ellsworth in business volume and if she invested her own savings as shrewdly as she did her clients', she must be in good shape.

She fantasized about Ruby's retirement party while the complaints continued in her ear. From long experience, she'd learned to let Ruby vent all her complaints with no interruptions save a gentle "Uh-huh," or "Oh, my goodness," until the woman simply ran out of energy.

"This morning he hasn't even shown up," she continued. "I've got a big client presentation I need his help on.

No call, no apology, nothing. I don't know what kind of—''

Sophie sat bolt upright in her chair, putting her stainless steel vacuum mug down on her desk with a thunk.

"Did you call Phil at home?" she interrupted, feeling a niggle of unease lodge in her belly. She hadn't slept well last night, worrying about what she'd overheard, but Detective Barker had all but ordered her to do nothing, and she had to assume the police would be watching Phil. Had they arrested him?

"Of course I did." Ruby's voice was scornful. "I ran this department long before we needed human resources counselors to tell us how to manage staff. I got his answering machine."

"Is he often late?" Sophie recalled seeing him a couple of times when she'd come in early to catch up. He'd always been cheerful and wide-awake, sucking on some revolting-looking health drink.

There was a pause, which was as good as a negative. "Well, no. But he's very unreliable." The niggle grew stronger. If Sophie hadn't overheard him yesterday blackmailing someone she would pass the call off as another example of Ruby's spite. But she had overheard that conversation yesterday, and then over and over again throughout the night. Was Phil even now packing his bags? Prepared to leave the country with money that didn't belong to him?

Detective Barker may have told her to mind her own business and stay out of whatever Phil was involved in. In fact the detective *had* told her in no uncertain terms to stay out of it. But how could she? If they'd arrested him, wouldn't she have heard about it?

She sipped coffee and stared sightlessly ahead. She'd hired Phil for the job that may have lured him into temp-

tation. He was only in his mid-twenties, far too young to
throw his future away. Surely she owed it to him to try to
talk him out of a life of crime. If she could convince him
to go to the police, it would be best for everyone concerned.

"I'll try to get hold of him, Ruby. Thanks for letting
me know. I'll be in touch as soon as I hear something."

There was a snort on the other end. "I certainly hope
I'll be hearing about a written warning going in his file."

Sophie pulled the receiver away from her ear and stuck
her tongue out. It was childish and rude, but it made her
feel better. "Let's find out why he's late first. Let me know
if you hear from him."

She took the second snort as a yes, disconnected and
then sat staring at the silent phone as though willing it to
ring with an apologetic Phil on the phone, calling with a
flat tire.

Except he bicycled to work. He liked the extra workout,
he'd told her. How hard could it be to change a flat bicycle
tire?

From her computer, she pulled up his address and phone
number and printed them out. Then she called his home,
but, like Ruby, she got a cheery recorded greeting.

With his personnel file still on her computer screen she
scrolled through his particulars. He was twenty-five years
old. He'd been subjected to a rigorous background check,
aptitude and personality testing, as were all their staff, and
he'd come out squeaky clean. A nice, clean-cut young
health nut.

She worked for half an hour, the sense of unease growing by the minute, then called again and once more got
the answering machine.

It wasn't her job to go chasing after white-collar criminals, regardless of whether she'd hired them, yet she did

have a professional responsibility both to the bank and to Phil. She hated feeling that he might be throwing his life away. Maybe if she talked to him...

Perhaps he'd open up to her. Maybe he had a good reason for needing money, perhaps he had an ill relative or...

Her own groan stopped her. She knew she had a bad habit of believing the best of people, but sometimes she was right. If he did need money and it was desperation that had driven him to foolishness, perhaps she could help him realize the error of his ways. He worked for a bank, for goodness' sake, if he needed financial help, didn't he realize they could probably work something out?

She might be impulsive, as the detective with the sharp eyes and clever lips had pointed out, but she wasn't stupid. She'd make sure her whereabouts were known. "Gwen, I think Phil Britten might be sick. He's not answering his phone and he doesn't have a car, so I'm going to his place to make sure he's all right. If I don't call you in thirty minutes, call me at Phil's, will you? Here's the number."

Gwen looked faintly puzzled, but glanced at the clock and wrote herself a yellow sticky reminder note and pasted it onto her computer monitor. "Sure."

One of the things Sophie treasured about Gwen was that she did what was asked of her without a lot of fuss or questions.

"Want a crust of bread so you can leave a trail?"

Sophie sighed, accustomed to corny jokes about her hopeless sense of direction. "No. I printed out a map from the Internet."

FORTUNATELY, PHIL LIVED not far from the bank in an area that she was familiar with, so she didn't take a single wrong turn. Feeling inordinately pleased with herself, she found a parking spot across from the West End low-rise.

Nothing she'd rehearsed on the way sounded right for talking a possible blackmailer out of a life of crime, so she decided to wing it. She'd counseled employees through various professional and personal crises, but this would be a first.

Her stomach did a flip-flop when she saw an ambulance outside Phil's apartment building, its lights flashing but the siren turned off. The apartment building's door was propped open. Had Phil had an accident after all? She stared at the ambulance again, but it appeared to be empty.

Turning her back on it, she strode briskly through the doorway. There could be a hundred people living in this building, any one of them could be in need of medical attention. It was probably nothing to do with Phil's absence from work. Still, she'd be happier when she'd spoken to him.

She almost ran into the building, and crashed into a warm body coming out.

"Oomph," he said on impact. There was a dull thud-thud as, one after the other, two crutches fell to the carpeted foyer. Detective Blake Barker teetered, and jammed his injured foot to the ground to stop himself tumbling after the crutches.

Instinctively, she reached for him to keep him upright and the pair of them staggered into the heavy plate glass of the building front. She was too scared to look at his face—she didn't need that much rage this early in the day.

Could her luck get any worse? It couldn't be coincidence that she kept bumping into this man. She must have done something really bad in a former life and this was her punishment.

She stared straight ahead at the fascinating view of the

top three buttons of his sports shirt. The first was unbuttoned and she was treated to a sexy glimpse of dark chest hair and tan flesh. A pulse thudded in his neck. If a pulse could show anger, this one did. Thud, thud, thud like a scolding voice.

Soon—much sooner than she would have liked—it was joined by the verbal scolding of Detective Barker himself, his voice low and menacing. "Just what the hell are you doing here?"

She jerked her chin up at that, which was a mistake. Big mistake. It pushed her gaze up until she was staring at one humdinger of an angry scowl. She could ask him the same question. "My job. I'm here doing my job."

His eyes narrowed in what she could have sworn was suspicion. The sexy and warmly exciting man who'd kissed her less than twenty-four hours ago was nowhere in evidence. "You're the coroner now?"

"Coroner? What are you—"

Just then the elevator doors slid open and two ambulance attendants emerged wheeling a stretcher.

"Oh, no. What…" She couldn't finish the sentence. She wanted to ask what had happened, but the words jammed in her throat as though by avoiding the question she could avoid the answer. Except, of course, the detective wouldn't let her.

"Your buddy. Phil Britten."

She stared at the approaching stretcher, hoping he'd suffered some minor accident, only to see that a sheet was pulled all the way over the body. No. Not a body. A body bag.

"It's not…" She began, then swallowed, her throat so parched her words sounded hoarse. "That isn't…" No more words came. She stared at Blake in mute appeal.

He answered the question she couldn't voice. "Britten's dead."

The floor seemed to tilt and her head felt as if somebody'd stuck it under Niagara Falls. Those warm hands of his gripped her tighter.

She tried not to look at the sad lump on the stretcher wheeling past where they stood. Tried not to think of the man who'd been so proud of his physique he did isometric exercises in the elevator.

One of the attendants stooped to pick up Blake's crutches and handed them to him with a curious glance.

Blake freed one hand to retrieve the crutches with a brief nod of thanks, his attention still on Sophie.

"Come and sit down." There was a rattan seating area to the right of the elevators, with one of those indoor fountains burbling and a few ferns. She knew the fountain was meant to be spiritually soothing, but in her frazzled state it sounded as irritating as a tap left running. She perched on the couch and Blake sank down beside her, his leg sticking straight out in front of him. He laid the crutches on the floor and turned to her. "Want some water or something?"

"No. I'm…" She couldn't say she was fine, that would be a lie. She'd never been less fine. She gripped her hands in her lap and stared at them. "What happened?"

"Why are you here?"

She rubbed her forehead, trying to dredge up the answer to his simple question. Why on earth was she here? "Phil." That's right, it was Phil. "I…he didn't show up at work this morning, or answer his phone. I was worried about him so I came to check…" She couldn't finish the sentence. She'd wanted to make sure he was okay, when he so blatantly wasn't okay. He wasn't ever going to be okay again.

He was dead.

"Do you know how he…what happened?"

He kept staring at her. His eyes not stormy, but still cold. "We won't know for certain until the autopsy's done but it looks like a drug overdose."

"Drugs?"

He had his detective face on now, she realized—his cold, serious face. Not at all like the sexy, passionate man who'd kissed her in the car yesterday.

"Drugs?" she repeated. "Maybe that's why he needed the blackmail money, because he was a drug addict." But even as she said them the words felt wrong.

Shock was like a glass wall between her and the rest of the world and it was tough to get messages back and forth across the invisible barrier. But even as detached and surreal as this whole thing appeared, it made no sense that the Phil she'd hired, with his bicycle and health foods, was a drug addict. "No." She shook her head, barely realizing she wasn't alone.

"What do you mean no?"

"Phil is…was a health nut. He wouldn't do something that harmful to his body. I'm sure of it."

"How are you sure?"

"Drug testing is part of the interview process at the bank. Phil was clean when we hired him four months ago. And he was into health and fitness." She called up images of Phil, but they all involved him doing something healthy or show-offy with his body. The only odd behavior since he'd started work was the phone call she'd overheard. "But…"

"But?"

"His boss complained that he was unreliable and mentioned unexplained absences, but I didn't think much of it. She complains about everyone. I can't believe he'd do drugs. Unless…'' She recalled a television special she'd seen once about amateur weightlifters and steroids. ''They weren't the performance enhancing kind were they? He was an amateur body builder.''

Blake shook his head, seemed as though he were debating with himself then shrugged slightly as though he'd come to a decision he wasn't entirely comfortable with. ''Heroin.''

Her eyes bugged out. ''Heroin?'' To go from slurping health drinks to shooting up heroin… ''This doesn't make sense.''

Beside her Blake blew out a breath. He didn't say a word, but she had the strong suspicion that he agreed.

''Heroin deaths are way up this year. There's a particularly pure grade coming from South East Asia. It's easy to make a mistake.'' He glanced at her, as though to make sure she was keeping up.

She nodded.

''I've read about that in the paper.'' Her stomach clenched as she recalled the article. ''Isn't there some new triad bringing the drugs in?''

He nodded. ''The Black Dragons.''

The name had a horribly familiar sound to it. ''The woman you almost arrested. Is she one of them?''

''Girlfriend of the top guy. Yeah.''

''Blake, I'm sorry.''

''I know.'' He patted her knee, a reassuring gesture that only made her feel worse.

''So, Phil had a connection to these people, too. What an amazing coincidence.''

He shot her an impassive cop glance. ''Looks like it.''

''Now what?'' she asked him, almost as though they were a team working this case together. ''With Phil gone, how are we going to find out what he knew?''

He quickly disabused her of any notion of teamwork.

"You'd better get your delectable ass back to work where it belongs. I told you yesterday, stay out of this." Once again a storm had blown in, reflecting gray over the icy green eyes.

In spite of the warm glow caused by him calling part of her delectable, she didn't appreciate his tone. "This *is* my business. Phil is…was an employee. As the human resources manager I'd say his demise was very much my business." Rapidly her brain began sorting all the tasks associated with the tragedy. "I'll have to arrange a memorial service, flowers, a message for our in-house magazine. I'll also have to hire a replacement."

He hadn't seemed to be listening all that closely to her litany of tasks, until the last part when he jerked to attention, his gaze once again firmly focused on her face. "That's right. You'll hire a replacement."

"I certainly will," she said grimly, determined to double up on screening tests and give every interviewee the kind of third degree that would reveal the slightest personality flaws.

"Good. Don't delegate to an underling."

She glared at him, thankful for the shard of anger that pierced her numb sense of grief. "Are you ever, for one second, not bossy?"

The corners of his mouth kinked, putting two deep creases in his cheeks. "What did he do? This Phil?"

"I told you yesterday. He was an assistant account manager in Private Banking. That division works with high net worth individuals, families and some companies. They help with investments, family trusts, estate planning, stuff like that. Phil was also a bit of a computer techie." She shrugged. "Outside of work, he was an amateur bodybuilder and health fanatic."

He shifted, rubbing his thigh absently. She watched one strong square hand massaging the quadricep muscle, saw it stop when it hit the top of the cast almost as though he'd forgotten he wore it. "Look, can you hold off for a few days on this? I'm going to talk to some people. It might be worthwhile getting somebody in the bank working undercover."

"Poor Phil. He must have been celebrating his big windfall with a drug party." She wondered if he'd received the money before he died. "He's probably got his financial records in his apartment. Maybe you can find out if he got his million dollars and try to track the payment." Even as she said it she knew how unlikely it would be that the blackmail payoff could be traced.

"John's up there now." His fingertips began tapping on the top of the cast, outlined clearly beneath the gray sweatpants he was wearing again. "What do you think? Could you get somebody in undercover?"

He was going to need a wardrobe full of baggy pants for a few weeks, she thought idly as she considered the logistics of bringing in an undercover police officer. "Without the approval of the executive committee?"

"We don't know who was on the other end of the call you overheard. It could have been anyone from the CEO to the janitor. Until we know the thief's identity and what he was up to, this stays top secret."

"I'd be putting my job in jeopardy, you know."

"You already did that yesterday, when you came to us. In fact, you seemed pretty fired up about your civic duty when I first...ah...met you." He glanced significantly at his cast.

She blushed, knowing he was right. If there was foul play going on at her bank she wanted to help stop it. Besides, there was an unspoken trade-off. He hadn't so much as hinted at it so maybe it was only in her mind. But she couldn't help thinking she owed Detective Barker a break on a case.

A break that didn't involve his bones.

She nodded and rose to leave. "All right, Detective, you have a few days before I do anything about hiring a replacement for Phil."

His voice stopped her. "Hey."

She turned back to him, brows raised in enquiry.

He glanced around the lobby, where a uniformed officer watched the door and a couple of apartment residents gossiped by the mailboxes. He grabbed the crutches and got to his feet, then made his way to where she stood halfway to the door.

Maybe he wanted to give her something else to think about, for he swung his body closer, so close his cast touched her knee and she could feel his body heat. "I'll call you."

She stared at him in surprise and was almost scorched when their gazes collided. She swallowed. "Will it be a business or a personal call?"

"Very personal. I'll be calling to find out what you plan to do about *us.*" He spoke in a low voice that sent entirely pleasant shivers racing down her arms.

She pretended to think about it, tilting her head to one side to study him. "I plan to stay out of cars if you're in them," she said.

He was so close she could see flecks of black in his irises, make out the specks of stubble he'd missed when he shaved this morning. "I think you want me."

Her brows rose, but it was tough not to fall for his charm when he bothered to turn it on. She had to stifle the urge to touch him, run her fingers through his hair or even just send him that certain smile she kept for special occasions. Her come-and-get-it smile.

But he didn't deserve it. Not yet. Every time they'd seen each other, she'd been the one to initiate it, albeit unintentionally. If the dishy detective wanted to see her on a personal level—as his passionate kiss and flirting words suggested—he'd better start making an effort.

"I want a lot of things that are bad for me. Dark chocolate, waffles piled with whipping cream, French fries loaded with ketchup to name a few." Now she did touch him, tapping the tip of her manicured forefinger against the end of his arrogant nose. "But I can resist. I have willpower."

She patted his cheek and turned away, heading once more for the door. The ball, she decided, was firmly in his court.

She drove back to the bank feeling more than a little unnerved. An employee she'd hired had turned out to be a blackmailer and a drug addict, and a cop had made a pass at her, and it wasn't even—she glanced at the dashboard clock on her rental—ten o'clock. It was shaping up to be quite a day.

7

SOPHIE OPENED THE DOOR almost as soon as he knocked, as though she'd been standing there, waiting for him to drop by. He grinned to himself, wishing that were true. "Hi."

"Detective?" Her eyes widened in surprise. She stared at his newly cut hair, then her gaze took in the rest of him. Sports jacket over the widest khakis he'd been able to find. "I'd never believe you were the same man."

"This is my usual look."

"How did you get my apartment number, Detective?" Her husky sweet voice made him think of an after-dinner liqueur. Sweet to the initial taste but with a wicked kick to it. He licked his lips, thinking how often she reminded him of sweet things to eat. And that naturally led him to imagine how sweet *she'd* be to eat. Every delectable inch of her.

"Sophie, I've had my tongue in your mouth. Don't you think we could move to a first-name basis?"

"That would depend on the nature of your call," she said, as sassy as a fresh bottle of soda.

"My call is of a personal nature," he told her, which was partly true. In his line of work he was accustomed to making truth fit his immediate requirements. Right now he needed her to cooperate with his investigation. But he also wanted to investigate her personally. Naturally, she'd need to be naked for him to do his best work.

"How *did* you find me? My name's not on the door."

"I know lots of things about you. I'm a detective, re-member." He recalled the DMV printout. "I know your birth date, for instance."

"Hmm." She sounded most unimpressed. "I knew yours first."

True. He could tell her her driver's license photo didn't do her justice, but that wouldn't be news, either. He went with a piece of information that had kept him awake part of the night while his leg had decided to remind him he'd overdone it all day. "I know that you wear lacy bras with practical cotton panties."

She drew in a breath. Had he offended her or intrigued her? Hard to tell. She had an appealing freshness to her, but also a certain attitude and way of looking at him that suggested she knew her way around men. And then there was the way she kissed...

She was wearing workout gear, and her face was still lightly flushed from exertion. She appeared relaxed, makeup free and her hair was in a stumpy ponytail. Her eyes were wary, though, and she didn't rush to open the door wider. "Does this personal call of yours have any other purpose than to pass judgment on my underwear?"

"Now, you're not being fair. I'm not judging you. Merely pointing out one way in which you intrigue me."

"Well, I hope you took a good look because that's as close as you'll ever get to seeing my underwear again."

He chuckled softly, enjoying her faux indignation as much as her breathy sexiness. "That sounded like a chal-lenge."

"Don't flatter yourself."

"Why don't I come in and we can talk about it." In the three days since he'd seen her, he was convinced she'd grown sexier. Or maybe she flaunted her sexuality under his nose merely for the pleasure of torturing him. He wondered if she had any idea how effectively it was working.

"You want to come in and...talk." Her voice registered patent disbelief while her tongue slipped out to touch her upper lip as though it were the cherry on top of a sundae.

He grinned, promising himself he was going to have her on her back very soon. He remembered his cast—damn, he'd have to let *her* get *him* on his back. He thought he could live with the change of plans. "We'll start with talk and see where it leads."

Still, she didn't invite him in, but sent him a glance full of satin sheets and quiet moans. "Might this talk lead to kissing?"

"I'd say that's a definite possibility."

"Then I'll have to decline your flattering offer." She started to shut the door.

There was one benefit to having a broken leg that he quickly discovered. When he forced the cast into the narrowing doorway, it made a nice wide opening. "Why?" He couldn't believe she'd tried to shut the door in his face. "You seemed to like kissing me four days ago."

"Oh, I really liked kissing you. That's the problem."

"I don't follow."

"Kissing leads to sex." The way her voice had dropped to a husky whisper had his hands itching to reach for her.

His own voice sounded like that of a three-pack-a-day smoker when he answered. "I like the way you think."

"I *think* sex would complicate an already complicated relationship."

She was right, of course, but he didn't care. A woman who appreciated the direct and preferably speedy connection between kissing and sex was his kind of woman. "What's complicated about it?"

"We don't even like each other."

"Like has nothing to do with it. What's going on between us is pure, high-octane lust. I want you, Sophie. I can't sleep at night for thinking about it."

A few strands of hair had fallen from her mini-ponytail to trail her cheekbones. In an absent gesture she lifted both arms and tucked the strands behind her ears. She wore pearl studs in her lobes, he noted, similar in size and shape to the nipples that beaded beneath her black workout shirt and caught his attention as she lifted her arms.

She might talk tough and disinterested, but her body was as hungry for him as his was for her.

He didn't need further invitation, but entered her apartment and closed the door behind him. Kathleen Battle's soprano soared from another room. This was good. A woman who listened to passionate opera when alone might be eased into passionate sex.

He stepped closer to her, and she tipped her head back, her eyes full of challenge. "Damn it, I want you." He pulled her to him and kissed her, not lazily exploring this time, but letting her feel his urgency and the need she'd ignited in him.

Her lips trembled beneath his, a mere hint of her taste trickling into him like water into a dehydrated man. Even as her body clung to his, she broke the kiss and pulled her head back. "You're arrogant, high-handed and aggressive," she said, the last word purring beneath his lips as he ran them down her throat.

"Uh-huh," he said, his voice vibrating against her sensitive skin and making her shiver while she clutched his shoulders.

"And those are your good points."

He nipped her lightly, just at the junction of neck and shoulder, where a hint of cologne remained. He was right about the recent exercise. He smelled the clean sweat of a workout, felt the warmth and relaxation in her muscles.

"You're impulsive, irrational, and…"

He drew back, eyes narrowing.

Insult and desire warred in her expression but desire was clearly winning. "And what?"

"And so sexy I can't keep my hands off you." To prove his point, he ran his hands over her breasts, enjoying the breathy gasp as his fingers closed over the soft mounds, barely restrained in a sports bra.

"And that's a bad thing?" She sounded as if she were torn between amusement and insult.

"The worst. You distract me."

She kissed his lips softly, almost as though she couldn't help herself, made a sound that was three parts sigh, one part moan. "You distract me, too." She gasped as his fingers closed gently on the firm points of her nipples, squeezing and pulling. He enjoyed her soft moans as her head fell back.

Her breasts swelled over the sports top, offering him irresistible temptation. He was almost embarrassed by how much he'd spent in the last few days thinking about Sophie and his plans for that mouth, and that body.

He leaned down, putting most of his weight on his good leg, and ran his tongue along the edge of her black top.

Response quivered through her and he felt her hands on his scalp, pulling him closer. When he got to the crease where her breasts met he licked between them and she emitted a strangled cry.

"I should shower," she said.

"Don't waste the water," he mumbled against her warm, creamy flesh. "I'll wash you with my tongue."

Her rising excitement and rapid breathing were very close to putting her sports bra out of a job. Those glorious, hard peaks were barely covered. He closed his lips over them, breathing warm, moist breath through her clothing.

"Oh, that feels so good," she cried and her shoulders rolled. He grinned against the rough, stretchy fabric knowing she was trying to free her breasts, as anxious to have his mouth on her naked flesh as he was to put it there.

He teased them both for a little longer until he could stand it no longer, then using his teeth, grabbed the edge of the exercise top and the bra together and tugged.

She cried even louder as the air hit her newly naked breasts. He would have cried out, too, except he'd lost his voice.

Not even his fantasies had prepared him for the sight of perfect, peach-tipped breasts thrusting forward proudly.

For a long moment he simply stared, then, as her clutching fingers became more urgent, he traced the puckered flesh around her nipple before sucking it into his mouth.

He thought she was going to go over the edge right there and then. Her hands were digging into his hair, then moving to his shoulders, clawing at his back. He held the nipple against the roof of his mouth, squeezing it with his tongue and she liked that so much she tried to thrust her hips against his pelvis.

Since his crutches were leaning against the wall, there was nothing to hold him up when she knocked him off balance, and, for the second time in a week, he found himself crashing to the floor, with Sophie sprawled on top of me.

Only this time he laughed and pulled her to him for a kiss.

But one look at her face told him she wasn't finding the situation at all humorous. She appeared shaken and angry.

"What are we doing?" she asked, rolling off him and struggling to her feet.

Since her naked breasts were bouncing in his line of vision, glistening a deep cherry red from where his tongue had wet them, he assumed it was a rhetorical question and used his energy to haul himself to his feet and grab his crutches.

She pushed her breasts back into her workout gear, where they seemed reluctant to go, and turned to him, looking flustered and aroused.

"You're investigating a case against my employer."

He kept his tone light, despite his own straining frustration. "At the moment, I'm investigating you. And I haven't finished."

She glared at him. "I don't get involved sexually with men I work with. We're working together."

He wasn't entirely happy with her logic. Especially as he had an inkling where this was going. "Theoretically," he hedged.

"It's a personal rule I've never broken."

Damn, the woman was throwing out challenges like they were last year's fashions. He could barely keep up.

"Oh, come on. This so-called working relationship is tenuous at best."

She shot him a professional-woman-in-business look. "Don't tell me you'd ever sleep with a colleague?"

One day she'd find out that his former longterm girl-friend answered to "Sergeant" and it wasn't a nickname. "I'm saying, that I want to sleep with *you.*"

"Is that why you came here? To seduce me?"

"No." His leg was starting to throb. Probably, he should have had that prescription for superstrength pain-killers filled, but he hated feeling groggy. He needed his wits sharp for this case. Especially now he had Sophie on the inside to worry about. "Could we sit down?"

She must have seen the him-trying-to-get-her-in-bed

part of the evening was over. No, not over. Merely on hiatus. He'd had his tongue on her breasts, heard her moans escalate along with her desire. Taking her to bed was only a question of time.

"Of course." She gazed about her entrance foyer, the black-and-white tiled floor, the art deco mirror reflecting soft gray walls, as though she'd forgotten they were there. "Come in." She led him down a short hallway to a square living area. It looked almost as though she hadn't been able to decide on a style so just bought whatever caught her fancy. An antique chaise in striped silk with a rolled mahogany edging was obviously her reading chair. There was a standard lamp with a beaded fringed lampshade about a century newer than the chaise, and beside it was an ultramodern small table in some kind of shiny black substance. A largish paperback—looked like one of those pseudo-literary novels book clubs loved so much—sat on the table.

A more traditional sofa that was somehow French with yellow-and-blue flowered upholstery, and an ancient green velvet wing chair surrounded the gas fireplace. A chunk of thick glass on a stone pedestal completed the furnishings. She obviously had a green thumb. Houseplants bloomed everywhere.

The opera, which now he recognized as *The Magic Flute,* spilled from a sleek but compact stereo with killer sound. As chaotic as the whole room seemed, it somehow worked. It suited Sophie. He swung himself toward the couch, passing a galley kitchen with modern appliances, granite counters and more of the black-and-white tile. "Nice place," he said. "Stylish."

She chuckled, pushing her hands through her hair nervously as though waiting for him to turn back into the sex maniac who'd done his best to ravish her in the entrance hall. He'd like nothing better, but it was clear she wasn't ready for that. Yet.

"Can I get you something to drink?"

"Nothing, thanks. Sit down."

She dropped the hostess role and came to sit opposite him on the wing chair, tucking her stocking feet under her.

Even though his breathing hadn't completely settled and he suspected it would be days before his Sophie-inspired erection completely subsided, he turned his mind to business. "The sergeant's assigned a detective to your bank to take Phil Britten's position. This person will work undercover and no one but you will know. Could you handle that?"

She sighed, a crease forming between her brows as the flush slowly subsided from her face and upper chest. "I've thought a lot about this. I suppose it is the right decision even though I'll hate doing something so underhanded. Tell me about the detective." Her sexy teasing was gone, and he knew he had her full attention as she focused on his face.

"He's pretty good with computers, and he's worked on some finance cases before, so he should be able to fake it for a couple of weeks."

"Uh-huh. So it's a man?"

"Yes."

"How old is he?"

"Thirty-two."

Her eyes flared for a second, but she nodded. "Has he ever worked in a bank?"

"He's helped bust a couple of money laundering operations, so he knows his way around the systems."

Even when she was completely focused on business, he wanted her. There should be a law against those exercise tops that showed half a woman's belly. Especially when

that belly was both slender and muscular, taunting him to
span it with his hands, to run his tongue over its firm lines
of muscle. To strip her naked and finish what they'd so
spectacularly begun. With an effort he pulled his gaze back
to her face and his mind back to the bombshell he was
about to drop in her lap.

"He's recovering from an injury so he's no good for
active duty. Sarge figures this will keep him off his feet
and out of trouble." In fact, Kimberly, his ex-lover and
current boss, had used words that were a lot harsher, but
that was the general gist.

This time not only her eyes flared, but also her nostrils.
"You mentioned a recent injury…"

"That's right."

"This recently injured undercover cop. Does he have a
name?" she asked in a voice drier than desert sand.

"Detective Blake Barker."

Her sigh was long and blustery. "I was afraid of that."
Her head fell back against the chair and she contemplated
the ceiling as though searching it for guidance.

Since she wasn't watching him, he let the grin out. "I'll
be a great employee. Trust me." Sophie wasn't the only
woman he'd had to convince. Kimberly refused flat out at
first, telling him he'd be out on disability until the doctor
said he was fit for active duty. The fact that he was the
only one who'd seen Wai Fung Li and could identify him
had allowed him to stay on the case. And, since this was
an office job where he'd be observing and passing back
information, it was the perfect assignment until he was
fully recovered.

Was Sophie really the lucky break she appeared or was
she more bad news?

"If I didn't trust you we wouldn't be doing this."

"They're putting together an identity for me. Something

close to the truth, but with things like banking experience added to the résumé and policing experience deleted. I'll get you a dossier as soon as it's ready."

She got over her fascination with the ceiling and faced him once more. "And I'll have to fake the hiring process, lie to the executive committee. I've never done anything so unethical."

"I'm sorry, Sophie. But somebody in your bank is a criminal. You being temporarily unethical is the best way to root out whoever that is."

She nodded, but the crease between her brows didn't clear. "Phil was an assistant account manager. He had an accounting degree."

"I've got a business degree."

"Real or fake?"

"Real." He shrugged. "I was planning to go into business, but I changed my mind."

She tapped restless fingers against the arm of her chair, then narrowed her gaze. "How do you calculate debt to effective equity on a commercial loan, Detective?"

"Minimum of two to one is acceptable."

"For this position you need a knowledge of RAROC methodologies."

He sighed, but he figured he'd be suspicious too in her shoes. "RAROC—Risk Adjusted Return on Capital. Like I said, I know enough to fake it."

She blew out a breath and stared at him until the same thing happened that always happened when they were together—the sexual heat started to build. He swallowed, resisting the urge to hobble over there and kiss her senseless.

She seemed to have other ideas. "Well, now that our working relationship will be a real one, there's no question of us having sex." Was that regret he heard in her tone? He hoped so.

She didn't even realize she'd upped the stakes and thrown out a challenge he couldn't refuse.

Apart from her tendency to cause him physical damage, Sophie Morton intrigued him more than any woman had in a long time. They'd be having sex all right. The question was simply when.

SOPHIE DIDN'T CONSIDER herself a particularly fanciful person, but she was starting to feel spooked.

She had the odd, prickly feeling of being watched. She knew it was ridiculous and all because she felt guilty about perpetrating her own fraud on the bank, albeit for a good cause, but she found the sensation unnerving.

Still, so far so good. Maybe that was what had her feeling uneasy. This undercover operation was going almost frighteningly smoothly. The most amazing thing being that Ruby hadn't made a single complaint in the three days she'd been overseeing Assistant Account Manager Blake *Brannigan.*

No way anyone could think there was anything untoward going on between her and Brannigan, either. He hadn't been near her since she'd "hired" him. She sniffed. Not that it mattered, of course. She'd been very plain with the detective that there would be no fraternizing with an employee, no matter how bogus that employee might be.

All right. She'd admit to herself that her feminine pride was stung that he'd taken her brush-off so well. Not that she would have wavered from her decision not to sleep with him, but it would have been nice to be tempted, if only to prove that she found him completely resistible.

She tapped her fingers on her desktop wondering just what the detective was getting up to in his starter office in

Private Banking. He'd promised her he could do the job well enough to pass muster, at least for a couple of weeks. Still, she always visited a new employee over the first few days of their tenure. It was a courtesy gesture—she hadn't even thought how odd it must appear that she hadn't made her welcome-and-how-are-you-settling-in visit to Phil's replacement yet.

If she didn't do it, and fast, people would start to talk.

"Gwen," she said, emerging from her office. "I'm going to visit the new assistant account manager in Private Banking."

Gwen glanced up from her computer and moaned softly. "He's such a hunk."

This wasn't surprising news. She'd noticed Gwen practically licking him with her eyeballs when he'd first come for an interview. From the office grapevine, it seemed all the female staff shared Gwen's view.

"We hired him for his banking skills, not as eye candy," she replied, surprised at the spurt of annoyance.

"I know." Gwen gazed at her with surprise. "But it's great he's both."

Sophie hoped he really did have some accounting talents in addition to his copious sex appeal—at least enough to get him through a week or two.

Taking no chances when she got to the private banking area, she enlisted a guide and was taken straight to Blake's office. He appeared huge in the small cubicle. She still wasn't used to his short hair and clean-shaven urban professional look. She found him as attractive, perhaps more so, but she doubted she'd have recognized him as the same man. He'd turned his computer chair slightly to make room for his casted leg. He was scrolling through a broker's report onscreen, she noted, seemingly engrossed in his work. He might not have a clue what he was doing, but she had to admit, she'd have believed he was authentic if she didn't know better.

"Excuse me, Blake," she said in a tone meant to be friendly but professional. "I just dropped by to see how you're getting along."

He glanced round sharply and gazed at her in a manner that was overfriendly and very personal. She scolded him with her eyes, but he merely winked at her.

She knew no one could see them, but still, his behavior rattled her and his teasing sexiness stirred her libido.

"Fine, thanks, Sophie," he said in a loud, clear voice. "Great place to work."

"Good." She eased into the cubicle in response to a come-here gesture. "You're finding your way around?"

"Oh, yes."

"How about the forms you need to fill in for the health plan and tax and so on? Any problems?"

"I'm glad you asked. There is this one section I don't understand. Right here." He reached for a file folder marked Personal on his desk and pulled out a standard company health plan form. "This paragraph confuses me."

In order to read the paragraph he was pointing at, she had to lean over his shoulder so their bodies almost touched. His warmth drew her in as did the clean soap and aftershave scent of him.

His lips brushed her ear and she shivered then realized he hadn't meant the gesture as a caress. He was whispering in her ear so softly she had to strain to make out the words.

"I need to get into Forsyth's office. Do you have a key?"

"This paragraph applies if you suffer an injury in the workplace," she said aloud, her index finger pointing to the word *when* in the document.

"After work tonight," he whispered. Aloud, he said, "But what about this provision?"

She nodded and continued talking about the health form while she thought rapidly. "I have to go now, but why don't you bring the forms to my office late this afternoon and I'll go over them with you then? We don't want you signing anything you don't understand completely."

He nodded and grinned at her. He was pleased she'd caught on, she could tell. Hmm. Maybe he wasn't the only one who could play detective.

"Thanks, Sophie."

"Don't mention it. See you later," she said and slipped out, her hands feeling suddenly cold and clammy.

8

"GOOD NIGHT, GWEN," Sophie called at last, trying to keep the relief out of her voice. She'd thought the woman would never leave, and couldn't help but think Gwen's frequent glances though the windows in Sophie's office had something to do with her sudden diligence. She and Blake had discussed the pension he was never going to collect until they were blue in the face waiting for Gwen to leave. Eye candy indeed.

Now her lusty-eyed assistant had gone and so, as far as Sophie could tell, had the rest of the fourth-floor staff. She knew it was an easy matter to enter the chairman's office since she had a key. Mr. Forsyth didn't always bother to lock his door, having a credenza and file cabinet that both locked. She also suspected he had a hidden safe, but it had never been any of her business—until now. Could he be proclaiming nothing to hide with an unlocked door while all the time salting away stolen money in a secret safe?

She hated the idea.

Still, she supposed it was logical of the police to start their investigation with the top brass at the bank. The executives had the most leeway with bank funds and the least scrutiny. Besides, as she couldn't forget, the last time she saw him alive, Phil had been with Mr. Forsyth.

"Everyone should be gone by now," she said nervously.

"Walk me to Forsyth's door then keep watch outside.

If the cleaners arrive early for some reason, keep them out of the way until I'm out."

The cleaners didn't start work until late evening so she felt fairly safe in agreeing. She didn't like the fact that she'd be so exposed playing decoy. But it was better than Barker getting caught, she supposed. She nodded.

Surprised, she watched him stash his crutches under her desk. "Walking cast." He pointed to his injured leg. They walked out of her office, chatting normally and strolled down the hall. His gait was halting, but she was amazed at how agile he seemed.

Nervous perspiration prickled her underarms and her hands felt cold, but other than that she was surprisingly calm.

Her gaze darted all around, as, she knew, did his. When they reached the heavy oak door of the chairman's office they both stopped. He leaned against the door, continuing to chat. To anyone viewing them they'd look perfectly innocent. He slipped a hand, with the key she'd given him, behind his back and eased the door open a few inches.

Then he was gone. If she hadn't watched him she wouldn't have believed how stealthily he slipped into the office.

He hadn't told her how long he'd be, or what he was searching for, and she hadn't thought to ask. He wouldn't be more than a few minutes, she hoped.

It was so quiet. Nervously, she glanced up and down the deserted corridor, wishing she were at home. In bed. With the covers pulled over her head.

Come on, come on.

Glancing at her watch every few seconds only reminded her of how slowly time could pass when you most wanted it to speed by. It couldn't be much longer. He'd already been two minutes.

Her eyes strained to see everywhere at once, her ears ached trying to detect any sound. She listened so intently she could hear her own breathing and the tiny sounds of a large building settling down for the night.

When the humming sound she'd most dreaded came to her ears, she froze.

The elevator.

Someone was in the elevator. It was most likely someone from a higher floor on their way home; the chances were minimal it was coming to four. Nevertheless she backed up until she was clutching the door handle to Mr. Forsyth's office, hoping and praying she wouldn't hear the *ping* that meant the elevator was stopping.

She held her breath.

The elevator pinged.

Don't panic, she ordered herself.

The elevators were around the corner so she couldn't see who got off, or where they were going. Please, please let them go the other way.

Forcing a relaxed expression to her face, she released her death grip on the door handle as she prepared to head off anyone who came near Forsyth's office.

A male voice spoke. "I'm glad I caught up with you." Ellsworth. She could fob him off easily enough.

But the other voice stopped her blood cold. "I'm glad to get your input on next year's performance targets," answered Henry Forsyth.

There was no time to think or plan. Certainly no way to stop the chairman going into his own office. She had a few seconds at most until the two men rounded the corner and saw her.

She did the only thing she could think of. She backed into Forsyth's office and shut the door behind her.

Blake's head rose with a jerk. He was bent over an open

drawer in the chairman's heavy rosewood desk. A small pouch of tools was open on the desktop.

"Forsyth's coming," she hissed.

He didn't so much as widen his eyes to show alarm, he simply scooped up his tools, then grabbed her hand and pulled her with him across the room. They were headed for Mr. Forsyth's private washroom.

"Not the bathroom, he's got a prostate problem. He'll go straight in there," she whispered.

He nodded, then opened the adjacent coat closet and shoved her inside.

The closet?

With no time to think of a better hiding place, she plunged into its depths. Musty darkness enclosed her and she almost panicked when she felt something rubbery hit her face, but there was no choice about going forward. Blake was pushing her deeper into the darkness, cramming himself in behind her.

It was dark in there and stuffy. She identified the rubbery thing as a raincoat, and pushed past it and a few other garments as far to the back as she could, but it wasn't a large closet. It had been designed to hold a few coats, not two fully grown adults and a leg cast. An overcoat brushed her face like bat's wings. She smelled galoshes and dry cleaning solvent and really, really hoped Mr. Forsyth didn't launch into one of his tedious anecdotes when he and his old friend Ellsworth settled down for a chat.

She heard the quiet click of the closet door and then felt the warm, muscular bulk of Blake Barker pressed up against her. Much too intimately against her.

It was a puny closet, granted. But did he have to squeeze quite so close? There was barely enough room to breathe.

"We'll wait them out," he whispered into her ear. He patted her shoulder in what she imagined was meant to be reassurance. Not that she needed any. This whole thing was farcical. She couldn't possibly be frightened, though in her head she understood there was a real possibility one of the men out there—God, maybe both for all she knew—was a crook.

But how could she be frightened with the smell of galoshes in her nose?

A mumble of male voices reached her and she pictured Ellsworth and Mr. Forsyth in there, chatting about golf, or planning strategy for the bank…or talking about offshore havens where they'd parked their illegal gains.

She strained her ears, but it was impossible to distinguish words in the conversation. With luck, whatever they said would be captured by the phone tap she knew he'd installed. For now, all she could hear was the quiet breathing of the man pressed up against her.

"We may be here awhile," he said, his lips just a whisper away from kissing her ear. She couldn't repress the shiver of awareness that ran through her.

It was warm in the closet and the woolen overcoat brushed against her nose. She would love to shove the hanger farther down the rack, but didn't dare make any noise.

The warm darkness was surprisingly familiar. She smiled to herself, remembering how she used to hide out from her brothers in the hall closet of their family home. She'd felt pleasantly sneaky, hidden and safe. And so superior, as she thought she'd fooled them with her cleverness. Now she looked back with her adult's vision, she realized they must have known she was there all the time. Probably they were only too happy to get rid of the pesky kid sister for a while.

She used to curl up and hide in that closet for ages. Funny how she'd forgotten. She could dream her dreams, make up stories in her head. It was a magic world. A world that existed only for her.

As she leaned back into the corner she found she could still weave fantasies in a dark closet. Only these were very adult fantasies. The man crowded against her had to be responsible. He was one big lump of testosterone calling out to her. Every place their bodies touched, she felt a current of awareness humming between them. His body heat seeped into her, centering like warmed honey in all her erogenous zones.

Her breasts felt heavy with it, her womb, her very blood as hot and slow moving as the air stirred by their mingled breath.

He shifted his body weight soundlessly, but she felt the movement against her and felt the response in every follicle and cell.

Did he feel it too? This intense connection? Her fingers ached to touch him, but she fisted them, keeping them at her sides. Hot images licked at her imagination, though. She imagined him kissing her, touching her in all her aching needy places.

A tiny sigh escaped her lips, and she could have sworn he nudged even closer. The voices in the outer office hummed distant and low, like a muted television set, while inside this small, enclosed space, the tiniest sounds seemed amplified in her head. The brush of his shirt against hers, the hush of their breathing. It felt as if there wasn't enough air to feed her pounding heart as scenes played in her head like a porno flick with herself and Blake in starring roles. Was it her imagination or had his breathing quickened also?

She couldn't stand much more of this. She had to get out of here or she'd do something foolish.

Mr. Forsyth was a garrulous man at the best of times.

He'd been a banker for thirty years, and every one of those years teemed with anecdotes, which he dispensed with the placid dignity of an elder statesman. It was more than politeness that had caused her to listen to his stories. She genuinely liked the man. How she hoped the investigation would reveal nothing more incriminating than that his best years were behind him.

She'd been in enough meetings with Mr. Forsyth to know that, as Blake had supposed, the two of them would be trapped in here a while.

Blake shifted again and she recalled that he'd left his crutches hidden in her office. It was probably too soon for him to be walking on the cast, never mind stuck standing in one position. Maybe, if she helped him, he could sit down.

She turned to suggest it, but in the pitch dark she hadn't realized his face was turned her way. Instead of his ear, her lips came in contact with lightly stubbled skin. She felt the shock of it through her lips. Had she brushed his cheek? There'd been a boniness and an indentation. His chin. Her lips had brushed his chin.

In the split second it took her brain to decode the shockingly delicious sensations, he'd dropped his chin and brought his lips down on hers. The humming shock jumped from her lips like an electric charge zipping around her body creating more sparks.

If he'd had any idea how hot and bothered she'd become, being in such close proximity, he never would have kissed her. The effect on her system was akin to splitting the atom. And he didn't know yet about her little problem. Oh, but he soon would if they didn't stop now.

But how could she pull away when his firm lips controlled her mouth with casual mastery? His hands, those wonderful, warm, capable hands traveled lightly up her arms, more to see her by touch, she thought, than in any intent to caress. But everywhere he touched her she did feel caressed. She wished she had a braille sign imprinted on her body for him to read. *Back off before it's too late.*

Her skin felt ultrasensitive, as though she could feel the blood pulsing, warm and full of life, just under the surface.

He brought his hands up to cup her cheeks, holding her head in place, his thumbs resting at the corners of her mouth.

She shouldn't be doing this. They shouldn't be doing it. He'd completely misunderstood her intentions, thinking she'd made a pass when she'd only intended to ask him if he was comfortable.

She should make him stop immediately.

She flicked his fingers with her tongue.

He needed no other invitation to deepen the intimacy. His lips increased their pressure and her whole body seemed to sigh as his tongue, hot and wet, entered her mouth. She met his tongue thrust for thrust, licking, nipping, nibbling at him all the while remembering to be quiet. So quiet.

Outside this warm and exciting cave, she was dimly aware of the low murmur of voices, but inside it was as dark as the deepest secret. Inside her body there was a hell of a racket going on: fireworks exploded, her heart pounded and her blood roared. But outside it was so quiet she could hear their clothing rub together, hear the soft inhalations and exhalations.

She felt the tide of desire rising fast—too fast, the way it took her sometimes so her reason went cloudy and she acted crazy.

Oh, she didn't care. She was always a model of propriety at work. Setting a good example, keeping her sex life well outside the office. So far in fact, that her last relationship had been a long-distance one with an engineer in California. The sex had been great, but ultimately there hadn't been enough there to make a future.

Her eyes snapped open in the dark. *Four months.* After a dry spell like that, no wonder she was acting totally and deliciously irresponsible.

It was too late to stop now. She knew that. Like a partyer who's had one too many and can't stop, so her desire had climbed too fast for her to tamp it down now.

She was squeezed so close to Blake in the tiny closet she felt as though she'd bear his imprint on her body for days, but still she couldn't get close enough. She was growing mindless and greedy with need.

Her hands reached for him, finding the silky spikiness of his hair, tracing the contours of his neck and shoulders. Oh, those shoulders. Strong and wide, as though he could carry the world and not topple.

Pushing her breasts into his chest only made them ache more. She rubbed them against him, needing the friction, even though her nipples felt like striking matches bursting into flame.

Whimpers of pleasure and need were crawling up her throat and she bit her lips to try to contain them.

Quiet. She had to stay quiet.

But it was so difficult with her body throbbing for fulfillment.

She rocked her pelvis against his, loving the feel of his erection against her neediest place. She felt empty, hollow without that glorious hardness to fill and complete her. A moan escaped her, cut off by his lips. He trailed a path of kisses to her ear and whispered, ''Shh.''

She should tell him, she should tell him now her shameful secret—that quiet wasn't an option when she was aroused—but then he'd stop.

And she'd die.

Getting caught going at it in the chairman's office closet seemed preferable at the moment to death from sexual frustration.

The murmuring voices outside the door continued, but in her foggy state they'd taken on the almost soothing quality of ocean waves in the background.

Her breasts were heaving as her breathing grew thick, not from panic, though. This was the opposite of panic, the tension that rises and rises only to burst in a great relaxing wave.

But her tension was building and building with no relief in sight. It was too tight in here to move. Besides, they hadn't exactly come prepared for this. Unless Mr. Forsyth kept a supply of condoms in his spare winter overcoat, lust among the galoshes seemed like it was going to be cut short.

Maybe she could be satisfied with kissing. Kissing Blake was one of the greatest pleasures she'd ever experienced. He acted as if he owned her mouth, and for the moment she was happy to hand over control.

His hand squeezed between them to cup a breast, kneading the aching flesh.

She moaned softly into his mouth and felt his lips curl in a smile. "Shh," he said against her lips.

He had no idea how restrained she was being. She might be quiet and professional at work, but she made up for it in the bedroom, as Detective Barker would be detecting before long.

He did a kind of pressing-pulling thing with her nipple that sent a hot spurt of desire spiking right to the core of her womanhood.

She couldn't stand it anymore. She slipped out of her

left shoe and her leg—the one that wasn't jammed against the back wall of the closet—climbed his castless one.

He wasn't slow to take advantage of a situation, she'd give him that. The hand left her breast and worked its way down to hike up her skirt and pin it between their bellies. Then his fingers plunged beneath her panty hose and into her panties.

His questing fingers must have figured out for themselves how very close she was, for he had the presence of mind to whisper in her ear, "Can you come quietly?"

Not a chance. She was a moaner, a yeller, a shrieker. Her vocal chords seemed to be under the impression that anything that good should be celebrated. But if she had to restrain herself or go without, she figured the woolen sleeve of a winter overcoat would make an effective gag. She nodded.

Even in the darkness she felt him gazing at her, trying to decide whether he could risk it. But the heat and tension emanating from him were clear indications he was as far gone as she.

She knew he'd made up his mind when he covered her mouth with his lips and began sliding his fingers over her hot spot, swirling her own wetness around and against that exquisitely sensitive flesh. The trembling began from deep inside her. He rubbed faster and she felt like one of those whirling fireworks that spins until it throws out sparks, then flames, then explodes into a million stars.

The trembling was becoming shuddering and she was jerking her hips back and forth in counterpoint to his rhythm. He thrust a finger inside her, still keeping to the same rhythm and she felt herself begin to lose control.

She had to be quiet. She knew she had to be quiet. God, it was too much, she wanted to scream. *But no. Have to be quiet.* She was panting with the effort to hold in her mounting passion. She pulled his head down and kissed him hard, but even from their sealed lips, she was certain her cries would be heard.

Two fingers inside her, up inside, pushing forward, found her G-spot. How could she not wail?

Frantic now, she pulled her mouth away from Blake's, and, with a mental apology to Mr. Forsyth, grabbed the sleeve of his winter coat, stuffed it into her mouth and bit down. She barely noticed the scratchy fibers against her tongue or the taste of damp wool as she gagged herself.

The pressure was building and building. A drop of sweat trickled between her breasts. She was going to blow like a volcano half a dozen centuries overdue for a good lava flow. Knowing her control was about to slip, she slapped both hands over her mouth, hoping the combination of heavy wool and her two hands would stifle her cries.

A thumb on her pulsing clit and she was gone. Explosion after explosion rocked her world, along with the cries of fulfillment spilling into the gag, and trapped by her hands. Mindlessly, her hips rocked and jerked and only as she came back to herself did she realize she'd been trying to climb his erection, to put him inside her.

9

"I WANT YOU INSIDE ME," she whispered, her voice half hoarse from the screams she'd stifled.

"If this closet weren't so damned tiny," he panted in her ear, "I would be." He sounded almost in pain as he said the words.

Feeling some of his pent-up tension, she reached between them for his zipper. "Why don't I—"

He grabbed her wrist. "Later."

He must have a lot more self-control than she did, she thought to herself as he glanced at his watch, the numbers glowing pale green in the dark.

Only now did she realize the sounds had ceased in the office. She hadn't even noticed, distracted by more immediate sensations.

"Can we go now?" she whispered, almost reluctant to leave the dark and musty confines of the closet. It seemed warm and safe in here, and after the intimacy she'd just shared with Blake, she felt shy about going back with him to the real world.

Her rather over-the-top sexual response embarrassed her. She'd read enough women's magazines to accept that she was lucky to have such exuberant orgasms, she only wished she could train her body to be less noisy about the whole business. Because of her little problem, she usually confined herself to having sex in her nicely cement-walled and well-insulated apartment or somewhere equally sound-proof.

The vertical strip of light startled her when it cracked the black darkness as Blake eased open the door. Slowly, the crack widened and black became gray as the overcoat in front of her took on shape and hue.

With a pang of embarrassment, she straightened the sleeve she'd bitten and brushed the fabric, though it seemed none the worse for the experience. Blake held her wrist in one hand as he pushed the door wider. He listened intently, then eased his head out rather like a reluctant groundhog not sure he's ready for spring.

Sophie felt no more eager to emerge from the closet. In the dark there'd been only sensation and need, but in the light of day—even the low-wattage night lighting in the office building—she'd have to deal with the man who'd pleasured her. Now that reality had intruded, her sanity made a belated return. She couldn't get involved with Blake.

The only way she could live with herself, sneaking an undercover cop into her bank, was believing she was doing the right thing professionally. But she knew she was on thin ice ethically. If she started sleeping with that same cop, how could she face herself in the mirror?

Much as she hated to do it, she was going to have to send him home sexually frustrated.

She glanced at him, but he was clearly unaware of her decision. He'd obviously concluded the chairman's office was empty, and now he pulled her out of the closet.

She blinked, feeling disoriented and stunned by the light and the change from erotic to professional. Clearly his mind was back on business, not sex, as he pulled her behind him to the door into the hallway. He opened this one just as stealthily as he had the closet door.

"I didn't finish my search. Keep a lookout."

She'd lost the taste for being lookout. She wanted to go home. Her glance must have told him as much for he said, "Give me five minutes," and swiftly kissed her before calmly crossing the room back to Forsyth's desk.

Sophie racked her pleasure-addled brain trying to think of some plausible explanation as to why she and a junior account manager might be in the chairman's office so long after everyone else had left.

As she walked back into the hallway and shut the door behind her, nothing occurred to her that was remotely plausible, but luckily she concentrated so hard on making up and discarding unbelievable tales that he was back by her side before she knew it.

Not until they'd collected his crutches from beneath her desk and were standing outside the elevator did she take a full breath.

"You okay?" he asked.

"Yes." Did he mean from the suspense or the intimacy? She wasn't sure. And hadn't in fact fully recovered from either.

Steadying one crutch under his armpit, he reached into his back pocket and pulled out a sheaf of papers. She recognized it as his pension form. At her raised brows he said, "I'll flap this around when we get near the security camera."

She nodded, but in truth she'd forgotten all about the security cameras on the main floor, where the retail operations of the bank were located. It would be clear she and Barker were in the bank much later than usual, so it made sense he'd flap his alibi under the camera's nose.

Surreptitiously she checked her clothing for traces of debauchery, but, as far as she could tell, their little escapade in the closet had left no outward signs. A quick glance at Blake showed him looking the same as always. She tried to appear calm and collected as they crossed the main foyer and took the parking elevator to the garage.

They passed no one, but it seemed to her the security cameras were malevolent eyes watching as she gestured to the company forms and kept up a pension-centered conversation as though the cameras had ears as well as eyes. Normally, she never even noticed the things, but now it took all her self-control not to glance at them nervously.

He helped her keep up the inane conversation until they'd reached the car park and her rental. Her own car still hadn't turned up, so she imagined she'd soon be shopping for another.

"So," he said, as they reached the beige sedan, "are you following me to my place or am I following you to yours?"

He'd acted so businesslike, she'd almost believed he'd forgotten all about what had happened in the closet. Now, a glance at his face revealed not only the hot blaze of desire, but a certain smugness.

While her body responded automatically to the former, the smugness acted like a slap in the face with a cold, wet washcloth and made her feel a lot less guilty about sending him home unsatisfied. "I'm certainly not following you home," she told him with high-handed disdain, marred slightly by the fact that she was blushing hotly. "And if you follow me home I'll have to call the police."

He grinned at her, looking far more dangerous than a man on crutches ought to look. "I'll give you my cell number."

"Not you," she told him, trying not to give in to six feet of temptation standing in front of her. "The real police."

He chuckled. "You're just pissed because I was right."

"What are you talking about?" She assumed a tone of outraged incomprehension.

"You told me you wouldn't have sex with me while we're working together. I just proved you wrong."

"I did not have sex with you."

He chuckled, low and wickedly taunting. "With a couple more inches to maneuver and no cast on my leg there would have been more going on upstairs than a little diddling."

"There most certainly would not!" she informed him. "I told you I don't have sex with men I work with." As if she had random near-sex encounters in closets every day of the week.

In fact, she'd love to go home with him. She still ached deep inside, her emptiness unfilled. But, just as in her childhood, the closet was a place of imaginary feats of daring where reality was suspended. An affair with Blake was a terrible idea, both for the obvious professional reasons, but also for personal ones.

"Anyway," she said, "if it happens in a closet it doesn't count."

He grinned at her in a totally unsettling way, as though he could see right through her airy excuses and into her heart. A heart that was afraid to trust. "I happen to have a very nice walk-in closet in my bedroom. Wouldn't count at all."

She rolled her eyes at him, trying not to let him see that she was tempted beyond belief by the idea. She couldn't tell him that men, even the most casual-seeming, had a disastrous habit of falling in love with her. She couldn't tell him about her two failed engagements and the way she started to feel panicky and trapped whenever she ended up in a serious relationship—as though she'd somehow taken a wrong turn and ended up in a blind alley. They had to work together under difficult circumstances and the simpler and more casual their personal relationship, the better for all concerned.

Oh, but why did he have to be the sexiest guy she'd met in ages? Why did her body have to pick now to remind her how much she loved sex?

Well, if she couldn't say no, she could at least turn this into a game. Games had rules, finite playing periods, and weren't to be taken seriously. Besides, she loved games. She had a feeling the dishy detective did, too. Maybe having sex while pretending not to was juvenile, but it was the best insurance she could think of to stop anyone getting serious. Besides, if he was busy inventing places other than the bedroom for sexual encounters, he'd be too busy to fall in love with her. And, she had a feeling they could both use some fun. Giving him her best you-can-do-better-than-that look, she said, "Use some imagination."

OH, IT COUNTS, BLAKE said to himself, watching her drive out of the garage. He relived the feeling of her body spasming around his thrusting fingers, heard her muffled yells of satisfaction. Oh, yes. That sexual interlude in the closet definitely counted.

He wouldn't have believed, from everything he knew about her, that she'd be so wildly and noisily responsive. He liked to see a woman enjoy herself, and if he was the one pushing her buttons, there was a little boost to his male ego that he was big enough to admit.

He'd driven her crazy, just as she'd driven him half-mad, her body straining instinctively to mate with his. Now why would a woman who so clearly loved sex be so skittish about taking their intense mutual desire to the next logical stage? Sophie's claim they were working together had been flimsy at best. Now she was throwing up new roadblocks to prevent him getting close to her. Why? It was a puzzle he was determined to solve, and a game he looked forward to playing.

Use your imagination, she'd said. He had no problem following that instruction. Those teasing words suggested it wasn't only clothes cupboards that didn't count. If he assumed everywhere but a regular bedroom "didn't count," his libido could have free rein. He was already dreaming up new places *not* to have sex with Sophie.

As he made his way to his own vehicle, he was restricted only by the bounds of his imagination, the law and the more hampering problem of a broken leg. Luckily, he was a fast healer. Already he was able to walk on the cast with almost no pain, but he'd keep up the pretense of the crutches. He liked appearing harmless to anyone who might be watching Phil's replacement.

He hoped they'd get something good from the phone taps that had been installed in the chairman's office, just as he hoped to find Phil's original computer. It hadn't taken him longer than an hour to discover his was brand-new, with no hidden memories to be dredged up.

He was neither a pervert nor a nervous Nelly, but in spite of Sophie telling him not to follow her home, he did, as he had been for days.

He couldn't have said what impulse had originally propelled his vehicle to take the same route, staying far enough back that Sophie wouldn't be aware he was tailing her.

He simply couldn't help himself. He was a cop. His job was to keep people safe. If he was being a little overenthusiastic in his current mission, nobody need ever know about it. He liked to see Sophie safe in her apartment before heading home to his own place.

There were a dozen shortcuts she could have taken to

get home quicker, but tonight, as always, she took the most obvious, and therefore the most congested route. The poor woman was so direction-challenged she took the same familiar route to and from work every day.

He shook his head, wondering why that struck him as so endearing.

He followed her through jammed traffic, red lights and busy intersections with a CD of *Don Giovanni* keeping him company until at last they approached her apartment. Her seventh-floor window was dark. He'd wait until the lights were on and she'd had time to make sure everything was as it should be, then he'd head home.

He watched her taillights disappear into her underground parking garage. Experience told him that in three or four minutes the lights would go on in her apartment. Without conscious thought, he checked the time: six forty-eight. He kept his eye on her dark window, his inner clock running.

A minute passed. Maybe half of another minute. He rolled his shoulders, tight from hauling himself around on those damned crutches.

Unfortunately, the cast wasn't for mere show. He'd begged and badgered, but he still couldn't shave so much as a day off the five weeks the doctors had incarcerated his leg.

He wiggled his toes aggressively. He knew what happened to a leg that was immobilized for five weeks. The muscles shrank, that's what happened. They'd take off the cast and a pale white noodle would emerge, slimy and shrunken, all the muscle gone.

It wasn't vanity that had him scowling, but the feeling that he needed all his muscles, as well as all his wits if he had a hope of doing serious damage to the Black Dragons.

In spite of his mental whining, he was fully aware that

almost two minutes had passed since Sophie's car had entered the underground garage. A couple of minutes more and she'd be home.

He settled back, letting the Mozart wash over him. Right about the four-minute mark her lights went on. He passed another minute or two out front, until he felt certain all was well chez Morton, then eased away from the curb.

CAFFEINE. NEED CAFFEINE. Sophie's system began sending unsubtle messages to her brain the next morning at the office. She imagined heavy smokers experienced something similar with nicotine fits. As soon as eleven o'clock drew near she began to get twitchy. If she went past the hour her hands would start to tremble and by half past she'd have the beginning of a headache.

She hadn't slept well last night, torn between horror that she was essentially acting as a spy in her own camp, and wishing Blake were there to finish what they'd started.

Since the office coffee fluctuated between bilgewater and tar, sometimes an intriguing combination of the two, she'd taken to running across the street to a family-run café.

She only had the one addiction, so she liked to make the most of it. Every day, just before eleven, she grabbed her refillable stainless-steel mug with the bank's logo on it and made the short trek across the street.

Traffic was moderately busy midmorning, but not busy enough to tempt her to walk a half block to the lighted intersection and crosswalk. With a quick glance both ways, she jaywalked. Well, jayjogged to be absolutely specific.

"Hi, Sid," she said to the coffee jockey with the bright green spiked hair. She'd long ago stopped asking for the usual. She just handed him her mug and watched him fill it with dark, rich French roast. Her nostrils quivered with pleasure at the scents of coffee, cinnamon and freshly baked carrot cake in the small café.

Sid handed back the warm mug and she took a long, life-restoring drink, just this side of scalding with enough caffeine to jump-start a corpse. "Ah," she said. "Perfect. See you tomorrow."

Back outside, she waited impatiently for a grumbling garbage truck to lumber past, then, with another quick glance right and left, stepped off the curb.

It was a beautiful autumn day with sun sparkling off the windows of downtown high-rises, heavenly after a week of nonstop rain.

Even as she trod briskly back across the street she sipped again, enjoying the dark smoky taste of the coffee.

What alerted her to danger she couldn't have said. One second she was swallowing coffee, enjoying the sun on her face despite a chilly breeze, and thinking ahead to the quarterly report she'd work on when she got back to her desk, and the next second she felt the hairs rise on the back of her neck.

Everything seemed to happen in slow motion and she felt as though she were watching herself from outside her body. She swung her head to the right, coffee mug still pressed to her lips, and saw a car speed toward her. It hadn't been there when she stepped off the curb, but like some vengeful monster it roared toward her now, black and deadly.

Her feet felt cemented into the roadway as the thing flew at her. She cringed, waiting for the honk, the squeal of brakes, for it to swerve into an empty lane, but it did none of those things; instead, it seemed as though the sedan picked up speed, almost as if it was trying to run her down.

As her panicked mind took in that fact, her feet finally accepted the frantic messages from her brain.

Move, move, move.

She took one forward running step, heard a scream in the distance, and, instinctively knowing she had only one chance, launched herself toward the safety of the sidewalk as though she were diving toward the deeper water in the middle of a swimming pool.

For a timeless spell she was airborne, flying, waiting, with a sickening dread, for the impact of the car hitting her. Then, tucking her head and putting her hands out in front of her, she hit the dirty gray sidewalk.

The diving fall onto concrete had a surreal familiarity to it, only this time there was no Detective Barker to break her fall.

Even as the pain shot through her hands, wrists, knees and hip she felt the whoosh of air and the heat of the car, smelled dust and grease and exhaust and heard the terrible screech of tires as it roared away.

Stunned, she glanced behind her, unable to believe the driver hadn't stopped. If anything, the car was going faster now. It turned, fishtailed round the corner and was gone.

"Jerk!" a woman's voice yelled. "Sophie, are you okay?" The anxious words seemed to come from far away and she had to force herself not to roll into a fetal ball and start wailing.

"Edna. Hi." She greeted the retail investment advisor shakily.

Was she all right? So much of her body ached that the only thing she could be certain of was that she wasn't dead. Dead couldn't hurt this much.

Something warm and wet pooled round her hip and thigh. Blood? Had she severed an artery? Was she bleeding to death and in too much shock to feel pain? But, when she stared down, the pool of liquid was dark brown and as runny as water. It wasn't until she saw her silver coffee mug lying on its side with the black plastic lid beside it and breathed in the pungent odor of French roast that she realized she was sitting in a puddle of coffee, not blood.

Edna was squatting by her side, patting her shoulder as though frightened to do more damage. "I can't believe that jerk didn't stop. Should I call 9-1-1?"

A small crowd was gathering and, as her initial pain faded, she felt foolish and embarrassed sprawled on the sidewalk like yesterday's trampled newspaper.

"No. I'm all right. Can you just help me up?"

"We should call the police. That driver was crazy!" With Edna's help, she struggled to her feet. One of the curious spectators handed her her coffee mug and she murmured her thanks.

Slowly they made their way into the bank building with Sophie gritting her teeth to keep them from chattering. "I thought you were going to be killed for sure," Edna exclaimed, which did not help calm Sophie's nerves. The minute they entered the building, Edna made a huge fanfare, telling the story to everyone she met on the way to the elevator.

Sophie did her best to shush the woman, but most of her energy was focused on holding it together. Her gray dress pants clung to her with a sticky wetness and once the doors closed on them, the elevator smelled like the inside of a dirty coffee cup.

While Edna rattled on, Sophie mentally calmed herself. She was fine. It was her own fault for jaywalking across a main street when sunshine blinded drivers. She'd have to get into the habit of using the lighted crosswalk.

"Are you all right?" Gwen rose from her desk, eyes widened, as Sophie appeared and Edna was only too happy to explain once more, in a louder-than-necessary voice, how she'd come to look this way. She ended the recital with, "Sophie was almost killed!"

In minutes, a small crowd had assembled in her office. Everyone from Mr. Forsyth to the internal mail guy filled the room exclaiming and fussing over her. She wanted to cry with the shaken-up pain of shock, instead she tried to calm the impromptu gathering.

Edna recounted the story once more, with all the relish of someone who lives a quiet life. "The car swerved toward her, I swear it. I lost five years off my life. How Sophie wasn't killed, I'll never know."

"It was just the sun in the driver's eyes," Sophie insisted with a forced smile. "Thanks for helping." She shot a glance of appeal to Ellsworth, who, pale and worried, was patting her shoulder as though to ensure himself she was still in one piece. Once she had his attention, she flicked a glance at Edna and widened her eyes. *Get her out of here!*

He nodded slightly, acknowledging her message and seemed to pull himself together. "Edna," he said jovially, "thanks for bringing Sophie back to her office. I know you've got work to do, we'll take care of her from here."

"Well, if you ask me, the police should be called."

"Did you get a license number?" he asked the older woman sharply.

"Gosh, it was going so fast...no."

"Would you recognize the driver again?"

"Well, certainly. He was wearing a woolen hat, pulled low, big sunglasses and..." She glanced at the faces all watching her, and dropped her chin. "No," she said. "I guess I wouldn't."

It seemed to take the wind out of her sails and she allowed Ellsworth to escort her to the elevator. Sophie could hear her excited voice right up until the elevator arrived.

"I'll lay you odds the entire building knows within half an hour," Gwen said.

Ellsworth returned alone.

"Thanks," Sophie said, sending him a tired smile.

He didn't return it. "She's right, you know. We should call the police."

"Ellsworth, you know how Edna dramatizes things. The sun was in the driver's eyes. He couldn't see me, that's all."

"Well, you should at least go home."

"I'll drive her home," a most unwelcome voice said from the doorway. Where had Blake come from? If there was one person she'd as soon not have heard about her escapade, it was him. His voice was as calm and decisive as though he owned her, which had everyone turning to stare.

She almost groaned aloud. A frown pulled his brows together and, with his hands shoved in his pockets and his body filling the doorway, he looked like—actually, he looked like what he was. A cop. Not an assistant account manager in Personal, Private Banking.

"What are you doing here?" she asked before she could stop herself. Then, before he gave them both away, she let her eyes scan the half-dozen executive floor staff crowded in her office. "More questions about your pension?"

He shrugged, seemed to pull himself in, like an actor changing roles, and then gave a damned good impression of a bewildered new recruit. "I heard you got hurt. Now I'm here, I might as well drive you home."

She started to glare at him then realized she couldn't do it without causing an even worse fuss than the one already swirling around her.

"That's not necessary," Ellsworth said, sounding mildly affronted. "I can drive Sophie home."

Blake shrugged. "I've got the time." His voice was mild, but the glance he shot Sophie, which only she could see, was insistent. If she didn't ride home with him, she'd only have to deal with him later.

Suddenly she was fed up with them all. "I don't need anyone to drive me home. I've got work to do. I'm staying."

Ellsworth looked patronizing, Barker barely contained.

Her knees throbbed, her ankle was grazed and the wet coffee-scented wool of her slacks was cool and sticking uncomfortably to her hip and thigh. "Oh, all right." She glanced at Barker. "I'll take an early lunch. I need to change my clothes. But I'll be back this afternoon." She glared around in case anyone was inclined to argue with her.

No one was.

She strode out of her office as though her entire body didn't ache, and pretended not to notice all the worried faces behind her gesturing to Barker to keep her at home for the afternoon.

She considered swinging round for the satisfaction of catching them at it, but in truth she felt shaky and a little frightened from her near miss with the front end of a speeding car.

Maybe spending the rest of the day at home wasn't a bad idea.

Why she chose Barker over Ellsworth as an escort she couldn't have said. Shock, probably. Also, she knew he'd browbeat her sooner or later, tell her it was all her fault, probably issue her a ticket for jaywalking. She might as well get it over with.

They were silent on the way to his car. Edna had been much more solicitous, she thought sourly as she limped on her own to Barker's car and slid into the passenger side.

Blake tossed his crutches in the back and eased himself behind the wheel.

He pulled out of the garage and into traffic and she couldn't help but notice how often he glanced into the rearview and side mirrors as though checking to see if they were followed. Must be some cop habit he couldn't turn off.

He didn't say a word.

Not a single word.

Not as they drove to her apartment, not when he ignored her flustered thanks and repeated assertions that she could manage from here. He didn't bother with the crutches as he escorted her right into her building. She tried once more to say goodbye outside her door and he shook his head.

He merely raised a brow and waited until, with a huffy, "Fine!" she let him in.

The door no sooner closed than he rounded on her. "Did you see the driver?"

She laughed. It was a nervous, frustrated sound. "You sound as hysterical as Edna. I crossed without looking properly. The sun was in the driver's eyes. He probably didn't see me."

"It was after eleven. The sun was overhead, and the way I heard it he was traveling west. No way the sun was in that driver's eyes."

West. Traveling west. How the hell did she know which way the compass needle had been pointing when she was almost killed?

Killed. The word made her shiver.

He gazed at her, his clenched jaw relaxing, his eyes turning greener before her startled gaze. He took a step toward her and she thought he'd reach out and touch her, but it seemed he thought better of it. His hands dropped to his sides. "Sophie, you should take a vacation."

10

"A VACATION?" SHE STARED at him, stunned. What kind of a stupid idea was that? "My vacation's already scheduled for next summer. I'm taking an escorted cycling tour of the Gulf Islands."

He seemed momentarily diverted from his purpose. "An escorted cycling tour?"

She'd rather he laughed at her than yelled at her. She shrugged. "I always choose escorted tours. Less chance of getting lost."

He wasn't so easily diverted, though. "You should take some time off, go away somewhere."

She grit her teeth wanting to kick him for being a jerk when she needed some TLC. "I need a hot bath and some liniment, not a vacation."

He sighed, and leaned against the door. As she gazed at him, with his rugged he-man good looks, the broad shoulders and head-to-toe muscles, she almost wished she could keep him there as a living, breathing safety system. Instinctively, she knew he'd step in front of a bullet or speeding car to protect her life. Any innocent life, she imagined.

After the shock of her almost-accident, a big strapping man standing between her and trouble seemed like an awfully good idea.

"Let's get you cleaned up, then I need to talk to you."

She glanced down at herself, sticky and wet with cold coffee, her knees grimy with stuff off the sidewalk she

GET FREE BOOKS and a FREE GIFT WHEN YOU PLAY THE...

Just scratch off the silver box with a coin. Then check below to see the gifts you get!

SLOT MACHINE GAME!

YES! I have scratched off the silver box. Please send me the 2 free Harlequin Blaze™ books and gift for which I qualify. I understand I am under no obligation to purchase any books, as explained on the back of this card.

350 HDL DRNH

150 HDL DRNX
(H-B-10/02)

FIRST NAME

LAST NAME

ADDRESS

APT.#

CITY

STATE/PROV.

ZIP/POSTAL CODE

7	7	7	Worth **TWO FREE BOOKS** plus a **BONUS** Mystery Gift!
🍒	🍒	🍒	Worth **TWO FREE BOOKS!**
♣	♣	♣	Worth **ONE FREE BOOK!**
🔔	🔔	🍒	**TRY AGAIN!**

Visit us online at www.eHarlequin.com

DETACH AND MAIL CARD TODAY!

didn't care to contemplate. She felt the incipient soreness of bruises bubbling under the surface of her skin, and imagined the contusion factory was working overtime.

Tomorrow she'd look like an overripe eggplant.

All she wanted was a hot bath, some aspirin and a chick flick. A day spent on the couch sounded like heaven. But somehow, she didn't think that was going to happen. The detective obviously had intimidation and browbeating on his agenda.

Giving in to the inevitable, she said, "Let me change, and I'll be back."

"I should take you to the hospital and have you looked at."

Frustration had her turning on him huffily. "But you won't, because I'm not going. I fell on the sidewalk. Tomorrow I'll have some bruises."

He limped toward her, his expression far from that of a trained healer. "I'm certified in first aid. I take a look at you or the hospital does. Not open to negotiation."

"You know what you are?"

"Losing patience."

"Pushy. You're pushy. Push, push, push…" she muttered as she stalked, stiff-kneed, toward the kitchen. "I'm taking two aspirin and I'll call you in the morning." She reached for the bottle of pain relievers she kept in the kitchen, filled a glass with water, popped the pills then drank the rest of the water thirstily.

"I'll go after I've checked you out. Put on a housecoat or something so I can see what I'm doing." His words were uttered in an everyday tone, but she felt a flush begin at her toes and work its way up.

Her body turned of its own volition to face him as she recalled the last time they'd spent time together. When he couldn't see what he was doing. Because it was dark. Inside a closet. Intimate, claustrophobic and sexy as hell.

Their gazes locked, and if he hadn't been thinking anything along those lines, the look on her face must have reminded him. The ice melted off the polar cap in seconds, blown apart by the volcanic heat in his eyes. "I didn't mean..."

"Didn't you?" Her voice was barely steady.

Maybe it was a reaction to the experience of almost being killed, but her body felt like it needed to celebrate life in the most fundamental way possible. Heat started to bubble inside her as he came for her, his limping gait not fast, but steady, purpose in his eyes.

It wasn't fear that had her stepping back, it was the need for a hard surface to brace herself against. She already knew that once their bodies collided she'd need the support.

He stepped toward her and she stepped back in a simple choreography, as though their blood pounded to the same beat. Step, step, step, his gaze locked on hers and she couldn't have broken the contact if she'd wanted to.

It was almost a shock when she backed into the kitchen counter.

She gripped the granite, cool beneath her heated flesh, bracing herself for the physical and emotional onslaught that was almost upon her. Close to two hundred pounds of irate, sexually charged male was advancing on her. He dragged off his light jacket and draped it across a stool at her breakfast bar.

Her chin rose slightly as he closed in on her. She had no idea why. It didn't make her taller and only exposed the vulnerable length of her neck to him.

Her insides began to quiver with heightened awareness

as he hit the kitchen, his foot and cast making a slap-thunk sound on the Italian floor tile.

Then he was there in front of her. Her chin tilted even more in order to maintain eye contact. She felt the heat pulsing off him, and his coiled tension. He invaded her personal space and she welcomed him. He kept advancing until he was flush against her and she whimpered, deep in her throat.

Her lips parted as his head lowered, but he didn't kiss her. He rested his forehead against hers, giving her a close-up view of the knife-straight bridge of his nose. She wondered dimly how he'd made it so far, given his lifestyle, without ever breaking it. Each of her brothers sported a bump or jog from rugby, wrestling or roughhousing. Blake either had straighter healing bones than her brothers or he was a better fighter.

"What am I going to do with you?" he said, knocking all thoughts of noses, straight or otherwise, out of her head. She'd been fairly certain she knew exactly what he was going to do with her. Have sex and soon had seemed the general idea, in his mind and in hers. Had he changed his mind? Before they even started?

She wished she knew him well enough to tell him how much she needed him right now. How much she needed to erase those terrible seconds of heart-stopping terror when she'd believed she was about to die. How much she needed the warm embrace of another human being, the temporary release from worry and tense muscles. And what the hell else was she going to do with the gallons of adrenaline still cruising her system looking for an outlet?

But she didn't know him well enough, so she simply asked, "What do you mean?"

"I mean, I should go."

She felt how hot his body was, and raised a trembling

hand to touch the crisp hair at the nape of his neck. "Are you going to?"

"No." The word was short and sharp, as frustrated as it was husky.

He tipped up her chin with one hand and lowered his mouth to hers.

She gripped the granite counter harder, to anchor herself as lust, pure, unstoppable lust, roared through her body. Dimly, she realized it must be a reaction from her earlier ordeal. Escape from near death seemed to have an aphrodisiac effect on her. Still, in the future she thought she'd stick to oysters.

His mouth plundered hers and she plundered right back, as greedy for sex as she was for life.

His tongue was insistent, thrusting in her mouth in a rhythm that had her moaning and her hips wiggling in anticipation.

"I can't believe what a terrible idea this is," he murmured as he reached for the hem of her clingy rose-colored cotton sweater and peeled it over her head.

"The worst idea," she panted, unbuttoning his navy shirt with urgent haste.

When she had the buttons undone she pulled the shirt from his pants and spread the two halves, catching her breath at the sight of his chest. Not so muscled as to look as if he spent his life pumping iron and popping steroids, but sculpted enough that his abs were taut, his pecs defined and covered with just the right amount of coppery-brown chest hair.

She caught him studying her chest with the same fascination, and the intensity of his stare had her nipples contracting and thrusting forward, puckering the silky fabric of her bra. As he lifted a hand to touch her through the silk, she took the opportunity to unbutton his cuffs.

He let her push the shirt off his shoulders, but shrugged out of the thing impatiently, returning immediately to her breasts the second his hands were free.

She loved the way his chest rose and fell with his breathing, and the steady bump of his heart beneath his skin.

Oh, and she loved the feeling of air and light on her skin when he removed her bra with practiced ease.

Even more, she loved his almost reverent intake of breath as he cupped her breasts in his big hands. "They're so spectacular, I thought I'd imagined them."

She chuckled. He wasn't the first man to call her breasts spectacular. Of course, she'd rather have a sense of direction, but she'd be lying if she didn't admit to being a little vain about her breasts.

"They're real," she assured him.

"I feel a sudden urge for us to join one of those remote tribes you see in *National Geographic,* just so I can watch these, loose and free like this, every day."

She let her gaze run up and down his half-clothed body. "I don't think I'd mind watching you in your loincloth—and spear," she said, with lustful silliness, staring straight at his crotch. If spear was extravagant, she thought billy club might be about right. Suddenly, she was feverish to know. What was he packing?

She'd felt his erection in the closet and had been thinking of it more often than she probably should. But now she needed to see it, hold it, taste it. But more than all these, she needed to feel him thrusting deep inside her body.

The relentless, wet wanting between her legs was becoming more insistent.

She reached for his belt. It was as though she'd put her foot to the gas pedal because that seemed to speed everything up. He mirrored her actions, his hands leaving her breasts with reluctance to head for the button of her slacks. They worked with quiet concentration, freeing each other of belts, buttons, zippers.

The coffee-stained wool snagged at her skin like a cold, damp sponge as he tugged her slacks and panties off.

Bright sunlight streamed into the kitchen—it couldn't be more different than the dark cramped confines of the closet where this had begun. She thought of the encounter in Mr. Forsyth's closet as foreplay, a teasing hint of what was about to take place.

A stronger woman might be able to resist Blake, but Sophie knew she couldn't. Not anymore. Having nearly been run down seemed to have diminished her scruples about sleeping with the cop she'd brought into the bank. Sure, she might end up losing her job, but right now, being alive and intimately connected with another human being seemed a whole lot more important.

She trembled as Blake hoisted her onto the counter, then gasped as she settled on the granite, so cold against her hot flesh.

Then he spread her legs and sank to his haunches.

Hands behind her on the counter, she braced herself, every part of her quivering for him. His head looked so dark between her thighs, the sun glinted off espresso-colored curls and a single gray hair stood out like a silver thread. She wanted to reach forward and touch the springy curls, but had a feeling she'd need to keep her hands planted behind her to stay earthbound.

She felt his breath, soft and erotic on the inside of her thighs, felt it waft against her own intimate curls like a gentle breeze through a wheat field. She ached for the touch of his tongue on her trembling flesh and it came, but not where she most burningly wanted it. He kissed the inside of her thigh.

"Mmm," she purred, her eyes drifting shut to savor the sensations. Probably she'd been this turned on before; she simply couldn't remember when.

He placed a row of kisses in entirely the wrong direction from where she so desperately needed him.

"Mmm-mmm." This time the sound she emitted was more a groan than a purr.

There was a time for teasing, a time for long slow buildup. Now was not one of those times. He didn't seem to have picked up on her obvious clues. The way her muscles were so tense, her hips strained to remain still, her breath started to hitch.

Little kisses traveled up to the front of her thigh, and then she felt his tongue. The shock of it lapping in such an odd place had her jerking her gaze to see what in the world he was doing. He lapped a faint brownish stain against her skin, then raised his head, as though aware of her perturbed gaze and shot her a killer grin. "I missed my morning coffee," he said and continued to lap.

"I'll make you a whole pot," she promised feebly. "After."

"But, I'm thirsty now," he mumbled against her thigh, and she felt the warm moist puff of air shivering against her skin as he spoke. He licked slowly up her thigh toward her hip while her mingled tension, frustration and desire mounted.

It was undeniably erotic, but there was a much more needy spot crying out for his attention. She wished she'd knocked the coffee into her crotch.

As though he'd read her mind, he raised his head once more. "I think some dribbled this way," and with his gaze holding hers, he took his index finger and tracked the supposed drop from her upper thigh, down the crease where her thigh met her pelvis. Closer and closer to her yearning, hungry core.

She wanted to hold still, but she couldn't. What those searing green eyes promised, and the single tracking finger hinted at, had her pumping her hips helplessly in the grip of desire. She wanted to tell him to hurry, but words seemed to have deserted her. Her only available communication seemed to be a kind of cavewoman grunting.

His finger touched her throbbing hot spot and she added moaning to the grunting.

Her head fell back and she shut her eyes, focusing all her energies inward, on the rising tide of excitement.

His finger, after that one brief touch, left her and his tongue tracked the course his finger had taken, from her hip, down the incredibly sensitive crease of flesh at the top of her thighs, to land, finally at her entrance, so hot and wet there could be no mistaking her need. His tongue traced her opening and she felt her body open wider in an unconscious plea for him to fill her.

But he didn't. "Not yet," he whispered so softly she barely heard him over her own escalating moans. In the closet she'd had to control herself. Here she didn't, and knew she couldn't if she tried.

His tongue trailed slowly up to the frantically throbbing bud. As the roughness of his tongue slid over the slickly smooth surface, she felt the warm wave build behind her eyelids.

She cried out.

He licked her again, not much more than a flick of the tongue. He seemed to gauge how close she was and was determined to drag out his sensual assault.

But need was greater than finesse, and she thrust her hips forward against his mouth. "Please," she gasped.

"Please!" And he, accepting she needed the release now, grabbed her hips and feasted on her.

Usually she tried to contain her embarrassingly rambunctious orgasms, but there was too much free-floating adrenaline, too much coiled tension in search of release, too much desire kindled by this particular man.

Her body was trembling so hard she felt she would tumble to the kitchen floor without his big strong hands holding her in place. His tongue drove her up mercilessly, exactly the way she needed it and her moans became cries, her cries, sobs, her sobs ululating wails. Finally, as the building wave crested and she felt her body thrown against the current like a tossed surfer, she screamed.

He held her through the mind-blowing intensity of the first explosion and eased her down through the aftershocks as her cries subsided to a final long drawn-out sigh of release.

But still, there was an unfulfilled ache deep inside her body, and Blake was still wearing his unzipped pants. They hung at his hips, so he was half-naked, but half-naked was not nearly naked enough. She slid her boneless body to the floor and this time she was the one to drop to her knees and strip him naked.

A smile of utter delight tugged at her lips once she allowed her gaze to dwell on him. He was as magnificent in the proudly upstanding flesh as her questing fingers had guessed.

She reached for him, but he stopped her. "Condoms," he all but spluttered, and she understood he wanted to be inside her, and fast. She wasn't about to get in the way of such a truly excellent idea.

"I have some in the bedroom, but I'm clean and on the Pill," she told him. "You?"

"Same," he muttered, already hoisting her back up

against the purring fridge. He must have realized how inane he sounded. "I mean. Not the Pill. Clean."

Then her hips were in his big, capable hot hands and her legs were round his waist. He kissed her, deep and hard and she tasted her own pleasure and a hint of coffee.

She felt his hardness probing and the shiver of appreciation as he drove high up into her body. The fridge was cold and hard against her back and Blake was hot and hard against her front, but it was the thrusting heat inside her body that had her going out of her mind.

Her hands, clinging round his neck, began to claw at his shoulders as their bodies thrust together, as primal and satisfying as a jungle drum.

She heard him groan, but it was more a groan of pain than pleasure and her eyes flew open.

"Blake. Your leg! Put me down."

"I'm not leaving your body until we both come." But he said it through gritted teeth.

She couldn't argue with his logic, but neither could she let him continue hurting himself. "Kitchen chair," she gasped.

"Floor." And he eased them down until he lay on the floor and she straddled him. It had taken some maneuvering from them both, but he was still imbedded inside her.

She grinned into his face, and then leaned forward and kissed him deeply. Her bashed knees protested when she tried to push up on them, so she lay flat atop him, put her legs between his and pushed her toes against the kitchen tile, rocking against him.

And she never stopped kissing him. He thrust his tongue deep in her mouth as she climaxed, swallowing the loudest of her cries and then groaning into her mouth as she felt the deepest, jerking thrusts and then the gorgeous rush of liquid deep within her body.

She lay sprawled atop him, her head against his chest, and started to giggle.

"What?"

"This reminds me of when we first met."

"I had a lot more fun this time."

She raised her head to smile down into his face. "Me, too. I thought somebody might pull the fire alarm the way I was screaming."

His deep chuckle rumbled beneath her. "You were smart to move into a concrete building. Good soundproofing."

"I should have warned you," she said, dropping her gaze to his chest and plucking softly at the hair there. "I'm kind of noisy."

"I like it."

"You do?" She raised her head in suspicion. Was he teasing?

"Sure. A lady in the boardroom, an animal in the bedroom. My ideal woman."

She chuckled herself, feeling ridiculously relieved. "You could go deaf. Next time bring earplugs."

A shadow crossed his face and she could have smacked herself. What on earth was she doing talking about next time? It wasn't as if they'd planned *this* time.

The atmosphere changed subtly, and she didn't know how to take it back to the comfort level they both clearly preferred. Fortunately, he did that for her.

"I think I just proved my point. You and I had sex, while we're working together."

A huge sigh of relief escaped her lips, followed by an uppity look. "No. We didn't."

"I had my cock inside you and we both climaxed." He nipped her lower lip.

"That absolutely did not count."

His lips quirked. "Why not?"

"We were standing up. Then we were on the floor. Besides, nobody has sex in the kitchen."

"Just for the record, let's say we were to have carnal relations in your bed. In the—" he scratched the emerging stubble on his chin and glanced at her like a poker player gauging what was in her hand "—missionary position."

"That would probably count," she had to agree. With a little prickle of unease she realized he could slip into her life and heart, just as easily as he could slip her into the missionary position. Or any other position he cared to name.

What had happened earlier could be put down to reaction from the stress and danger of almost being hit by a car. If they carried on and made love all afternoon in her bed...

She glanced at the kitchen clock before he did anything that would crumble all her willpower. Something really underhanded. Like kiss her. Or touch her. Or even look at her with that sexy expression in her eyes.

She was strong, but she had her limits.

"It's after one," she told him. "We should get back to work. Can you wait for me while I change?"

"You're not going back to work today." The bright green eyes were telegraphing "storm warning," and with a pang she realized their sexy idyll was over.

"That hit-and-run was no accident. Somebody tried to murder you."

Murder. That was a word for grisly novels, TV dramas and sensational newspaper headlines. It wasn't a word for people like her, ordinary women who worked in banks. "In your line of work, you must see murders all the time. But honestly, it doesn't happen in my world."

11

"SOPHIE, THIS ISN'T like your sex game, where you can choose whether it counts or not. This is serious. You were almost killed today, deliberately. Take a vacation."

"It was a crazy driver, that's all." With her free hand, she tightened the purple terry robe she'd put on after they made love. "I know it seems like a bizarre coincidence—I overhear a blackmail conversation, then the blackmailer dies, and now a car almost hits me—but coincidences do happen."

"Phil Britten was murdered." He hated having to tell her now, when she was feeling vulnerable, but he had to make her understand her life was in danger.

Truth was, he didn't want Sophie going on vacation and he didn't want her working in a company he was investigating. He wanted her to be a woman he'd met and liked. A woman he could take to bed for the pure bliss of moving inside her body. Of enjoying her utter enthusiasm for the deed. And going half deaf from her outrageous yells of completion.

But it wasn't that simple. He brushed her sex-disordered hair off her forehead, wanting to give her the comfort of his touch. Wanting to feel her, warm and alive.

Her head jerked up and she stared at him, her rosy cheeks paling before his eyes. "Murdered? But—but you said he overdosed on heroin."

He shoved a hand through his hair, wondering how

much he could tell her. Enough to get her on the first plane, bus or bicycle out of town, but not enough to put her in more danger. Or compromise the case.

"He was hot-capped."

He saw her puzzled expression and explained. "Britten didn't self-administer that dose. He was murdered with it. I met with my handlers yesterday—John and another guy you don't know. The toxicology report came back and there was ten times the normal dose in Britten's system, and it was the dope the Black Dragons have been peddling. They'd planted some stuff in his place to make it look like he was a user, but he wasn't."

"Oh, my God. So, it wasn't a coincidence after all? But…" She glared at him, as though realizing he'd been holding out on her. "You'd better tell me everything."

He'd hoped he wouldn't have to. He didn't want her having information that could endanger her, but now it seemed she was already in grave danger. "The Black Dragons are using your bank to launder money, Sophie. We've been interested in the Investment Bank of Vancouver for a while."

Once more a flush mounted her cheeks, but this time it was anger, not sexual satisfaction causing the glow. Her eyes sparkled with outrage. "This gang is using our bank to launder money?"

"Yep."

"But that's—"

"Hard to believe, I know. We've thought for a while they must have someone on the inside. Maybe several someones."

She rose, and he stepped back to give her space. She paced the kitchen floor in her bare feet. "So, Phil must have found out who their inside person is. That's what the blackmail was about. And instead of paying him off, they killed him.''

He nodded. ''And today you were almost killed. Are you convinced now that you need a vacation?''

She poured two glasses of water and handed him one. He didn't think she was thirsty so much as stalling for time. ''You think someone would try and kill me right outside my office in broad daylight?'' She shook her head. ''It's not logical.''

He understood she wanted him to make her believe that her life wasn't in danger, and he wished like hell he could do that. But she *was* in danger. Maybe if her close escape from death hadn't made him sick with worry and anger, he could have left her alone, but he hadn't been able to resist when she'd turned to him. Now that they'd made love, he was doubly determined to get her safely out of the way.

But, instead of being reasonable and cooperative, she was being her usual stubborn self.

''If that was a hit-and-run, why did they do it in broad daylight when people were all around?''

He shoved his hands in his pockets and went to work convincing her. ''Okay. How would you do it?''

Her forehead creased in puzzlement. Then she stared at him as though she had serious doubts about his sanity. ''You mean how would I plan a hit-and-run attack on myself?''

''Yeah.''

''Well, I'd get me alone on a deserted street late at night, and—''

''Where do you typically go late at night that's deserted?''

She looked up at the ceiling for a minute. ''Sometimes grocery shopping. Maybe out to dinner with a friend…''

"There's no pattern to it. A killer would have to track you for days looking for an opportunity."

She wrapped her arms around herself as though she were finding this exercise macabre. Which it was. But necessary. "What about the parking garages?"

"They're both secure. Sure, he could hit you, but there's no way it could be made to look like an accident, like Phil's death." The official word on Britten's death, the one given to the media and circulated at the investment bank, was that another unfortunate accidental overdose had occurred.

"You go for coffee across the street every single day about the same time." He hated to rub her nose in her own fear but he had to. "Anybody at the bank could pass on that information to the triad."

"Anybody at the bank," she said in a hollow voice. "Like the person I overheard Phil talking to. He must have passed on to the triad that Phil was trying to blackmail him. And they killed poor Phil."

He squeezed her shoulder. She didn't need him to confirm what she'd already figured out for herself.

"But why would they want to kill me?"

He'd been wondering that ever since he'd heard the garbled reports of Sophie's near accident and he'd raced to make certain she was all right. "Maybe they found out you overheard the conversation. Or it was enough that you went to visit Phil the morning he was found dead."

She sent him a cool glance. "Or we were seen going into the chairman's office when you searched it."

"Yeah." He liked that possibility least. It meant he'd dragged Sophie into danger. "If Forsyth's office has a surveillance camera, it's a sophisticated one and it's not hooked up to the central security system." Which suggested Forsyth had private surveillance. Blake had taken a quick look before searching the office, but he hadn't found anything. Didn't mean there wasn't something there, though.

"So far, everything we've picked up from the phone tap and bug has been legitimate work or personal business, which means that Forsyth is innocent, or he knows his office is being monitored."

Sophie seemed to be thinking deeply. He hoped she was trying to decide between the Caribbean and Europe. Then she shook her head. "I had a hard enough time thinking Mr. Forsyth could steal from the bank, but I'm certain he wouldn't take money from drug dealers. In any case, he's well-off, and I believe his wife comes from money. He's on all sorts of charity boards."

"You'd be surprised the trouble people can get themselves into."

"Well, if the triad's on to me, they're probably on to you, too."

"I'm trained for this stuff. You're not. I'm telling you to take a vacation." He couldn't keep the frustration out of his tone. Couldn't she see he wanted her safe?

"Is that a cop or my lover talking?"

If she'd kicked him in the privates she couldn't have more effectively taken his breath away. Because she was right. Physical attraction clouded the judgment and completely changed the dynamics between them. Would she argue with John like this? Or Kimberly? "Sleeping with you was a terrible idea," he groaned.

He felt her stiffen, and immediately realized his words weren't exactly going to win him any romantic-man-of-the-year awards. He looked down into her sexy-sweet face. "Hey, Sophie—"

"I'd say your lunch hour's over," she said.

"Look, I didn't mean… The sex was great. Fantastic. But I'm a cop on a case. I'm not your boyfriend."

"I don't recall asking you to be my *boyfriend.*" She gave the word the emphasis of a whiny high school student.

"Please, take a vacation."

Her blue eyes seemed to focus inward. After a full minute, she shook her head. "I don't run and I don't quit. Besides, you need a partner inside. Maybe I could have done more to help Phil, maybe I can stop other people from dying. There are decent people working for the bank. Decent people invest with us. I'm staying."

"But you're in danger."

She turned to him. "Now that I know there's danger, I'll be extra careful. Besides, you're a cop. It's your job to protect me."

"CAN'T YOU GO BACK OVER Phil's recent files and see if something looks suspicious?" Sophie asked Blake. They'd *accidentally* bumped into each other when, just as she was about to cross the street for her coffee, she saw him swinging toward her on crutches, balancing a huge take-out cup.

He'd got her coffee for her. The gesture was domineering, high-handed, interfering and so sweet she wanted to kiss him right there on the sidewalk.

Blake rubbed the back of his neck. "I've been through everything. Plus Ruby's assigned me a bunch of her bureaucratic busywork and spends half her day checking up on me."

"Welcome to banking," Sophie said, unable to hide her smirk at his grumpy face. She sipped her coffee and took a step back toward the bank building. "Thanks for the coffee."

"Wait. I want to ask you a couple of questions."

She glanced up and down the sidewalk. "I don't want anyone getting any ideas. They might think we're..." She flushed uncomfortably.

"We're what? Seeing each other? Having sex? You can explain that it doesn't count in a closet," he dropped his voice to a husky almost-whisper, and moved a step closer until his ugly green tie was hanging in her personal space, "or if we do it standing up."

Suddenly there didn't seem to be enough air in downtown Vancouver. Warmth pooled in her belly at the images his words evoked. Still, she was at work and this was her career. "I don't want people getting ideas about us."

He snapped his fingers as though he'd just discovered the answer to a baffling question. "Sure we do."

"Do what?"

"We want people getting ideas about us. Thinking we're an item. Don't you see? It means we can chat privately without anyone thinking it odd that the manager of HR is whispering to a lowly assistant account manager. If they think it's sweet nothings..." He shrugged.

"What about my reputation? My career?"

"You're missing the best part of the plan. In a couple of weeks, when this is over, I quit my job. Giving as my reason my growing attachment to a fellow employee. We'll look so damned noble you'll end up with a promotion."

"I have a strict personal policy—"

"We won't really do it." The devil danced in his eyes. "Not in a way that counts."

She was trying to disengage her brain from her pelvis when he leaned forward and kissed her lightly on the lips, thereby shutting down her brain completely.

She wasn't at all sure about Blake's brilliant plan to "pretend" they were an item when she was spending so much of her personal mental energy pretending they weren't.

The truth was, he got to her. He seemed as uninterested as she in being tied down. Not that she really knew much of anything about Detective Blake Barker. He had a bad temper, liked to drive and was great in bed. Well, she amended, he was great in the closet, against the fridge and on the floor. It seemed a fair assumption that he'd be great in bed if they ever got that far.

Not much to build a character assessment on. She couldn't even search his personnel file for clues because that was fake.

This whole thing was starting to feel fake. Like some bizarre reality TV show. And if Blake Barker had his way, she'd be voted off the show, sent on some bogus vacation while the plot heated up.

She wasn't a particularly brave person, but she wasn't so poor-spirited as to run away at the hint of trouble. Perhaps the car had meant to hit her, or perhaps it had meant to scare her, or maybe it was merely a case of her jay-walking in front of a crazy driver. Whichever it was, she was on her guard now. That had to count for something. She'd be extra careful. But how much danger could she be in? She had a bona fide cop working with her all day, security parking and she lived in a safe building.

She'd stay away from dark alleys, make sure she didn't stray too far alone, and look both ways before she crossed the street.

"What did you know about Phil at work?" Blake broke into her thoughts.

She considered his health, the isometric exercises he'd been doing in the elevator. "He was kind of obsessive. About everything. He was into extreme fitness, and, even though he hadn't worked here very long, he was very ambitious. Drove Ruby crazy. She wants a real assistant, not someone who's nipping at her heels for her job.''

"Ambitious." He grabbed her arm and stepped back as a bike courier hopped onto the sidewalk in front of them to bypass a bus. "Obviously willing to use any methods, including extortion, to make a buck."

She nodded, thinking again of that conversation she'd overheard. He'd sounded gleeful as he calmly asked for a million dollars. "He was supposed to try to bring in new business, but what if he went poaching? Trying to steal business from other account managers?" She shrugged. "It happens. The more business you bring in, the better you'll do. Maybe, while he was trying to steal their business, he found something—a loan that didn't conform to our policy, money coming in from suspicious sources."

"Well, if he was anything like me, he did a lot of work on Ruby's accounts. Maybe I'll do a little poaching myself. I'll start snooping around her biggest clients and work down to the smaller ones. Maybe something will jump out."

Edna emerged from the building behind Blake's back. Sophie hated what she was about to do, but she had to admit, if they were going to be seen together a lot, Blake's plan to pretend they were an item made sense. She put both hands on his cheeks and went up on tiptoe to kiss him as though she just couldn't help herself.

She watched his eyes widen, and warm, but before he could say a word, she said brightly, "Hi, Edna," knowing yet another story about her would be circulating around the bank in minutes.

She didn't like the idea of posing as Blake's girlfriend, but she had to admit, the deception smoothed the way for her to be his accomplice in crime-solving. Still, there was something unnerving about such a pretense.

She shook her head. They were two people having an affair, pretending not to have an affair, except at work where they were going to pretend they were having an affair. The whole thing sounded like a bad farce.

BY FRIDAY, BLAKE KNEW that Ruby was a lot nicer to her clients than she was to her drones. She had some nice, fat accounts, but, in spite of all his digging, every one of them still appeared legit. The only intriguing information he'd uncovered was some e-mails that made him suspect Ruby and Ellsworth had a thing going, or maybe she simply had a crush.

He pulled up across from Sophie's apartment, having followed her home once again without her knowledge. He was frustrated things weren't moving quicker on the money laundering investigation. As he sat waiting for her seventh-floor window to light up, he knew he was equally frustrated that pretending to have a love affair for the benefit of the office was giving him lots of kisses and cuddles at the office and no post-work follow-through.

While he sat there, gazing at her dark window, he imagined her entering her apartment, maybe going to the bedroom, shucking her clothes, stepping into the shower.

He was trying his damnedest to respect her wishes and stay away, but he couldn't stop himself wanting her.

He couldn't have said what it was that made the hairs on the back of his neck stand on end. Premonition? A sixth cop sense? Or had he seen something that hadn't registered at the time?

All he knew was that something wasn't right. That this night, of all the nights he'd surreptitiously followed her home, was different. She'd been inside her building almost four minutes. Normally her lights would flip on about now.

He'd been a cop too long to ignore his instincts. He was

out of the car, leaving the crutches in the back seat, and hobble-sprinting for Sophie's building before he even realized he meant to do it. He heard a sound, like a low moan building in intensity and then the explosion. Glass shattered and flames billowed from a window above. He didn't have to look up. He knew which window it was.

No time to waste. He was hammering on the doors of her apartment building to get the attention of a startled-looking older woman gazing at the ceiling with her mouth at half cock. His banging on the door seemed to rouse her from her rapt contemplation and slowly she shuffled toward him.

"Come on, come on! Fire!" he yelled at her through the glass door.

After she opened it, he barely stopped to tell her to evacuate before bolting for the stairwell.

The fire alarm was already blaring and, as he raced up, cursing his cast, he dodged stunned residents streaming down—mothers with children, people still chewing their dinners, an old woman clutching a yapping poodle.

As he ran his head was clear and calm. For now, he was a cop doing a job. But that didn't stop the sickening sense of dread in his belly or the sweat that popped out all over his body.

12

As he pounded up the stairs, he kept asking, "Sophie Morton? Has anyone seen Sophie Morton? Blond woman lives on the seventh floor?"

The residents who streamed past shook their heads, or stared at him blankly.

The fire alarm echoed shrilly in the staircase. The more distant, but equally shrill fire engine siren added another note of urgency to the silent wail in his head. *Sophie!*

His lungs burned by the time he reached seven. He smelled smoke even before he yanked open the metal door.

He didn't want to go through the fire door, afraid to face what might await him in the devastation of her apartment. He discovered, to his surprise, that his hands were cold and trembling. Maybe he'd wait here for the emergency crews.

But what if she needed him?

What if she was alive and trapped in there? It was that thought that had propelled him upward on his weak leg and it pushed him on in spite of the dread pitching in his gut.

He grit his teeth, shoved the door open and stepped through. The smoke wasn't too bad by the fire door but it billowed from her apartment doorway as though pumped out by a carnival smoke machine.

He was a cop. He'd seen death and destruction. He had a protective barrier he slid into place—knowing if he let emotion take over he was useless. But still, his mind couldn't stop silently yelling that one word. *Sophie.*

Where he'd pounded up the stairs, flight after flight as though a pit pull was snapping at his heels, now that he was on her floor everything seemed to slow.

All he could think about was how full of life Sophie was. He saw her in a fast series of photographic images. Her lying on top of him that first day when she broke his leg. Even stunned and in pain, he couldn't resist her sexy beauty. He saw her prim and proper in a business suit, then naked on her own kitchen counter—glorious and spread out for his delight, the sun highlighting her milky flesh, glowing off her pink-tipped breasts.

"Sophie!" He yelled aloud the name he'd been silently screaming all the way up the stairs.

He saw a shadowy movement from inside the cloud of smoke.

He squinted and made out a shape, a female shape. He felt goose bumps rise on his arms as he identified legs, arms, blond hair, and then the mist seemed to swirl around her so she disappeared.

"Sophie!" he yelled hoarsely, hope and fear warring in his chest.

The apparition turned and, with a stumbling step toward him, took solid form. There were tears on her cheeks. He didn't know much about spooky stuff, but he didn't think ghosts cried.

He ran down the hall toward her, once more cursing the cumbersome cast that slowed him.

She didn't move toward him, but stood rooted outside her apartment—or what was left of it. The door had blown out and the inside was a mess of flames, dust, debris. Her leather bag was hanging from the crook of one arm and in the other hand she held a newspaper.

"My apartment," she said.

He'd reached her by this time and all he could do was grab her to him, needing to feel her warmth and soft flesh, feel her heart beat and her breath move in and out of her body.

She hugged him back automatically, but it was clear she was in shock. "My apartment blew up," she said in the same stunned, blank voice.

"Let's get out of here. It's dangerous," he said as gently as he could.

She hadn't even started trembling yet. All the trembling was coming from him.

She was alive. And he had one thought and one thought only. He had to keep her alive.

"Come on," he said gently, turning her toward the fire escape. The smell of smoke and dust was making his eyes water and his throat close up.

"We've got to go." He squeezed her shoulders. "It's dangerous to stay." He dragged her down the hall as fast as he could, but they were both coughing when they got to the stairwell.

"I'm so glad I don't have a pet," she said, her voice hoarse. "We're allowed to, you know. Have pets in our building. I thought I might get an abandoned cat from the pound and give it a home."

"That's nice," he said, holding her hand as they walked down the stairs.

"If I'd saved a cat it would have been killed in there." She sniffed. "Blown up."

She looked so lost and stunned that he gave in to the impulse to kiss her. A quick, hard kiss that tasted of smoke and tears.

Where it had been crowded on his way up, the stairway was now empty. The fire alarm was starting to sound like it was tiring, but he assumed that was his ears growing accustomed to the din.

Down they went, slower than he would have liked because of his damn cast, but he didn't urge Sophie to go ahead, knowing she needed to hang on to him.

By the time they got to the ground-floor lobby, fully suited firefighters were entering the building. Through the door he glimpsed the milling residents, looking like confused bees forced out of their hive. They were being ushered across the street while emergency crews cordoned off the immediate zone around the apartment building.

He headed for the door, Sophie tucked under his shoulder, then stopped and cursed under his breath. Like rats sniffing out food scraps, he saw the media had arrived. The last thing he needed was to blunder into a scrum, maybe get his picture in the paper.

Blake ushered her not toward the front entrance, but to an inconspicuous exit that led to where garbage Dumpsters were stored.

She followed him, never questioning their movements. He opened the door a few inches and scanned the area. As he'd hoped, it was empty. All the excitement was at the front of the building.

Pulling her outside, he slipped his arm round her once more and headed down the paved alley, hoping to look like a couple strolling out for dinner or a movie.

How he wished that were true.

His vehicle was parked too near the front entrance to risk getting away unseen by cops he knew, firefighters he knew or journalists he knew. He shuddered at the thought and kept going. He hauled out his cell phone and called a cab to pick them up, naming an intersection a few blocks away. Then he called John to tell him what happened, asking him to alert the firefighters that there was no one inside Sophie's apartment.

The yellow cab was waiting when they got there and they were pulling up at his place within a few minutes. But it was a world away from the noise and confusion, the smoke and destruction of her apartment.

He helped her from the cab, paid the fare and they entered his own Yaletown apartment building.

She remained silent until he'd ushered her into his place. After their conversation about cat adoption, she'd fallen silent and stayed that way. He'd never known Sophie to be quiet for so long before and he was starting to worry.

He flicked on the lights and she shuddered.

"Cold? I'll put on a fire."

"No!" Panic lit her eyes. "No fire."

Stupid! Why don't you suggest some fireworks while you're at it?

He led her in and sat her on one of the leather couches, tossing yesterday's newspaper onto the antique pine blanket box his sister had bought him for a coffee table.

Sophie turned to stare out the window. He didn't think she was seeing the view of the harbor, though.

He left her alone with thoughts that had to be grim and went to find a bottle of wine. Maybe hot, sweet tea was the textbook remedy for shock, but in his experience a decent red wine did the job nicely.

He eased the cork out of a Bordeaux with a quiet sigh, then flipped through his CDs until he came to one of those reedy female soloists he kept around for times when he needed to impress a woman. It wasn't that he wanted to impress Sophie, he realized, he simply thought the music would relax her.

Turning the volume slightly lower, he poured the wine

and brought it over to where she was still sitting, staring out the window. "Here," he said gently.

She turned back to him and he was pleased to see a bit of color in her face. She even smiled. She started to reach for the wine, then glanced at the newspaper she was still clutching as though wondering how it got into her hand.

Carefully, she placed it on the blanket box, putting her leather bag on the floor beside her feet. Then she took the glass and as she sipped her hands weren't shaking too badly.

"Do you have a paper bag?" she asked him. Her color was fluctuating and she sounded breathless.

"A paper bag? I think so."

She was zipping open her leather satchel and starting to wheeze. "Never mind," she gasped and pulled out a crumpled paper bag. "Panic attack," she whispered, then stuck the bag over her nose and mouth and stared at the glass of wine as though it were the most important object in the universe.

He didn't know what to do. Should he go over to her and pat her back or would that make things worse? He decided to give her a few minutes and see what transpired.

He took the chair across from her and sipped his wine, which he'd opened mainly for her, wishing it were a scotch. He wanted to take somebody apart for what they'd done to Sophie and instead he had to pretend to be Assistant Account Manager Blake Brannigan, who'd so far uncovered absolutely nothing to help put the drug-dealing murderers away before they got Sophie.

She pulled the bag away from her face and slumped back. "Sorry," she said, glancing at the bag still clutched in her hand. "I feel like an idiot. In my head I know a paper bag doesn't stop the attacks, but, as my therapist said, whatever works." She was still breathless and he could see her chest continued to jerk with her unsteady breath, but, it seemed, the worst of the attack was over.

"Is there any chance that was an accident?" she asked.

"Sure, there's a chance. Why don't you tell me exactly what happened?"

She sipped deeply, then tilted her head back, resting it against the couch. "I opened my door, flipped on the light switch, then turned back to get the newspaper. I'd forgotten to pick it up. Sometimes the kid who delivers them is careless and the paper's nowhere near the door." She took a deep breath. "I remember thinking I was going to complain about it one of these days. I left my key in the door, took about two steps and...and next thing I knew there was a bang and the door flew open. Then flames came out." Her voice wavered as she hit the last sentence, then stopped, pressing her lips together.

"Thank God you weren't inside." It was a stupid, inane thing to say, and he hadn't planned to interrupt her, but right now he wanted to find that paper carrier and give him the biggest tip of his career. His carelessness had saved Sophie's life.

She seemed not to have heard him, anyway. "I was on the floor, my shoulder jammed against the wall." She massaged her left shoulder vaguely, as though she'd only now realized it was sore. "I guess the explosion threw me and I didn't notice. I got up. The fire alarm went off—I remember that—and then people started coming out of their apartments. We've had false alarms, but it was pretty obvious to anyone on my floor that this was for real. A couple of people asked if I was okay and then went for the stairs."

"Did you see anybody you didn't recognize? Before or after the blast?"

Her blue eyes sharpened. "You think it was deliberate, don't you?"

When she turned those transparent blue eyes his way, he wanted to soothe her. But he couldn't lie. "Yes."

She nodded. Not surprised.

"I'm sorry, Sophie."

She started to set her wineglass down then paused. "Do you have a coaster?"

"I don't usually bother."

"This is an antique. You should treat it with respect." She shivered and all at once he knew she was imagining her own possessions. He didn't imagine you could treat anything with less respect than to blow it up. If it made her feel better to fuss over his possessions he supposed he could let her.

"I've got some somewhere. Hang on." He got up and rummaged in the drawer where he kept his corkscrews and odds and ends. There was a set of London pub coasters his dad had bought him from a trip to England.

He brought over a couple and she set her wineglass down at last. Then she looked at him and he was surprised to see the old Sophie was coming back. Maybe not completely; she was still pale and there was a definite tremor in her hands, but the blank expression was gone. Her warm vitality was returning. He hadn't realized how much he'd wanted to see that again.

"We've got to get more aggressive in our investigation at the bank," she informed him in the kind of tone she'd use to up morale in the office.

He couldn't believe what he was hearing. "Sophie, you've got to see that your life is in serious danger. You'll e-mail your resignation and then disappear. We'll help you. Nobody, and I mean nobody, will know where you are until this thing is over."

The color he'd wished to see in her face was back now with a vengeance as an angry flush mounted her cheeks.

"I'm not a coward, Blake. Those bastards won't get away with this."

"It's too dangerous."

"What if you don't find them? Huh? Then what do I do? Hide from my shadow for the rest of my life? There are women in policing and the armed forces who risk their lives every day, fighting monsters like these thugs, and you want me to run and hide?" She thumped the pine with her fist, making the glasses tremble. "I will not run away from these scum."

He admired her, even as her courage made him fear for her. The truth was that he was involved and that made it difficult to be objective. "I don't want to lose you," he said, giving her the truth.

Her anger softened and her smile was full of sexy sweetness. "You won't lose me. We'll do a better job of working together so we can clear the vermin out of my bank."

"This is not open for discussion."

She sipped more wine and seemed to think things over, while he waited for her to see reason. "All right," she said and rose to her feet.

He couldn't believe she'd caved in so fast. His eyes narrowed suspiciously. "Where are you going?"

"To a hotel for tonight."

His mind raced through possibilities. He nodded slowly. "If we get you in without anyone seeing you, using an alias, you'll be safe enough for a night. Tomorrow we'll figure out a safe place for you to stay."

"You said this wasn't open for discussion, so I'm not discussing it. I'll see you at work Monday."

"No."

"You can't stop me, Blake."

Fury welled within him along with the fear that he might

fail to keep her safe. "You're not going to work if I have to tie you to that bed in there until it's safe."

Her chest rose and fell in a quick, jerky breath, and he wished he'd come up with some other threat. Now the image of her, lush and naked, staked out for his pleasure, was interfering with his intellect. "That's not what I—"

"It's a tempting offer." Her voice had a taunting, seductive quality that spoke right to his inner caveman. He couldn't blame his ancestors for clubbing women over the heads and dragging them to their caves, not if they were as infernally stubborn as this one.

And, like the caveman, when reasoning had ceased to impress his thickheaded cavewoman, he advanced on her, his eyes narrowed.

She must have known what he was thinking for she took a step backward, possibly to protect herself from being dragged by the hair to his cave for some hot and dirty sex. He imagined after a few rounds with Sophie, his cave paintings would resemble an early issue of *Playboy*.

He put his hands on her shoulders and felt the tension in her muscles.

Her eyes stared up at him and he could tell that now her body was coming back to life, she was having the same post-danger high she'd experienced after her near miss with the hit-and-run.

If Blake knew anything about women, Sophie wanted him. And she wanted him now.

13

BLAKE LEANED FORWARD TO kiss her, but apparently he'd misread her cues, for she pulled back. "I smell like a dirty ashtray," she said. "Do you think I could borrow your shower? Can't go to a hotel smelling like an arsonist."

She grinned. Amazingly, she grinned. And somehow, he couldn't help grinning back. He kept forgetting how much tougher she was than she appeared. "I'll lend you my bathrobe, then we'll talk."

"Thanks."

"We need to eat. Pizza okay with you? There's a brick-oven place around the corner that delivers."

He fetched her a couple of clean towels and showed her to his bathroom. "You're in luck. The cleaning lady comes Fridays." He could have led her to the guest bathroom, but his shower was bigger. Besides, he loved the idea of Sophie naked and wet in his shower. If it weren't for his cursed cast, he'd be sorely tempted to join her. Instead, he fetched some clean clothes from his room, made do with a sponge bath, and washed his hair in the laundry sink.

By the time she emerged, wrapped in his bathrobe, her hair clinging to her head in damp ringlets and her feet bare, he'd had a chance to calm down. Although he felt less than relaxed when he realized she had to be naked under his robe. He cleared his throat. "I ordered the pizza."

"If pizza's first, what's second?" Her lips savored each

word and he was mesmerized by the sensuality of her mouth.

Knowing it was hopeless to try to resist, he went to her, dipped his head and kissed her, slowly and thoroughly. She smelled of his shampoo and tasted of his toothpaste.

"Second, we talk. Like it or not you and I are a team. We have to start acting like one." He traced a finger up one side of her neck and twirled a wet curl.

"And third—" He dipped his head again, taking his time, tasting her, deepening the kiss until she was clinging to him, her hands delving into his hair, pulling him closer.

"On the other hand—" he raised his head for a panting breath "—I might have got the order wrong. About that pizza..."

"Screw the pizza," she murmured and pulled him back down to her mouth.

As much as he wanted to rip his robe from her body and take her with the flaming urgency that consumed him, he was also conscious of a desire to touch and savor slowly. To kiss each inch of her so miraculously spared by a paper carrier with a bad aim. To touch and caress her and watch each nuance of her expression as her passion built, to feel the warmth rise on the surface of her skin, watch her various pulse points as they picked up speed until they were racing in a dead heat for the finish line. And when that finish arrived, he wanted to watch the abandoned way her head fell back and she let out her own rebel yell of victory.

Above all, he wanted to bury himself in her body. Spill his seed inside her. Pill or no pill, he was self-aware enough to recognize his primal roots in that burning urge to pour his life essence into her. If his forebears were all like him, it was no wonder his bloodline had flourished.

His hands dropped to her belly, touching the flat, firm

abdomen, and the idea of her blooming, heavy with his child, added an extra degree or two to the roaring heat in his blood.

He didn't freak, as he normally would have done, to find himself fantasizing about the woman he was about to make love to getting pregnant. He accepted it for what it was, a basic instinct to celebrate the escape from death with the creation of new life.

But there was a tiny part of him that wondered if that's all it was.

He didn't bother analyzing his feelings any more than he tried to talk Sophie into his bed. He simply led her to his leather couch, pushed her back so she toppled, giggling, in a sprawled, sexy heap, and yanked open the tie at her waist. Beneath the masculine black robe, her body was all female. Rounded and pink, the nipples on those amazing breasts blooming beneath his gaze. He reached for his wine, stuck a finger in it and rubbed the dark red liquid first on one nipple, then on the other, while she moaned and twisted beneath him.

Of course, being a wine lover, he had to lick the stuff off, pulling each dark red point deep into his mouth to suck and savor. Half laughing, half moaning beneath him, she grabbed at his shirt, plucked at his belt in a totally uncoordinated attempt to undress him.

He rose and did the job himself, in no mood to waste time.

She ran her gaze up and down him, a siren's smile on her face and then, before he saw it coming, she'd pulled him off balance so he landed beside her on the couch.

While he tried to rearrange his limbs in a less dorky pose, she reached for the wine, took a mouthful and, with a teasing glint in her eye, knelt over him. Then she took him into her mouth and his hips jerked helplessly as the wine swirled around his engorged, sensitive flesh. She sucked on him in some fantastic way that sounded as if she were inhaling the remains of a soft drink through a straw. It felt like a miniwhirlpool against his cock and he delved and thrust helplessly, approaching bliss much faster than he wanted to.

She swallowed the wine with a noisy gulp and rose up to sit in his lap, taking him in hand and guiding him into her body. He leaned forward and licked the trail of red wine that dribbled down her chin.

They were as silly as kids, but this was a celebration of the most fundamental kind and even as they played and teased, their thrusts grew harder, her gasps louder, until he couldn't stand it anymore and grabbed her hips, pulling her down even as he thrust up, always deeper, as though he could thrust through to her very essence.

She was sobbing, her head thrown back as he felt her inner muscles clench around him. He pulled her down faster, delved farther, and there it was, the high-pitched scream that was just about the sexiest thing he'd ever heard.

He let go, feeling his own life essence pump into her.

Afterward, they lay slumped and panting in each other's arms and would have slept had the pizza not arrived. He borrowed his own robe, deliberately leaving her naked. When he returned with the fragrant box, he shucked his robe and they ate—naked and greedy—feeding each other, sharing wine, both determined not to talk about or think about the earlier disaster.

But, eventually the pizza was gone, the wine bottle empty and the sky outside was dark.

She sighed. "I'd better call a cab and get myself to a hotel."

"Stay here." he heard himself say. The minute the

words were out he felt the rightness of them in his belly
and some of his coiled fear for her safety eased. If he kept
her under his roof, he could protect her. While he let her
think about the idea, he didn't waste his mouth's proximity
to the swirl of her ear, but traced it with his tongue, then
breathed lightly, enjoying the shiver that rippled through
her.

"You want me to stay here tonight?" Her voice was
vague and foggy and he had the impression that while their
spent passion gave his mind an odd, racing clarity, it had
fogged hers over so she was having trouble thinking co-
herently.

"Not just tonight." The wonderful straight line of ten-
don that stretched from her ear to her throat beckoned. He
traced it with his tongue, pausing here and there to nibble
gently. "Stay here until we catch the bastards."

She ran her hands through her hair, making him want
to follow suit. He loved its random curls, especially now
they were tossed all over the place, still damp in places,
gleaming with hints of gold, platinum and copper. "You
mean move in with you?"

A shaft of panic speared him. He'd avoided that trap for
years. Was he now snapping the jaws shut on his own
freedom? "Not permanently," he assured her.

Her breasts, rising and falling rapidly, called to his aching hands, but he could see she was trying to think so he
pulled away and stared at the floor, trying to get his own
breathing under control.

"I've got friends I could stay with," she said, sounding
uncertain.

"Don't push it, Sophie. The only way I'll consider letting you go back to work on Monday is if you agree to
stay here with me until this thing is over. We live together,

commute to work together, spend every damn minute of the day together.''

She glared at him mutinously for a moment, then nodded.

His relief was tempered by determination to watch her every second. Sophie wasn't going to die on his watch.

To move in with Blake, even temporarily, was to enter dangerous territory. A girl with no sense of direction could end up seriously lost making a move like that. Hopelessly and permanently lost. Sophie sucked in a deep breath. ''Where will I sleep?''

Cleaning the criminal scum out of her bank had to be their first priority, and she knew if she climbed into his bed, it would be a very long time before she climbed out again.

She was so happy she'd started that silly no-bed equals no-sex rule because now it seemed it would come in handy. Sharing Blake's bed—living together, for goodness' sake—sounded way too permanent. She didn't do permanent. Permanent was for people like her parents, who found the perfect partner for life and lived happily ever after. It wasn't for a commitment-phobic modern woman who'd never had a relationship that didn't end up making her feel trapped.

His narrowed eyes told her he'd guessed what she was thinking. Still, he tried. ''I have a king-size bed in my room. Plenty of space. I think it was recommended by the American Chiropractic Association.'' He tapped his spine. ''Very good for the back.''

She held back her smile. He was so adorable when he turned on the charm. They'd both need visits to the chiropractor if they did half the things she wanted to do with Blake in his bed. With regret, she told him what he'd probably already figured out for himself. "If I stay with you I can't share your bed." She must sound like a crackpot, but she couldn't explain to him how she felt.

"Why?" He sounded more like a petulant four-year-old who'd been denied a treat than a grown man.

"Because I don't particularly want to die. I do want to, one, get the bastards who tried to kill me, and two, get the bastard who's using my workplace for criminal activity. We won't be able to concentrate if we spend all our time in bed."

He sighed noisily. "For someone who likes sex as much as you do, you put up a lot of barriers."

She decided to put up another one, and retrieved his bathrobe from the floor and snuggled into it. It smelled like him, so she hugged it to her, taking strength and comfort from the robe just as she did from the man. Since she was thinking about sex anyway, she might as well get the whole subject dealt with at once. "I think we should have a few ground rules about living together."

He scowled at her and began shoving his clothes on. "If you're thinking about some kind of dorm roster of who does the dishes and who cooks meat loaf on Thursdays, you can forget it."

"I'm not worried about food. I'm worried about sex," she snapped back.

Miraculously his scowl lifted. "Honey, you've got nothing to worry about. Lie back and leave everything to me."

She chuckled. God, he was cute. Arrogant, but cute. "That's a perfect example of what I'm talking about."

"What?"

"Sexual innuendo. Come-ons. No come-ons while I'm staying here. It's not fair."

"Because your willpower is so frail?" he taunted.

He must know that was true. She was a sexual powder keg and he was a blowtorch. "Yes."

"Agreed."

"No walking around naked or half-dressed."

"Does my naked body arouse you that much?"

He was really getting her goat. "Yes! And don't think I'm happy about it."

"Well, it goes double for me." He looked her up and down as though she were an oasis and he'd just crawled through a thousand miles of desert. "So the same rule applies. You wear a ski suit in this apartment or I'm not responsible for the consequences."

She shot him an evil look. "And none of that, either."

"None of what?"

"Those steamy come-to-bed glances. I'm only human."

"Yeah, well, do you have some kind of bra that doesn't show your nipples? Maybe something in iron?"

She glanced down, appalled at the blatant way her breasts were telecasting her lust, and crossed her arms over her chest. "It's not going to be easy, is it?"

"No, ma'am."

She cleared her throat. "Should I sleep on the couch?"

"If you're sure..." He glanced toward his bedroom, where visions of king-size chiropractic-approved mattresses danced in her head and she frowned him down. Oh, Lord. How were they ever going to get through this? "I have a guest room. Come on, I'll show you."

She hadn't noticed a second bedroom. In fact, she hadn't noticed much of anything when she first arrived, but now that the shock had subsided, she found herself looking around his apartment for the first time and taking it in.

It was nice.

Much nicer than she would have imagined—a decent-sized loft in a trendy part of town. She didn't know much about police officers, but she didn't think they earned this kind of money. Unease stirred within her. "This is a very nice place," she said.

He must have heard her surprise for he chuckled softly. "You can thank my sister."

"Your sister?"

"Yeah. Tanya talked me into buying it when they first started converting these old warehouses into lofts. She was in real estate then and she told me it was a great buy." He shrugged. "She was right." Sophie knew enough about real estate in Vancouver to hazard a shrewd guess that if he'd bought in Yaletown before it became ultratrendy, his apartment had easily doubled or tripled in value. A good buy indeed.

"Do you always do what your sister tells you?"

"Pretty much," he said with no irony that she could see. "She's a lot smarter."

This was the first time he'd mentioned a sister, or any family. Once again she realized how little they knew about each other. He was so bossy with her it was hard to imagine him taking advice from a sister. "She must be something," Sophie said almost to herself.

"Oh, she is."

"Is she still selling real estate?"

"No. She's a financial planner now."

She shot him a quick glance, and took another look around the apartment, only now taking in details that didn't seem consistent with a cop's salary. The apartment itself may have been a steal, but he hadn't furnished it with junk. The leather on the couches was butter soft, the appliances she'd glimpsed in the kitchen were top of the line, there was art on the wall that didn't look like prints. Even the wine had tasted expensive, now that she thought about it.

"She's your financial planner, isn't she?"

His eyes twinkled with lazy amusement. "Yep."

"Blake, are you rich?"

He chuckled. "Tanya's rich. But I'm in good shape for a rainy day."

Somehow, her world kept getting stranger and stranger. "Show me my room."

He led her down a short hallway. The guest room was surprisingly nice for a household run by a bachelor. The double bed was made with a cheerful chintz spread, there was a pine dresser with a nice-sized mirror and a night table with a lamp and a clock on it. "Your bathroom's through there," he said, pointing to a door.

They wouldn't be sharing a bathroom then. Thank goodness, that was a major source of anxiety gone. There'd be no bumping into each other half-naked on the way to the shower. No middle-of-the-night meetings on the way to the washroom.

Which suddenly made her realize she didn't have so much as a pair of pyjamas. "I don't even have a toothbrush," she said.

"There's some girl stuff in the bathroom," he said vaguely. "A couple of unopened toothbrushes, and some clothes in the closet that will probably fit. We can do some shopping tomorrow after we check in with John."

She might have bristled over his bossy ordering of her day, except she was too busy bristling over his casual mention of women's clothes in his guest-room closet and "girl stuff" in the bathroom.

"Taken up cross-dressing?" she asked sweetly.

His cocky grin made her wish she'd kept her witchy comment to herself. Now he probably thought she was jealous. "It's my sister's stuff. She stays over when she's in town."

It was plausible. Anyway, it wasn't as if she owned the

man. They'd had "doesn't count" sex a few times, but they both knew things were too complicated to risk getting involved.

So why was she itching to check out the clothes and decide for herself how sisterly they looked?

14

"Do you feel like Thai?" Blake asked. "Or better still, do you feel like cooking?"

They were strolling along Robson Street, a hefty selection of shopping bags between them—though all the contents were hers. It was amazing how much stuff she had to replace.

Sophie was torn between enjoying his company and his Sherpa services, and feeling irritated that he'd insisted on accompanying her everywhere today. He was easy company, if she ignored the wariness in his eyes. She sensed that he was assessing every car that went by, every pedestrian they passed, from a group of Korean language students, to German tourists to locals out shopping.

As much as his solid bulk made her feel safe, his bodyguard act was making her edgy. John and the fire inspector had paid a visit this morning and she'd been forced to relive the experience of coming home to an exploding apartment. As though she hadn't relived it all night in her brief spurts of sleep.

There'd been a gas leak, they told her. Something had sparked and caused the explosion. It could be accidental, they wouldn't know for certain until the fire investigator's report was complete. But the subtext was clear; given the suspicions of money laundering and the all-too-recent death of Phil Britten, nobody believed it was an accident.

Including Sophie. No matter how hard she tried, she

couldn't stop herself from imagining what would have
happened had she been standing inside, instead of outside,
her apartment when it blew.

As grateful as she was for Blake's protection, she
wished she didn't need it. She wanted him walking beside
her because he was crazy about her. She wanted to be able
to stop in the middle of the sidewalk and exchange a light
kiss, like the couple not far ahead of them.

With an internal groan she realized she didn't want
Blake to be a brief fling that should never have happened.
She wanted him as her lover until they wore each other
out.

She stopped dead. Right in the middle of the milling
throng. Oh, Lord. She wasn't feeling twitchy, or hemmed
in, or wanting to bolt as she'd imagined she'd feel the
minute she agreed to move in with Blake. Instead, she
wanted him to act like a lover even after she'd specifically
told him not to. How weird was that?

Blake had walked on three full steps before he noticed.
His head jerked back and she saw alarm flash in his eyes
until he spotted her. He was at her side in an instant. "Everything okay?"

"Yes," she said, handing him a carrier bag. The sooner
they could solve her bank's problems, the sooner they
could both start acting like normal people.

OVER SEAFOOD FETTUCCINE and white wine, she said, "If
we were seen going in to Mr. Forsyth's office, then why
aren't you being targeted, too?"

"I don't think the chairman's office had anything to do
with the attacks on you." He rubbed the back of his neck.
Lines of tiredness spiderwebbed from the corners of his
eyes. "Everything we've overheard has been benign."

"Well, that could happen if we were seen, right? They

wouldn't want you to know you were on to them, so they'd act innocent.''

"Then why blow up your apartment? It can't go both ways. If it's Forsyth, and he knows he's being watched, he's incredibly stupid to make attempts on your life and try to make them look like accidents.''

She nodded. "And if it's not Forsyth, then we're back to who's involved in the triad and why they're trying to kill me.''

"Yeah. You're the key. You've seen something, or have information you don't know you have.''

"I hate this. Everything that happens at work, I wonder. Every conversation, every e-mail, I'm wondering. Is it them? Are they involved? I need to do something to make this go away. I've searched my memory for anything odd or out of the ordinary, but my life was fine until I overheard that conversation and everything's been crazy since then.''

"Then the person being blackmailed, the person we have to assume is the same one working with the triad, must have seen you and thought you overheard the conversation.''

She felt sick going in to work, but she felt even more sick at the thought of running away. "Will you try really hard to keep me safe?''

"Yeah. If you insist on coming to work, your best defense is to act like you're crazy about me.''

She choked. She'd been thinking she'd have to take a crash course in karate, carry an arsenal of secret gadgets, conduct cryptic conversations with possible murderers, and all she had to do was moon over a co-worker? "I have to tell you, I think that idea sucks.''

He touched her cheek with one finger. "Fake it. I hear you women are good at that.''

"Oh, you hear that, do you?"

He grinned at her and the awful band of combined fear and anger eased off her chest. "I certainly don't have any recent experience. Nobody could fake what you do."

She was half amused and half embarrassed. "Nobody'd want to."

"Are you kidding? It's sexy as hell."

"So," she said, determined to ignore the way he'd eased his body closer to hers while they spoke, until there wasn't more than an inch between them. She felt his warmth, saw his chest rise and fall with his breathing. She knew it would be the easiest thing she'd ever undertaken to pretend to be gaga over him. "Apart from pretending I've lost my mind and find you irresistible, what else do I have to do?"

"Keep your eyes and ears open. Do nothing out of the ordinary. Everyone at work knows you and they talk to you. Maybe something will slip. And you'll be crazy about me, coming to see me whenever you can in the day, we'll have lunch together, leave together, giving you plenty of opportunities to pass on anything you hear."

She knew he was determined to protect her 24/7, and she had to admit to being relieved. Still, she wanted to help, to speed up the investigation in some way. "That's it?"

"If you and I are a hot and heavy couple, I'll have more freedom to move around. I can go anywhere and tell people I think you're lost and I'm looking for you." He winked at her and she smiled perfunctorily.

"As a human resources manager I have to tell you this whole crazy-for-each-other business is extremely unprofessional and I would never normally act that way."

"I know. And I'm sorry."

"You'll only bring suspicion to yourself if you're seen with me."

"I don't think so. I'm the new guy with the gimpy leg. Nobody's looked at me twice."

She decided not to let him in on how many of the female staff she'd seen ogling him. Still, she had to admit, no one seemed suspicious of him. "Because you've been doing your job. Start acting strange and they'll notice all right."

"I'll be in love. Love always makes people act strange."

She smiled, but there was a pang in her heart at his words. Probably stress and fear were messing with her brain but she wondered what it would be like if they weren't pretending.

"YOU DON'T NEED TO ESCORT me to my office," Sophie insisted for the seventeenth time.

"I can't stand to be away from you for as much as a minute," Blake argued, holding the door open as they entered the bank building.

"You know, I never go out with guys like that," she informed him, in case he ever truly decided to pursue her.

"Guys like what?" he asked as they trod the marble foyer together to the elevators. Of course, he'd chosen to arrive at the busiest time of the morning, so the maximum number of bank employees would see him with his arm around her shoulders, using his weak leg as an excuse to treat her as a human crutch.

His arm felt like a warm shackle. "Guys who cling," she told him, trying without success to shove his arm off, "and don't give a person any space."

"That long-distance relationship must have been perfect for you. Lots of hot sex when you saw him, and the rest of the time your life was your own."

He'd figured it out so exactly, she was stunned at his perception.

''Those messages on your machine last night weren't all from your sister,'' she reminded him.

Maybe it was in an effort to underscore that this relationship was pretend, but they'd spent Sunday evening talking about their previous lovers.

It was strange. It hadn't been in the spirit of sharing, but more like, *here are my warning signs.* She'd flashed hers. Told him about her four-year long-distance relationship with the man in San Francisco. They'd been split up only a few months and she was appalled at how little she missed him. She missed the sex, but not the person.

Her warning placard was raised: *I go for sex, not intimacy.*

He'd retaliated by telling her about how his friends had stopped setting him up, letting her see the neon sign flashing: *confirmed bachelor.*

That had been over coffee after dinner. By the time she was yawning for bed, they'd been through a litany of all their friends who'd started out in love and were now divorced or split.

How they each had parents who'd been married forever. Too bad nobody was doing that anymore. Must be modern culture.

She told him the only thing she'd ever really stuck with was her job.

He told her his job stopped him from getting involved with women. Sometimes he disappeared for a while when he was on a case. There were things he couldn't talk about.

Clearly, he wasn't a monk, though, as the phone calls from different women proclaimed.

The third time she'd raised her brows as the bubbly voice of a flight attendant in town for a couple of nights chirped over *La Traviata* playing in the background.

He didn't look a bit abashed. ''A guy's got to live,'' he

informed her. His gaze rested on her and she felt the heat even through her sweater and jeans. They were both trying so hard, she knew, to keep things light and casual, but there was nothing casual about the expression on his face. It was his come-to-bed look. Did he even realize he was wearing it? Probably not.

She was only human, and her body had woken from its sexual hibernation famished. Any man would probably make her feel this way, she tried to convince herself, even as she licked her lips and answered his hungry gaze with one of her own.

The heat that smouldered constantly between them flared to life and she moved toward him, wanting to touch him, needing his overwarm flesh rubbing naked against hers.

The phone rang.

"Leave it," she ordered, leaning over him to run her tongue across his bottom lip.

She heard a husky female voice leaving a message, and Blake pulled away to answer the phone. Then, with a glance of apology, he took the portable phone with him into the bedroom and shut the door.

It was nothing to Sophie, of course, but she was irritated at his lack of manners. When he emerged a few minutes later and said, "I have to go out for a while," she'd blurted what was in her mind, without stopping to think.

"I might not be looking for permanence, but at least I stick with one man at a time."

He turned on her and she was surprised to see a spurt of anger disturb the glassy green surface of his eyes. "I don't screw around indiscriminately, either. That was a...source. Whatever is going on with us, I'll see it through."

"Nothing's going on with us," she assured him, feeling somewhat light-headed.

"Bullshit."

"Good night." She rose.

"Does my language offend you?" he called after her.

She turned back. "No. Your attitude does."

Since she'd gone to bed then and hadn't heard him come in, they'd been polite but distant with each other this morning. Until they arrived at work and he turned into octopus-arms Brannigan. She tried once more to shake him, but he merely smiled and kissed her nose, leading her into the elevator.

The minute they were alone, she shook off his arm and moved a pace away. "If you ever kiss my nose in public again, you'll be eligible for a boys' choir."

He sucked in a breath. "Ouch."

"Do you have any idea how many people are talking about us right now?" she all but wailed as the elevator rose silently.

"The more the better."

The indicator light for the fourth floor lit up and he closed the space between them, putting his arm around her waist this time. "It's showtime."

She could either leave her own arm flapping around in the air like an outdated fashion accessory or she could copy his pose and wrap her arm around his waist.

It galled her, but she didn't have much choice. Just as the elevator doors opened she gave the flesh at his waist a good pinch.

"Ow," he said in her ear. "What was that for?"

"Nose kissing."

It didn't matter that the low conversation between them was composed mainly of insults and promises of retribution, to anyone watching them with their heads together and arms wrapped around each other, the conclusion would be obvious.

Sophie, the most discreet employee the bank had ever hired, had embarked on a sloppy, public, childishly moronic affair with a colleague.

She might go along with playing kissy-face, but inside she was seething. On top of ruining her apartment and trying to kill her, her unseen enemies had forced her to compromise her own career.

Just when she thought Blake was about to leave, he grabbed the front of the white shirt he'd watched her iron not an hour ago at his place. While her mouth opened in outrage and her hand went up automatically to beat him away, he pulled her toward him in a gesture that was irritatingly Neanderthal and excitingly suggestive.

He brought his lips down to cover hers and her body forgot this was pretend as shock waves of excitement danced across her skin.

He took his time, seeming to savor the touch and taste of her.

The hand that had risen to bat his away, clutched at his fist instead. Holding it against her heart.

He raised his head at last and in that second before he released her, she saw emotion flit across his eyes. A mix of attraction, pure, physical want and an unsettling something that had her yearning for time together away from the distractions of their work.

He let go of her shirt slowly and she exhaled, a stuttery, fluttery breath.

"Whenever you have a minute, Sophie." Ellsworth's voice seemed to come from far away and she was surprised at how peevish he sounded until she came back to herself and realized he'd witnessed the unprofessional smooch that Blake had no doubt arranged for his benefit.

She hoped Ellsworth would mistake the flush of anger sweeping her cheeks for embarrassment. When this thing was over, she was going to insist that the chief of police write a letter to her company explaining that Sophie was acting on police orders when she started kissing a fellow employee in the workplace.

"Morning, Ellsworth," Blake said cheerily.

"Blake." The older man nodded curtly.

"I'll come get you for lunch, Soph," Blake said then turned and headed for the elevator.

Soph? Her jaw dropped. She turned to find Gwen's mouth similarly gaping and Ellsworth looking green around the gills.

She'd put up with a lot, but Blake had crossed the line.

"You've got some messages, *Soph*," Gwen informed her with a barely-straight face.

"It's a new relationship," she said. "He hasn't totally figured out all the ground rules yet. Like my name is Sophie."

"Well, whatever your name is, I don't know what you've been up to, but you've got police, fire department and your insurance agent all trying to get hold of you." Gwen spoke lightly, but with an edge of real concern.

Sophie tried for the upset tone of a woman whose home had blown up accidentally, rather than the flaming anger of a woman who knew it had been done deliberately.

"There was some kind of gas leak at my apartment Friday that caused a fire."

"Oh, my gosh. Are you all right?" Gwen's face paled and her eyes widened. Good acting or true shock? Someone was in on this and it could be anyone at the bank.

She glanced at Ellsworth and saw him flush bright red then pale to the color of chalk. "My God, you should take some time off. Go home...'' He shot her a questioning look and she shook her head.

"I can't go home. It's a bit of a mess.'' In fact it was a total disaster, but she didn't want whoever was behind this knowing how close they'd come to getting rid of her.

"Have you got somewhere to stay?''

She nodded. "I'm staying with Blake temporarily.''

"Every cloud has a silver lining,'' Gwen mumbled, handing Sophie her messages. "If it doesn't work out with the hunk, you're welcome to stay with me.''

"Thanks,'' she said, touched that Gwen would offer. Of course, the woman who'd been her assistant for two years wasn't a murderer. She'd better get her head together or she'd never find out anything useful.

"Those bastards!'' Ellsworth said with feeling, and she glanced at him sharply. How did he know there were bastards involved? Maybe his shock was feigned.

"What are you talking about?''

"Those bastards at the gas company. What are they thinking putting faulty lines in buildings? You could have been hurt. Maybe worse.''

Her heart rate slowed. She'd completely misunderstood Ellsworth. He couldn't be a criminal any more than Gwen could. Why, the man was a top producer with a sterling reputation, had been for years, why would he get involved in dirty money? And she was wasting valuable time that would be better spent tracking down the real criminal. "Well, I wasn't hurt. I lost some stuff, and my clothes smell like they belong to a chain smoker.'' She made a face.

"I won't bother you now, Sophie. You'd better sort out your apartment. But please, if there's anything I can do. You know Lillian and I would love to have you stay with us.''

She thanked him, and didn't encourage him to stay. He was right, she did have a lot of calls to make regarding her apartment explosion. After she'd returned all the calls, she closed her door and went to her computer. She pulled up loans and investments over half a million.

She and Blake had decided to concentrate on the obvious laundering practices first: venture capital, phony loans, large deposits. A few weeks ago, she'd never have believed anyone in her company would go against both ethics and the law by turning a blind eye to dirty money. Now, she had to admit, she was convinced. She and Blake were splitting the work of trying to track down any suspicious activity, but still, talk about your needle in a haystack.

15

"*SOPH?*" SHE YELLED THE minute the door to Blake's apartment shut behind them, letting some of her frustration out after a day of unsuccessful snooping.

"Hey, I gave you the key to my place. Something I've never given a woman before, except my sister. Don't I get some leeway?"

"Soph is beyond leeway, it's right out there in the middle of the ocean. Unless you want me coming up with some adorable little nickname for you."

"Lighten up. It's part of the job."

"Okay, cuddlebutt."

"Very funny."

"No. I'm serious. I thought about it today while being teased by every second employee in the bank. Cuddlebutt is perfect."

"Don't even think about it."

"But you have a great butt. The women's bathroom committee all agree."

A horrified groan had her smirking in bitchy amusement. "All right. I won't call you Soph anymore."

"Great decision, CB."

While she unloaded the groceries for tonight's dinner, he set the table. "You know, I'm starting to feel like an old married couple." Except she didn't think many old married couples spent their days tracking money launderers. And Blake hadn't had any more luck than she.

After dinner, the door buzzer sounded. "Are we expecting anyone?" she asked.

"John and my other handler, Mitch, for our regular briefing session."

"I'll give you some privacy and go take a bath."

When she emerged, she picked up her new lavender-scented body lotion and squeezed some into her hand. She crept to her door to listen, but there were no voices, so John and the other man must have left.

She felt tired and dispirited. Loan after loan, deposit after deposit, they all looked fine to her. What had Phil discovered? And why couldn't she and Blake find it, too?

She'd never before realized how utterly tedious detective work was. Her eyes were strained from staring at the computer all day, her shoulders were tight from concentrating. As she rubbed the lotion into her skin, she realized how tight she was, and how much she needed a break. The lotion sliding against her flesh was making her feel womanly and sexy, and the very best mini-holiday she could think of was outside in the living room.

Right now, she didn't want to talk about blackmailers and bank defrauders and murder.

She wrapped herself in her new baby blue bathrobe, picked up the bottle of lotion, then opened her door and walked out to the living area.

Blake was sprawled out on the couch, reading the paper, his cast resting on one arm, his other bare foot resting on top of it and his head comfortably propped on the opposite arm. He fit the thing so perfectly, it crossed her mind he'd had the couch custom-built.

"Blake?" she said in her best sultry, come-to-bed voice.

"Mmm?" he answered in a classic male I'm-reading-the-sports-page-don't-bother-me tone.

She smiled to herself and said, "Blake, can I show you something?"

"What?" He turned his head.

Putting the lotion down on the blanket box, she unbelted her robe and let it drop to the floor so she stood there naked, still slightly damp and warm from the bath, the scent of lavender hovering in the air.

"What am I going to do with you?" he groaned.

"I hope you're going to make love to me," she said slowly.

"That," he informed her, dropping the paper to the floor, "is the best idea you've had all day."

"No, wait. I've changed my mind."

She watched his Adam's apple bob as he swallowed. "You have?"

"Yes." She paused for a moment, taunting him. "I've decided *I'm* going to make love to *you*."

A slow grin lit his face. "Just to prove I'm a sensitive New Age guy, I'm going to let you."

She kissed the grin right off his face, then ran her fingertips across sandpapery stubble at his chin, to the soft smooth skin at the base of his neck where a pulse beat strong and fast. Down to the curly dark hair on his chest. She unbuttoned his shirt and spread it.

She loved his chest. The ridges and furrows, the coppery nipples, the secretive darkness of chest hair.

She pressed her lips to the pulsing hollow in his neck and flicked her tongue against the warm flesh.

His shiver had her smiling against his skin. She moved down, kissing and licking. He tossed restlessly as she took a small hard nipple into her mouth. It tasted like more so she continued her leisurely trip down his chest to his belly.

He started to struggle off the couch, but she pushed him back. "You look so comfortable there. Don't get up."

She unfastened the wide-legged khakis, and he raised his hips for her so she could slip them over his cast.

She rose to inspect him, naked, his erection looking ready to burst.

"You're still overdressed. When do you get the cast off?"

"Is it cramping your style?"

She thought about that for a moment. "Not really. In fact, it makes you just helpless enough to suit me."

Feeling the power she had over him, she smiled down. "I'm going to have to punish you."

"For what?" he said, not looking nearly scared enough.

She narrowed her eyes. "For wrinkling my freshly ironed shirt when you mauled me this morning." She placed her bathrobe on the blanket box and sat on top of it, right across from him so he'd have a great view, then picked up the lotion.

"Will it be bad?" He sounded more excited than nervous.

"Not as bad as the punishment for making me look like a lovesick fool in front of my colleagues," she told him, warming to her theme. She squeezed a big dollop of cream on her hands, stared at his erection long enough for him to think it was the intended target, then, with a sneaky smile, put her hands to her own breasts, rubbing the cream into her skin while he watched.

"Don't forget I called you Soph," he reminded her in a husky tone.

"Oh, I haven't forgotten," she said, and her own voice had grown hoarse. She pulled on her nipples, slick with cream, while he lay there, watching her. "For that I'm devising a special torture."

"Will I survive?"

She smiled at him. "I doubt it " She squirted more

cream, this time applying it to her belly in long, smooth strokes, lower and lower. She slipped her legs apart so he had a great view of her own rising excitement.

"But I'll tell you one thing, you'll die happy."

He reached for her, but she evaded him. His hand fell back to his side. "You're killing me already."

She chuckled softly. "I haven't even started."

She worked all around her throbbing core, knowing she'd blow apart if she so much as touched herself there, wanting him inside her when it happened, but he didn't have to know that. So, she teased while he watched, his hands fisting with frustration, his hips rocking as the desire built.

Her plan, such as it was, had been to cream his body as thoroughly as hers, but it was hopeless. She didn't think either of them could survive that much delaying torment. Instead, when her body was so thoroughly moisturized it glistened, she straddled him, keeping her eyes on his while she slowly lowered herself onto him.

She cried out as he filled her body, hot and hard within her. His hands, deprived of her earlier, made up for it now, rubbing and sliding over her cream-slick breasts, her back, hips, everywhere he could reach, while she moved on him, setting a pace that kept them both on the edge until she had no more control left.

She bucked and rocked, then she screamed. Finally, shuddering and spent, she held him through his own climax.

"HOW LONG CAN YOU KEEP working on this case?" Sophie asked when they'd recovered their breath. She plucked at his chest hair as though she was weeding a flower bed. "Obviously, the unproven bank fraud and a suspicious

death aren't going to hold a busy detective full-time forever."

He placed a hand over hers on his chest, feeling the fine
bones beneath her skin, the slight flutter of nerves. "I'll
be around as long as you need me," he promised, wondering how long that would be.

She gazed up at him from under her tousled blond hair,
her eyes both trusting and nervous. "But, if you don't
discover anything working undercover…"

"We will. They've got a guy from commercial crimes
working this from the other side. I send anything that both-
ers me his way. There are some files of Ruby's that check
out, but still seem kind of funny." He hugged her to him,
her naked body feeling so right tucked against his. "I'm
not going anywhere. This is only one aspect of a complex
investigation. These things take time. We'll get these guys,
I promise you."

He might preach patience to Sophie, but he felt like
throwing his computer out the window as, again and again,
he hit a dead end.

Their frustrating investigation proceeded. Day after day,
while they checked and rechecked files, loans, trade orders,
looking for anything out of the ordinary. In the four weeks
since Sophie's apartment fire, he'd helped Ruby land another big client, which made her almost nice to him. He
was also pretty certain Ruby and Ellsworth were doing
more than flirting by e-mail. Other than that, Blake was
becoming bored and frustrated and more glad than ever
that he'd chosen policing over banking as a career.

When the stress grew too great, there was always inventive love play to be had—everywhere but the bedroom.
He was starting to fantasize about Sophie in his bed. He'd
lie there at night, his body drained from whatever crazy
new place they'd found *not* to do it, and want her with a

fierceness that had him gritting his teeth to stop himself yelling for her to get her butt in here.

Sure, the sex was great, but so was turning over in the night to find a warm woman to snuggle up to. Waking early in the morning to lazy, half-asleep loving.

Damn it, all he wanted was a normal affair. Was that so much to ask?

As they were driving home from work, he decided to see if he could start nudging her in that direction.

"I have a surprise," he said, trying for a light tone.

"A good surprise or a bad surprise?" He couldn't blame her for asking. She'd received too many of the latter over the past few weeks.

"A good surprise. Tickets to *Tristan and Isolde* for Saturday night. I thought we'd do it right and have a nice dinner somewhere afterward."

His distraction worked even better than he'd hoped. She wriggled with excitement. "A real date? Blake, are you asking me for a real date?"

"I'm asking you to the opera."

She grinned at him, blue eyes sparkling. "I accept."

SOPHIE GLOBBED ON AN antistress mud mask she'd found in the bathroom that she assumed was Blake's sister's. It was from a local spa, so she could replace it, and, the way her life was going, she needed any kind of stress-reliever she could find.

Having slapped gray, gooey mud all over her face she tried to lie down and relax but that just brought the tension roaring to the forefront of her mind. She removed the cucumber slices, somewhat the worse for wear, from her eyelids and hoisted herself off the bed.

Blake had been on some mysterious errand all afternoon, after which they were going on their date, the opera followed by a late supper. Since she didn't want her stomach rumbling louder than the baritone, she decided a late-afternoon sandwich was just the thing. It would give her something to do besides obsess over her problems, the bank's problems, or the world's economic crisis she'd read about in this morning's paper.

These days, stress was drawn to her and she seemed to be sucking it up as avidly as her skin was supposedly sucking up the moisture and free-radical destroying enzymes in the facial mask.

She pulled out a fresh loaf of rye, sliced turkey breast, cheese, lettuce, sprouts—was that overkill? Lettuce and sprouts? Ah, the hell with it. Tomatoes, pickles, mayo. Avocado? She shrugged. Why not?

She stacked the layers on a cutting board and pulled out a chef's knife to cut her towering creation when she heard Blake's key in the lock. Odd, he always knocked first before entering his own apartment—a courtesy which endeared him to her.

Unease prickled at the back of her neck. He'd said he wouldn't be home until five. It was only three o'clock. And he hadn't knocked. The person crossing his foyer made a *clack-clack* sound, not *clack-thunk.* Two shoes, not one shoe and a cast.

The knife handle grew slippery in her grasp as she clutched it tight and backed up against the counter. She then edged to the doorway so she'd see whoever was coming in before they saw her.

Was it a member of the triad sent to kill her?

She held her breath. Could she do it? Could she stab someone if she had no other choice? Sophie didn't know, and she didn't want to find out. Her best plan was to wait and hope the intruder checked out the bedrooms first, then she'd make a run for the front door.

Whoever was in the apartment was either a very bad assassin or so cocky they didn't care if she heard them. They made no attempt to creep about, but walked, with a steady tread down the hallway that would pass the kitchen doorway.

She saw a slim shadow. She grit her teeth and raised the knife just as the shadow became black-clad reality.

The intruder must have seen or sensed the movement for they turned.

And screamed.

Sophie screamed, too. The knife slipped from her sweaty grip and clattered to the kitchen floor.

The woman, for Sophie's overloaded senses had made out that the person was a woman, cried, ''Where's Blake?''

Sophie registered details: the intruder wasn't much older than she, with shoulder-length straight brown hair, black leather jacket, black T-shirt and black hip-hugging pants over chunky black boots. She was Caucasian, not Asian.

Then, Sophie realized what she'd said. Oh, my God. It wasn't her they wanted. It was Blake.

The women glared at each other for a long moment. Sophie fixed her concentration on breathing, and wiped her damp palms on her housecoat, ready to dive for the knife if the other woman made a move for it. But she didn't. And after a second, Sophie realized she was as pale and trembling as Sophie herself must be.

''Who the hell are you?''

''I'm Tanya,'' the other woman said. ''Blake's sister. Who the hell are you?''

Sophie's mouth dropped open. ''His sister? Oh. I'm Sophie. Blake's ah…''

The woman sagged against the counter. ''Remind me to call first, next time I'm in town.''

"Oh, God. I'm sorry. I thought you were an intruder." She held out a trembling hand. "Sophie Morton."

The other woman clasped it with her own cold and shaky hand.

"Can you ever forgive me?" She might have been tempted to ask the woman for proof of her identity, but the resemblance between Tanya and her brother was striking.

Tanya cracked a grin. "For half that sandwich and a glass of wine I might be tempted to forgive you. I'll even stay away from bad jokes about backstabbers."

Sophie winced. "I'd appreciate it." She bent to pick up the knife and placed it carefully in the sink, taking a clean one from the knife block.

"How's the antistress mask working?" the other woman asked with almost a straight face.

Her hands flew to her mud-encrusted cheeks and her eyes widened in horror. She thought about running to the bathroom to wash the stuff off, but what was the point? She moaned. "I have a real talent with making a great first impression around your family."

"No kidding?" Tanya reached across the counter and grabbed a slice of pickle. "You swept Blake off his feet by attacking him with a knife?"

"No. I broke his leg."

Tanya choked, and Sophie didn't think it was from pickle juice.

"It was an accident. I didn't know he was a cop."

"Evidently."

Realizing how insane that sounded, she tried again. "I'm not saying I break men's legs who aren't cops." She sighed noisily. "It's a long story." One good thing she could say about the antistress mask was that it covered her blush.

"I've got all afternoon." Tanya rose, and now that she wasn't in terror for her life, Sophie noticed the easy, athletic grace of her gait and a firmness to her jaw that was like her brother's. Tanya had green eyes too, but hers were a lighter green, more reminiscent of spring meadows than a winter storm at sea.

Tanya knew her way around Blake's place, Sophie noted, as his sister pulled a bottle of white wine from the glass-fronted temperature-controlled wine fridge and opened it with the same kind of smooth efficiency as her brother.

Sophie cut the massive sandwich in half, put the halves on two plates, then pushed one toward Tanya, accepting a glass of wine in exchange.

"So, you're living with my brother and I've never heard a word about you. What's that about?"

Sophie damn near spewed her wine in the other woman's lap, which, she figured, would pretty much cement this promising friendship. After choking for a while and gulping more wine to get her breath back, she wiped her eyes on a napkin. "You don't believe in beating around the bush, do you?"

"Nope. He's my brother. You hurt him and I'll have to hurt you."

Sophie glanced up startled, to see serious intent behind the glint of humor in Tanya's eyes. The woman was bold and obnoxious but also straight up, a quality Sophie admired. And she obviously loved her brother, which meant she couldn't be all bad.

"We're not living together." How much could she tell this woman? She didn't imagine Blake wanted her blabbing his undercover secrets, not even to his own sister. On the other hand, she didn't want Tanya getting the wrong idea about their relationship.

"You're in my brother's apartment in a mud pack. I'm guessing intimacy has occurred," Tanya said, spearing Sophie with a gaze, in much the same way she speared another pickle with the glinting blade of her knife.

"Would you give me a minute? I don't think I can have a serious discussion in a face mask." And, in the time it took to remove the mask, hopefully she could decide just what to tell Blake's sister about their relationship.

Ten minutes later her skin gleamed with a notable absence of free radicals, but it was the free radical out there at the breakfast bar that really scared her. No mud bath would neutralize Tanya's prying. And yet, being a sister herself, she understood, even applauded, the impulse to protect a much-loved big bro.

Leaving her face free of makeup, she pulled a brush through her hair and swiftly dressed in jeans and a T-shirt before going back to face The Sister.

Tanya had polished off her sandwich by the time Sophie returned and was sitting, apparently at ease, with her wine. But there was a puzzled expression on her face when they were once again facing each other, and her sharp gaze searched Sophie as though seeing her for the first time, which, in a way, she was. "You went into the guest room. Was that for my benefit?"

She hadn't even thought about how odd that would appear to Tanya. "No. I'm staying there." She huffed out a breath and picked up her own wine. "Look. I don't know how much I'm supposed to tell you, but Blake's and my association is...professional."

"I'm guessing you're not a hooker."

At Sophie's indignant splutter of protest, she grinned. "You're a cop?"

Oh, the hell with it. If Blake hadn't wanted her to tell his sister anything, he should have warned her the woman had a key to his apartment. "I'm the human resources director for a bank. I've had some...um...problems. Blake's been assigned to the case. If you want to know anything else, you'll have to ask him."

"So you're not sleeping with him?" The patent disbelief mixed with indignation in her tone had Sophie doing the grinning this time. She knew where The Sister was coming from. When you thought your own brother was God's gift to womankind, it was tough to imagine any woman not wanting him.

"No. I'm not sleeping with him. We just have sex."

"Excuse me?"

Sophie rose. "I should do these dishes before—"

"Sit!"

She squeezed her eyes shut in the vain hope that she could open them and find Tanya had been a figment of her imagination. A bad dream. A demon from her subconscious. But when she opened them, the woman was still there, looking determined to yank all Sophie's secrets out of her, by torture if necessary.

"Your brother's a very...well, we're attracted to each other. And we've got carried away a few times." Understatement of the century. "But we're trying to keep the relationship casual."

She glanced up, hoping to see female understanding in Tanya's eyes, but all she saw was puzzlement. There was hostility, too, but she was obviously holding it at bay until she got the whole story. And she might be the absolute worst person in the world to unload to, but Sophie realized she desperately wanted to unload to someone.

"You see, I have this policy of not sleeping with men I work with. I think that's only professional, don't you?"

"Sure. But my brother's not a banker. He's a cop."

Sophie sighed noisily. "That's how he sees it, too. But

right now…well, it's complicated. And I'm no good at relationships. I always screw them up. So I stopped having them.''

"You stopped having relationships?" The woman looked as though she was struggling to keep up.

"Right. I was engaged twice but I couldn't go through with it. It's like—I don't know—I felt like I was getting trapped by these men into a marriage I didn't want. I couldn't breathe.'' She huffed with noisy indignation. "Everybody else in the world seems to have casual sex with no problem, but with me, they always fall in love and want to get married.''

"Maybe you haven't found the right man yet?"

"Or maybe I'm not meant for it. The trouble is, I love sex. I really love it. Before Blake, I had a long-distance thing with this guy in San Francisco. I thought that would be perfect. Long distance, snatched weekends—could my intentions be any more clear?''

"What happened?"

"He proposed.''

"You can't trust men. What about Blake? Is he in love with you?"

The question took her aback. "Oh, no. He's not that kind of guy. He's like me. Well, he thinks I'm an idiot to sleep in the guest room, but he's dealing with it. No. He's not in love with me. He only wants to protect me to death.''

An earthy chuckle caused her to glance sharply at Tanya. "What?"

"I think things are going to get very interesting.'' She smoothed a perfectly manicured hand down her thigh. "So, when is my adorable brother expected back?"

"About five. We're going to the opera.''

The other woman's brows rose. "Is he forcing you at gunpoint?"

She laughed. "No. I love opera."

The smile on Tanya's face had a distinctly smug edge. "Well, well. I might just have to stick around for a while."

At the words, Sophie gasped, her hand flying to her mouth. "Oh. You sleep in the guest room when you're in town. I forgot. Look. I'll move my stuff out and sleep on the couch. And I know that was your mask. I was planning to replace it."

Tanya stuck her hand in the air like a referee. "Forget it. I've already booked into a hotel. I'm doing some business while I'm out here. It's easier from a hotel. Really."

Of course Sophie didn't believe her. But she knew she'd do the same if she waltzed in to her brother's place and found another woman staying there. She ought to be the one going to a hotel. She'd discuss it with Blake when he returned.

"I'm staying at the Waterfront. Tell the rat to call me."

"Are you sure you won't stay?"

Tanya rose, in one elegantly fluid move. "Positive. That was a great sandwich. It was…interesting meeting you."

Sophie couldn't hold back her chuckle, part mortification and part genuine amusement at the woman's dry humor. "Sorry about the knife."

"No problem. Oh, I know he's a slob most of the time, but Blake treats a trip to the opera like a personal audience with God. Make sure you dress." Tanya narrowed her eyes and perused Sophie from head to toe. "Your boobs are bigger, but other than that we're probably about the same size. Help yourself to anything in the closet."

"Thanks. But I bought a dress." A real smasher, too. She had no idea why, she'd simply wanted to spend one over-the-top night without worry or stress, enjoying

Blake's company, and Wagner. She could hardly wait. The dress was simple, but devastatingly elegant. She'd taken one shocked peek at the price and shoved her credit card at the saleswoman.

"Ooh. Can I see?"

Feeling girlishly excited, Sophie nodded.

"Put it on."

So she did. Sighing with pleasure when the silky black fabric caressed her skin as she slipped it over her head. The neckline didn't plunge, but it hovered on the brink, with a generous hint of breast on display. The fabric lovingly outlined her curves, ending in a flirty flared cocktail length.

"Oh, it's fabulous. Where did you get it?"

They launched into an instant female bonding routine as they exchanged favorite stores and designers. Watching its effect on his sister, Sophie could only imagine Blake's reaction to the dress. She felt feminine and desirable, and the way the fabric teased her flesh when she moved, she had a feeling it would turn her on just wearing it. In combination with sitting next to Blake and listening to opera… Mmm.

Tanya took a slow turn around Sophie, looking like a very critical—and young—fairy godmother. "What about jewelry?"

She hadn't told Tanya about her apartment blowing up, so she said, "I picked up some chunky costume stuff. Want to see?"

Tanya shook her head slowly, then said, "Wait here," and ran out of the room.

Sophie heard a zipper being opened in the front hallway. She'd been right, then. His sister had planned to stay. Tanya returned with a small leather jewelry case. She opened it and pulled out diamond-and-ruby drop earrings and a matching necklace of webbed gold studded with diamonds and rubies.

"Oh, how gorgeous."

"Try them on. I think they'll be perfect with that dress."

"Oh, but I couldn't. What if I lost them?"

"They're insured. And with Blake beside you, nobody would dare steal them."

Even as she hesitated, Tanya was fastening the necklace and holding the earrings out to her. The gold felt cool as it settled onto her chest, but soon warmed. She walked to the mirror in the guest room and Blake's sister followed. Once she had the earrings in place, they both considered her reflection in the mirror.

"Perfect," said Tanya, echoing her own thought.

She touched the necklace with gentle fingertips. "Are you sure?"

"Absolutely. Look, I've got to run, and you've got to get ready. Have a great time."

On impulse, Sophie hugged Tanya. "Thanks."

"Oh, one other thing."

"Yes?"

"Ditch the panties. The lines show through the dress."

16

"HEY, SOPHIE. SORRY, I'm late, but I have a surprise for you," Blake called cheerfully as he came in the door, hanging his dry cleaning in the hall closet so he had his hands free to kiss Sophie. Thinking how nice it was to have her there.

"I have a surprise for you, too."

"I got my cast off."

"I got a new dress."

They spoke at the same time. He emerged into the living area as she stepped into it from the direction of the guest room.

"You got your cast off? That's great. Did it hurt?"

He could only stand and stare. Answers, conversation, thought of any kind was suspended. Oh, the synapses were firing all right, but he imagined them in a riot, making a fireworks display of his brain as he reacted to the sight of Sophie looking like his personal sex goddess, every glorious curve of her glorious body touched and teased by a dress that only made him impatient to strip it right off her.

"Blake?"

There was a time for words, and a time for action. Since Blake currently had no words more recent than Paleolithic-man grunts, he settled on action. In two strides he was in front of her, pulling her to him so he could kiss her.

He felt the air leave her body as he brought her close, his blood so hot he feared he'd scorch her. But after the first huff of surprise, she responded in kind, answering his plundering tongue with her own as they stole each other's breath, tasting, lapping, needing more. Needing to be closer.

He feasted on her, nipping, biting, sucking at her lips, her tongue while the need to take her beat inside him. He grabbed her butt and pulled her hard against his pulsing erection.

She moaned, deep in her throat, and he felt her heat even through his old tearaway pants and her new dress. He angled his hips to nudge at that warmest spot of all.

"The opera," she gasped, sounding like a drowning woman coming up for the third and last time.

Probably no two other words could have stopped him.

The opera was Wagner. *Tristan and Isolde,* star-crossed lovers who died in each other's arms. He felt a sudden kinship. To call him and Sophie star-crossed would be a gross exaggeration, but their path wasn't a smooth one, either.

There were obstacles. A gang of international criminals were easily as threatening to true love as any operatic squabble. He would protect Sophie, whatever it took, but there was yet another obstacle between them. Her own skittishness. As long as she kept up the pretense that they weren't emotionally involved, there was no future for them.

The irony wasn't lost on him. Normally he'd be over the friggin' moon to have a free-spirited, sexy woman giving him some of the hottest sex of his life then pretending the whole thing had never happened.

It was your basic guy's wet dream. No "we have to talk," no hints about the future, no ticking biological clock. She only wanted him for sex.

So how crazy was it that he found himself thinking

about the future, wondering how long this thing would last before their hot passion cooled, or they ran out of places other than the bedroom to have sex.

He shrugged. He wasn't a man to turn away from something this great. But sometimes he wondered…

Tonight, all he was wondering, with hot anticipation, was whether she'd go along with the surprise he'd planned.

Would she let him combine his two greatest loves? Sex and opera?

He took a shaky step away from her, knowing it was his last chance. If he didn't get his hands off her right now, they wouldn't be seeing any opera. Maybe if he could hoist her off those ridiculous heels and march her into his bed, he'd say to hell with *Tristan and Isolde*. But he'd made the most stupid bargain of his life and he tried to be a man of his word.

If he couldn't have sex with Sophie in his bed, he'd go with his original plan. Or give it his damnedest.

He was on his way to the shower. An icy one if he had any chance of getting out of this apartment in the next hour. But first, he leaned closer to her, not close enough to touch, which would have been the end of him, merely close enough to whisper in her ear. She wore perfume tonight. He didn't ever recall her doing so before. It was so subtle, he could only smell it when he put his face mere inches away from her. "I have a surprise planned for later."

He pulled away to look at her face and her expression was sexy and mischievous. "I love surprises."

Then he took off for that cold shower.

His first shower since he'd broken his leg—just his luck it would have to be a cold one. Not even frigid water pounding against his skin could cool his blood. He tried to focus, not on the dress that made him think of Sophie's

beautiful body naked, but on the opera. The music began
to swell in his head. Without conscious effort, his brain
downloaded the *Liebestod*, the wonderful, passionate aria
from the final act.

He felt it build inside his head, mounting like a woman's
passion, growing in intensity, the focus shifting inward as
she sang of a love so great it could cross any barrier, of
the—

His eyes flew open. It was like a five-minute long vocal
orgasm.

He climbed out of the shower, dried swiftly then shaved,
brushed his teeth and dashed to his room to dress. For her.

She deserved a tux, but he didn't own one. He put on
the Hugo Boss suit his sister had appropriately bossed him
into purchasing with one of the shirts she'd had specially
made for him as a Christmas gift and added a wild tie in
Popsicle-colored stripes that made him feel less Wall
Street.

He'd planned this evening carefully, and he couldn't
wait to get started. The seats were the best. The champagne
would already be chilling when they reached the restaurant, and, since he never allowed himself to drink and
drive, he'd ordered a car. Well, a limo actually, but what
was the point of a healthy investment portfolio if you never
indulged? Most of his likes were simple. But a night at the
opera—not to mention a night with Sophie—cried out for
decadence.

Her eyes widened when he emerged to find her comfortably lounging on his couch, feet curled beneath her.
"Wow," she said. "You clean up good."

He had a view down the top of her dress that made him
swallow before he drooled.

Fortunately, at that moment the telephone rang to say

his car was waiting. "Shall we?" He extended his hand
to her and she placed hers in his palm.

She didn't comment on the limo, beyond shooting him
a glance from under her lashes. Did she think *this* was his
surprise? Humping in the back of a limo? Well, it could
be fun, but not tonight. Tonight he'd already made his
choice.

THE LIMO SMELLED OF leather and the seat was cool beneath her, reminding her she wore no panties beneath her
dress. She considered leaning over to whisper the fact in
Blake's ear, but she had a sneaking suspicion he'd find out
for himself before the night ended.

She settled back against the upholstery and he took her
hand, holding it idly on his thigh, their fingers linked.

She stared at their two hands, hers pale and slim in
contrast to his darker, sturdier one.

"How's your leg?"

He admitted it was a little stiff and he was already
scheduled for physical therapy, but he was happy to have
the cast off. She could see for herself his movement was
much freer and her thoughts turned immediately lustful as
she considered how much more mobile he now was.

It wasn't only lust, though. Here they were on a date.
She could pretend the sex they'd shared didn't count, but
no way a night on the town complete with limo and tickets
to the opera could be considered anything but a date.

She glanced at him under her lashes and caught his gaze
on her, so hot she was surprised her dress didn't scorch.

He opened his mouth and she tensed, waiting for some
provocative suggestion, but he said, "Do you know the
story of Tristan and Isolde?"

"Let's see." She tried to remember. "Tristan's escort-
ing Isolde to marry his king. They start out hating each

other, but fall in love. His duty and somebody's treachery separate them. They're reunited in the end, but they both die. Isn't that it?''

His voice quivered with humor. ''In a nutshell. There's this one aria in the final act that gets me every time. It builds slowly as the soprano sings of her passion.'' His eyes darkened and his voice grew husky. She could swear it was playing right now in his head, she knew the piece, heard it begin to play inside her own head. His fingers tightened on hers. Did he even realize it? ''It builds and builds until this kind of sweeping intensity takes over and you can feel the entire audience being swept up in it and finally, when you think you can't take anymore, the wave crests and crashes, and slowly subsides. It's like an unbelievable orgasm.''

She smiled, her eyes half-closed, listening to the music in her head and hearing his interpretation of it, feeling so aroused, she crossed her legs, only to be reminded of her pantyless state.

''The *Liebestod*,'' she said.

''You know it.''

''It always makes me cry.''

They'd reached the opera house by this time, and Blake helped her out, while the uniformed driver held the door. The driver handed Blake a printed card. ''Call me, sir, when you're ready to be picked up.''

Then they were inside the plush opera house, and some of the tension she'd been carrying night and day since she overheard that fateful phone call dissipated as she gazed at the opulent theatre with its chandeliers and red-and-gold decor. Patrons milled around, some sipping drinks and wearing ballgowns and tuxes, some in jeans and hiking boots.

"Thank you for this," she said, turning to him impulsively.

As though he'd read her thoughts, he said, "I think we both needed a break."

She'd seen Blake in jeans and a scowl and thought he was gorgeous, but in a designer suit, which he wore with the same careless grace he wore jeans, and without the ungainly bulge of the cast, he was more than gorgeous. He looked elegant and sophisticated, but the rugged appearance of his features, a sense of the watchful warrior within him, and banked fires in his gaze, added a more earthy appeal to his looks. The combination made her breath hitch.

She loved the veneer of sophistication, but she also couldn't wait to strip it off and mate with the animal beneath. He put his hand on her lower back and she let his warmth seep into her.

"Do you want a drink?"

"Sure." Maybe something cool and wet would put out some of the flames licking her insides as she tried to work out where and how his surprise would take place.

Drinks in hand, they wandered among the eclectic crowd. It was one thing to hear *Don Giovanni*, or *La Traviata* blasting from his home or car CD player, that was surprising enough, but to see him here, in the opera house, dressed in designer clothes, tickets to *Tristan and Isolde* in his pocket, was…stimulating. And disconcerting. It was like finding one of those beefed-up entertainment wrestlers had a degree in advanced mathematics.

He must have sensed her puzzlement as she looked him up and down. "What?"

She shook her head. "I thought cops drank beer and watched football."

He slipped a finger under a spaghetti strap, the lightly

calloused pad scraping erotically over her sensitive skin. "And I thought bankers wore blue suits and smoked cigars."

"I guess it's the contrasts that make us interesting."

"That and the hot sex we're *not* having."

She bit her lips to prevent herself from retorting. Their game had become so second nature she'd forgotten she'd started it to stop either of them from becoming emotionally involved. Of course it was crazy, and of course they were having sex. Some of the best and most inventive sex of her life. But it wasn't making love. And that's the only thing that kept her from running screaming into the night. Sex she could handle. Love was like nuclear power. Maybe it could be harnessed for useful purposes, but one slipup and... She shuddered.

"Cold?" His arm round her shoulders warmed her instantly. "Let's go inside."

The seats were perfect, and somehow she wasn't a bit surprised. When he undertook a task, whether protecting her life or choosing theatre seats, he did it well. When the task was pleasuring her, she had to add a juicy adverb. Like *superlatively* well. She glanced at his hands as he ushered her into her seat.

She settled into her seat with a sigh, feeling as twitchy and on edge as though those superlatively talented hands were already on her body.

Opera was about passion and she'd never felt more in tune to the wild swings of emotion. Had never believed in the absurd idea that two people who started out despising each other could fall so deeply in love they'd sacrifice anything, even life itself. But tonight, she thought perhaps she did.

While the sounds of rustling dresses and muted conversation combined with the squeaks and thuds of an orchestra tuning up, Blake leaned over to whisper in her ear. "Go to the bathroom and remove your panties, then bring them to me."

A sizzle of excitement skittered through her system along with a silent thanks to Blake's sister, which allowed her to feel smug, knowing she was about to wipe the cocky expression right off his face.

She leaned in, so close the ends of his hair tickled her nose, and whispered breathily in his ear, "I'm not wearing any underwear."

She trailed her tongue softly in a question mark along his ear, ending the point at his lobe, which was too inviting a target not to bite.

"What are you wearing under that dress?" he asked in a strangled whisper.

She smiled at him, wiggling her toes and fingers. "Nail polish."

Whether from the nip on his ear or her pantyless state, she wasn't sure, but he dragged in air as though he'd just reached the summit of Everest. One hand went to the knot of his tie as though to loosen it.

Feeling, under the circumstances, that he deserved to suffer even more, she angled her pelvis so her weight rested on her right hip and her left reached for the ceiling, leaving her backside, clad in nothing but the filmy black fabric, tilted provocatively in his direction.

"I ought to arrest you," he all but growled into her ear, the arousal and frustrated wanting in his tone generating a corresponding want in her belly. She felt the heat of his gaze penetrate the dress and felt as exposed as though she were naked.

"What for?" she asked over her shoulder.

He rested a hand on her hip and her eyes widened at the heat coursing from his palm and spreading through her body to tickle and tease every sensitive nerve ending. ''Torturing an officer of the law.''

''Sorry, sir,'' she said meekly, glancing at him from under her lashes as she shifted until she was sitting properly. Or as properly as a woman without underwear can sit.

For a while she held the upper hand in this most exciting of sexual power battles. She'd thrown him so far off course he was sprinting to catch up. But he managed it, one-upping her nicely. Once more he leaned in, speaking in the same intimate tone he used when he was inside her body. ''When I give you the signal, I want you to go to the ladies' room. When you're the only one in there, open the door for me.''

She bit back a moan as her body tingled and tightened. ''What's the signal?''

''I'll squeeze your knee. Like this.'' He demonstrated, smoothing his palm down the length of her thigh until it met her knee. Then he squeezed, gently but firmly, turning the area into a blazing erogenous zone. ''Understand?''

Incapable of speech, she could only nod. The lights went down, but he didn't remove his hand, merely rested it on her thigh, warm and connected, a constant reminder that she'd agreed to make a trip to the bathroom at his whim.

Then the overture began playing; *Tristan and Isolde* had begun. Sophie sighed, so conscious of her naked thighs pressing together, of her sex pulsing with insistent arousal. Blake didn't do anything so tacky as try to caress her in the darkness; there was only his hand resting open-palmed on her thigh. But it was enough. A constant reminder of their unconventional rendezvous planned for the ladies' room.

When would his signal come? Every time he shifted, she wondered. Would she ignore him? Or would she do as he'd asked and traipse off to the bathroom? Her brain hadn't quite decided yet, though her body clearly had its own agenda.

And then Wagner seduced her mind and nothing mattered but the music flowing around her and in her. In quiet harmony, she felt the hum of desire, of connection, flowing back and forth between her body and Blake's.

Tristan was taking Isolde to marry his king. They didn't like each other, and yet... There was a potion that was supposed to be poison. They both drank it, but it was a love potion. Dislike, animosity turning to love. Could it happen outside of a dark theatre? Was it in fact happening here and now?

Tristan presented Isolde to his king, but, in spite of the danger, they couldn't stay away from each other and made love, thinking they were safe in the darkness. But night ended, and still they clung together until they were discovered.

Sophie was caught up in the haunting beauty of the music, the passion of the lovers, knowing the opera would soon be over, when she felt Blake's hand move slowly and deliberately down to her knee. In the darkened theatre she turned to him, saw the dark glow of his eyes, so hungry for her she felt faint.

There was no question of ignoring his need, it reflected hers so perfectly, the driving obsession to be together, now, while they still could.

She rose as quietly as possible and slipped past him, up the aisle and out into the lobby. There were lights there, and the grand emptiness of a foyer between intermissions. For a second she was disoriented, then she remembered where she had to go. Her shoes tap-tapped across the marble foyer in counterpoint to her pounding heart.

The door to the women's washroom was heavy and ornate, her arms weak and shaky as she pushed it open.

She gasped as she saw herself reflected in the gold-framed baroque mirror that sat above sinks set into what looked like an antique buffet. Behind her was a plush red Victorian settee and behind that stretched a discreet hallway with a dozen or so bathroom stalls which women would spend the entire intermission lining up for, but now were blessedly empty.

She took a moment to calm herself then realized she'd need several hours for that, with Blake nowhere in the vicinity.

The opera house had thoughtfully placed speakers in the bathrooms, so she could hear the opera almost as clearly in here as she could from her seat. Isolde began to sing. Softly, sweetly.

Sophie breathed deeply, feeling as though her blood were flowing in the same rhythm as the aria. Her eyes opened. The *Liebestod*. Of course. Two years of college German wasn't much, but she thought that translated to love in death. Which naturally made her think of the French term, *le petit mort*. The little death of orgasm. Which naturally reminded her that Blake was at this minute outside the door with love and death on his mind.

She crept to the door and opened it.

Blake slipped inside like a shadow.

There were no words. They needed none. Isolde sang to her lover, and Blake pulled Sophie to him, wrapping his arms around her and bringing his lips down to meet hers.

Tiny explosions burst and popped throughout her body as they kissed, straining together, almost as if they wanted to climb into each other's skin.

Blake turned her until she was facing the mirror, then stepped behind her. She gazed at their reflection. Her eyes looked huge in the mirror, her lips wet and pouty. She watched him watching her, almost felt the impact of his gaze like a physical touch. He only had to stare at her breasts, rising and falling with her rapid breathing, and they swelled and budded, aching for his touch. His gaze moved lower, to where her panties ought to be, and the heat settled there, intense and urgent.

The music swirled around her full of passion and forbidden desire. She saw herself in the mirror, on display for him, watching, wanting, waiting. His touch still shocked her when it came. His fingers running down her throat, so her soft moan hummed against them, tracing her breastbone and then slipping, so slowly, beneath the straps of her dress to caress her aching flesh.

She saw her eyes darken, her nipples harden and her breasts rise and fall with each shallow, panting breath. It was like having a panic attack, except it wasn't panic, but excitement stealing her breath and sending her system into chaos.

With one hand she held on to the back of the settee, needing the support to remain standing. With the other, she reached behind her to skim her hand along Blake's thigh. She watched herself touching him in the mirror, her nails painted with cinnamon-colored polish; her fingers, long and pale against the dark wool of his suit pants, trailed from the outside of his thigh, skimming over the hard quad muscle, reaching the softer inner thigh. His breath was almost as uneven as hers when she slowly and deliberately cupped him, running her curved hand up and over the gorgeous hard length of him.

Breath hissed out between his teeth and she glanced up to see an expression almost of pain cross his face. Still without a word, he took her arm and led her down the corridor to the last bathroom stall on the left and pulled her inside.

And the music was rising, gaining in intensity. She quivered with need, the feel of him imprinted on her palm. Her hips were moving, she couldn't seem to stop them, caught up in the music, in the driving need to have him inside her and moving to the same passionate rhythm.

He shut and locked the stall door, kissed her once, long and slow and deep, then turned her slowly until her back was to him. She whimpered with frustrated longing.

"Shh," he whispered, dropping soothing kisses down the length of her neck that didn't soothe her a damn bit, as he must have known.

The ache in her womb was growing. Since the high heels pushed her hips out, she was able to exaggerate the pose by tipping her pelvis up and back until she found his groin. Then she swayed, teasing him as her bottom swept back and forth across his erection. The only trouble was, as much as she knew the movement was driving him wild, it was driving her just as crazy.

She felt a breeze against her calves, the fabric trailing mistily against her flesh as he raised her dress. *Oh, yes.* She slipped her legs apart in anticipation, felt the cool metal of the stall partition against her hands as she braced herself. She bit her lips, almost weeping with the need drumming inside her, becoming part of the rising music.

Cool air hit her where she was so very wet with anticipation and she gasped at the shock of sensation, then the gasp turned into a long, wailing moan as she felt his erection slip between her legs.

He entered her so slowly she felt each inch stretch and widen her clinging passage. Her legs were trembling, and, when he was buried all the way inside her, his hips pressed against her backside, she felt his trembling, too.

Of course, he was totally overtaxing his barely healed leg, but she didn't think that was responsible for all the tremors.

With her dress bunched between them at her lower back, his hands were free and he let them roam until one hand touched and squeezed her breasts, the other slipped down to touch her clitoris, so swollen and sensitive she cried out. It was just the first cry. She knew there were lots more louder cries lining up in her throat. She felt like a champagne bottle about to blow its cork. Fortunately, the music was so intensely passionate—and loud—she thought she'd get away with her own special harmony.

She smiled at Blake's foresight in bringing her here.

She waited for him to start thrusting in earnest, giving him a little nudge with her behind in case he was somehow waiting for her, but he surprised her by putting a hand over her mouth. It was the hand that had been between her legs and she could have wept with frustration at having that sensuous touch disappear.

She felt her own wetness against her mouth, inhaled the scent of her own desire. Couldn't he tell she was too close to play games? She nudged at him with her hips. Why wouldn't he let her go? Let her outsing Isolde as desire overtook her. What kind of sadist brought a woman so close to mind-blowing satisfaction and then shut down?

Then she heard the click of metal on metal and her eyes flew open. Someone else was in the bathroom. He must have noticed what her desire-fogged brain couldn't.

They waited, still and quiet, though her pounding heart sounded like a jungle drum in her chest, and she couldn't control her heaving breaths. He felt huge inside her and so warm. He didn't thrust, but made tiny rocking movements that kept them both on the edge. She could have sworn his penis had a built-in G-spot detector the way it kept nudging her just there. Luckily he kept his hand over her mouth, muffling her tiny sobs of pent-up excitement.

The toilet flushed.

She had to get a grip before she lost all control and embarrassed the poor woman out there. She watched her own hands, fingers splayed against the cool beige metal of the bathroom stall, the cinnamon-tipped nails shiny and sophisticated, completely at odds with their position, the pair of them bare-assed in a public toilet.

She'd never been so turned on in her life.

Beneath the glory of the building soprano, she heard the more mundane sound of the taps going on and she pictured the oblivious woman out there washing her hands.

She felt his erection twitch inside her, and she squeezed her inner muscles around him. Kegels should be done every day, she knew, to keep her vaginal muscles toned. Great preparation for childbirth, and, since that was still far in the hazy future, she could enjoy the fringe benefits of a toned pelvic floor: increased sexual pleasure.

Of course, she hadn't done her Kegels in a few days. Now seemed like the perfect time to practice. She pulled up and in, sucking him with her vagina. She felt a ripple against her back and smiled wickedly, glad Blake couldn't see her face. Rhythmically she continued her kneading, pulling movement, toning her pelvic floor so thoroughly she could give birth to triplets about now and bounce right back into shape.

Luckily his building excitement caused him to squeeze the hand still on top of her mouth because he wasn't the only one suffering. As she squeezed and pulled her inner muscles around him, her own excitement mounted almost unbearably.

Her ears strained, waiting for the woman to leave. What was she doing out there? Sophie pictured her applying lip-

stick, fixing her hair, completely oblivious to the torment
going on in the last stall on the left.

After an eternity, Sophie heard the door whoosh shut
and in the next instant Blake pulled out and thrust into her,
a long, hard thrust that made her cry out as the inner muscles tightened once more, this time with no conscious help
from Sophie.

She pushed back against him even as he thrust into her,
and now she understood why he'd called this piece a verbal orgasm. The intensity was building, almost more than
she could bear. She felt the tightness of tears in her throat
at the intense sweetness, the soaring notes. The same ele-
mental passion that soared around them was echoed by the
harmony of their bodies moving in unison, reaching up,
straining for the peak.

His hand left her mouth and once more found that magic
spot between her legs, stroking her even as he thrust with
urgent, ancient rhythm into her body. She was sobbing as
the sensation built, so she had to cry out or explode. She
sang her own savage, instinctive aria that rose and blended
with the soprano.

And then the peak, the long note, impossibly high, held
impossibly long, on and on while she sobbed, everything
in her responding. She was the passionate lover, she was
the song, her body was part of the music, part of the story.
She arched and strained, hitting the perfect note, so perfect
it had no sound.

Behind her, she felt Blake stiffen, felt his teeth sink into
her shoulder, not hard enough to hurt, more, she thought,
to muffle his own groan. Then he shuddered, pumping his
life force into her as the waves of passion and music
crested and slowly ebbed.

Blake's thrusts followed the same instinctive rhythm,

bringing her down gently through all the aftershocks that rocked her body.

Spent and shaken, she leaned against the metal wall then felt him leave her. She heard him straighten his clothing and zip up then he turned her until she was facing him. Only when he touched her face did she realize it was wet with tears. She couldn't look him in the eye, didn't want him to see inside her, to where she'd laid herself bare for him. Not now. Not yet.

So she kissed him. But the kiss was almost as intimate as the loving and she felt he could see all the way inside her to her deepest self even though she had her eyes tightly shut.

His kiss was so gentle and sweet that fresh tears stung her eyelids. When he finally let her go, he looked at her for a long moment, but all he said was, "I'm getting out while the coast is clear. I'll see you back at our seats."

She took some time to clean herself up. Then she dried her tears and fixed her makeup. But nothing could cover the shattered expression she saw in her own eyes.

Applause. The sound made her jump. The audience was clapping, loud, then louder as enthusiasm built for the performance.

She stood there, surrounded by the sound, realizing she'd finally done what she thought she was incapable of. She'd fallen completely and forever in love.

17

"YOU'RE GETTING A reputation at the bank as an aggressive backstabber," Sophie informed Blake after another fruitless day of digging for leads.

He shrugged. "I'm trying to follow in Phil Britten's tracks. The best way I can think of to track down bogus money is to pretend to be poaching the business from my colleagues."

"Well, some of our legitimate clients are telling their own account managers about your calls, and they complain to me." She shot him a grumpy look. "Of course, they tell me unofficially. Maybe I could slip a word in your ear, they say with that smug expression that means they think I'll whisper cautions in your ear after a bout of hot sex."

"No, really. You should try that," he said, then laughed as she launched a shoe at him.

He looked to be ready to retaliate when his cell phone rang. Not the cell phone she'd seen him carry at work, but a smaller, more high-tech-looking gadget. She knew it was his "real" cell, the one he used for his police work. His voice, his entire manner took on a more serious aspect when he answered. He spoke softly and rapidly, checked his watch. "I'll meet you at the usual place. An hour."

"Isn't it easy to be overheard on a cell phone?" she asked when he folded his and returned it to his pocket.

He seemed miles away. "Hmm? Oh, it's secure."

"I guess that means my phone's insecure. Maybe it needs therapy."

Her weak joke couldn't keep the flutter of nerves from her stomach.

"I've got to go out for a while."

"Meeting with your female snitch?"

Disconcerting humor flashed briefly in his eyes. "An informer. Yes."

She didn't know what made her do it, but she crossed to him. Putting her hands on his shoulders she stared deeply into his gray-green eyes. Into the eyes of the man she'd gone and fallen madly and hopelessly in love with. "Be careful," she said, and kissed him.

"Did Tanya put you up to this? I had a feeling you and my sister would hit it off, but not that she'd turn you into a worrier."

In spite of their unconventional meeting—or maybe because of it—she and Tanya had indeed hit it off, and Sophie felt as though she had a new friend.

"I like your sister a lot. She's like you, only tougher." She grinned at his expression. "But she didn't start me worrying about you. I just got a weird feeling when you took that call. I can't explain it."

She would have pulled away, but he didn't let her. She felt one of his hands push into her hair while the other held her lower back, warm and sure. First he mimicked the soft brush of her lips against his, giving her back the caress. But she felt the building storm of desire swirling dark and dangerous just below the surface. "You going to wait up?" he asked, softly teasing, but somehow she knew the answer mattered.

"Yes," she whispered back. She would wait up for him, just like an anxious police wife. It felt natural somehow. As though it were part of her destiny.

Then he deepened the kiss, letting some of his passion and need off the leash, so it nipped and jumped at her.

Oh, yes. She'd be waiting up for him all right.

When he let her go they were both shaking. "Don't cool off," he said, brushing her lips lightly one last time.

Minutes later, he was gone.

He hadn't paid any attention when she was salvaging clothes from her apartment, so he hadn't seen her tuck the midnight-blue silk nightgown into the bag. Because it was her favorite, and had been ridiculously expensive for something so small, she stored it in a padded, scented silk bag the lingerie store had sold her, and the bag had protected the gown from the smoke.

It wasn't much to salvage from an entire apartment, but the simple fact that one of her treasures had survived unscathed lightened her heart considerably. And visions of how her nightgown would affect Detective Barker had a smug smile curving her lips.

Maybe it was time to stop running in new directions. Maybe it was time to stop and settle down. The first thing she needed to do was let Blake know she loved him. And she knew exactly how she was going to do it.

She spent the evening in humming anticipation, bathing, shaving her legs, getting her hair just right, so it tumbled in sexy curls round her face, then she slipped on the nightgown.

The silk whispered against her skin like seductive promises as she waited for Blake, trying to tamp down the nerves skittering in her stomach. It was ridiculous to feel nervous. This wouldn't be the first time they'd made love.

She sighed as she brushed out her hair and repositioned the candles one more time. It would be the first time they'd made love when she knew she was in love with him. That was an extremely significant event for Sophie, since she'd never felt this way before. Somehow, she knew it would be different this time. Sweet and tender as well as hot.

He'd been gone for two hours. A flutter of worry snuck in among the nerves. He hadn't said how long he'd be, but surely two hours was plenty.

She hung freshly ironed blouses in the closet, poured herself a glass of wine, and, gritting her teeth against unreasonable fear, turned on the gas fire. Nothing exploded, but still, her hand shook slightly as she picked up a newspaper to pass the time.

The minutes continued to tick by and she made a lot better progress emptying her wineglass than she did consuming the news.

She'd gone from pretending to be relaxed on the couch to out-and-out pacing—and she figured she was about one minute from hand-wringing when she finally heard his soft knock and then the key in the door.

Without any thought at all, she ran through the apartment to the front foyer and, satisfied at a glance that he was still in one piece, launched herself into his arms.

"Hey." He half laughed, but still scooped her into a tight embrace. "What's all this about? You're trembling."

"I was afraid something had happened to you. You were gone so long."

He buried his face in her hair and she nuzzled in closer, inhaling the warm comforting smell of him. Somewhere he'd encountered cigarette smoke, for she smelled that, too, and the faint whiff of beer. She pulled back slightly, wondering if she'd worried for nothing. "You met your source at a bar?"

He shook his head and then sighed. "A cheap hotel room."

She could tell from his wary expression that he wasn't

sure how she'd take the news, but she discovered she trusted him completely. "Your snitch is a hooker?"

"Yeah."

"Was it worth it?"

His smile gleamed as lethal as a hunter's blade and sent an involuntary shiver through her. "It was worth it. An unknown person will be meeting with my friend Wai Fung Li to buy a new identity."

"But, I thought you were after the triad for drugs?"

"He's already wanted for murder and drugs."

"Murder? I thought those big shot mobsters had their henchmen do the killing?"

"He does, but Li also enjoys killing people." He rubbed his hands together. "We know where he'll be tomorrow, and I can identify him. Sophie, this is it."

He kissed her, but instead of desire, she felt fear. Her heart bumped uncomfortably in her ribs.

Taking her hand, he led her into the living room. He blinked when he saw the gas fireplace blazing, but didn't say anything. Instead, he flopped back on the couch, taking her with him so they both tumbled against the soft leather and she ended up with her head resting on his chest.

"Do you want something to eat or drink?"

"No." He ran a hand through her hair and she sighed with pleasure, feeling the individual pads of his fingers pressing lightly against her scalp until she rubbed her head against him, resisting the urge to purr.

"When's the meeting?" she asked, fighting the nerves that tightened her muscles.

"Tomorrow at six." He tweaked her ear. "Don't worry, Ms. Human Resources Manager. I won't miss a minute of work."

She tried to smile, but the nerves were tightening. She couldn't explain why, but she had a bad feeling about the meeting. "You're undercover. Can't someone else go in your place?"

"I've been working this case for two solid years, nothing's keeping me away from the biggest break we've had. Besides, I'm the one who can identify him."

"But your leg…"

"I'm a fast healer. It's fine."

Running out of logical arguments, she went with the truth. "Please, Blake. I can't explain it, I just have a really bad feeling about this."

"Women's intuition?"

"Maybe." Or maybe this unreasoning fear was a normal byproduct of loving a man. If so, it was a heavy burden to carry, worrying so much about his safety.

"I'll wear a bullet-proof vest just for you. How's that?"

"Bullet-proof head-to-toe armor would suit me better. You not being there would suit me perfectly."

"Hey, what's got into you?"

You. She wanted to tell him. She'd been smart to stay away from love all these years. She must have known deep down how painful it would be to care this much for another person. And when that person was a cop chasing the deadliest criminals, she could have smacked herself upside the head for her own stupidity.

Instead she asked another question. "Where is it?"

"In a club in Chinatown."

"Which—"

"I've already told you too much. Let's talk about something else."

"I love you." The words were out before she could stop them. Once again she cursed her own impulsiveness. This wasn't how she'd planned to tell him, it had slipped out.

His entire body went rigid. "Huh?"

"You wanted to talk about something else. It slipped out. I love you."

"If you love me how come you sound so miserable?" There was a glimmer of a smile in his eyes.

"I am miserable. You're the last person I want to love. You're not my type. You're pushy, bossy and arrogant. Half the time I don't even like you. You work in a dangerous job. You could be killed." She started out strong, but her voice was shaking by the end.

"I'm a cop. But I'm a careful cop. I won't get killed tomorrow." He brushed her hair back off her forehead. "I promise."

She snorted, fighting the wetness gathering in her eyes. "And if you break your promise, I'm going to have a tough time collecting. You can't say 'I told you so' to a dead man." She hated the way her tone wavered as she tried to get the words out. "I've never been in love before. I hate it."

He kept a soothing rhythm, brushing the hair off her forehead and down the side to her neck then he'd start the process over again. Somehow he seemed to understand she needed the physical contact.

"Sophie," he said softly and gently, in a tone she'd never heard him use before. Her heart held its beat. Her lungs held their breath. It was coming. He was going to admit he loved her, too. Somehow she'd talk him out of going into danger tomorrow. And they could start planning a future together. "You don't love me."

Her breath expelled as though her lungs were spitting. Anatomically incorrect, but that's just how it felt. Her heart began beating again, too. Hard and fast, pushing angry blood into her cheeks. Surely she hadn't heard him correctly. "Pardon?"

"It's this crazy situation—the danger, losing your apartment, you staying here. It's making you irrational."

This time she didn't even try to stop the tears pooling. He didn't love her. Worse, he didn't believe she loved him. "You may not love me back, I understand that. But do me the courtesy of letting me know my own feelings. I wish I hadn't fallen in love with you. It's very inconvenient, but I'm stuck with it. If you don't feel the same way, that's fine."

She tried to struggle off the couch, but he held her back, turning her face to his. "I feel a lot of things when I'm with you. We're both bewitched." Then he pulled her into a kiss.

And not just any kiss. A kiss of such intimacy and sweetness she felt as though it were a different Blake kissing her.

She ought to pull away and go to bed alone. But tomorrow he was going into danger and that made tonight doubly precious.

It was time for her to stop playing games.

She pulled away, breaking the contact with regret and rose, but only to reach her hand down to grasp his and pull. He got to his feet and followed her.

The nerves playing jump rope in her belly went at it double time as she followed her instincts and her heart. Right into his bedroom.

The bed was already turned down and she'd placed candles and matches about. She began lighting them, focusing her attention on each flame as it sprang to life.

She heard him behind her, but didn't turn. Couldn't. For the moment she felt utterly vulnerable.

When all the candles were lit and candlelight danced upon the walls and bed, she turned.

He was leaning against the wall, watching her, his eyes

unreadable in the wavering candlelight. "Are you saying what I think you're saying?"

"I'm saying, this time it counts," and, putting both hands on the hem of her nightgown, she pulled it slowly and deliberately over her head.

18

BLAKE DIDN'T THINK HE'D ever seen a sight quite as beautiful as Sophie naked in candlelight.

No. It wasn't just that. It was Sophie, naked in candlelight, *in his bedroom.* Her crazy pretense that their sex didn't count had begun to rankle. Now, she was willing to admit it did matter. And he found that as erotic and exciting as the sight of her limbs, naked and luscious in the wavering silver-white candle glow that spun her hair gold, tipped her nipples with deep rose and drew his eyes to the dark mystery between her thighs.

She said she loved him, but he knew that wasn't so. She'd become carried away, that's all. Homeless, chased by killers, she'd turned to him, both sexually and emotionally. They were even living in the same apartment, no wonder she was having fantasies.

Once this was over and she was back in control of her life, she'd feel a little awkward that she'd fallen into the common trap of falling in love with her protector. He'd seen it happen dozens of times—more than once to him.

The things a woman said in times of crisis were like the cries she made at climax. Not to be taken seriously—and words a gentleman tried not to remember.

Still, if he'd ever come close to making the same foolish mistake himself, it was with Sophie. She got to him as no woman ever had. Thank God he was trained to recognize the signs of a temporary infatuation caused by stress.

Her declaration he'd ignore. But her naked body, moving toward him with long-limbed grace, he couldn't dismiss. Probably this affair was the product of stress and temporary infatuation, too. There were probably men in the world who could have resisted becoming intimate with Sophie.

He was not one of those men.

He needed her in his bed with a fierceness that surprised him. And because his hunger was so fierce, he vowed to treat her gently.

He reached out and touched her hair.

She nipped his lower lip and made him gasp.

Slowly, slowly, he reminded himself, as with restrained gentleness he let his fingers skim the underside of her breast.

She grabbed the neck of his shirt and, grunting with effort, ripped it open, sending buttons flying. She clawed at his jeans in her haste to get him naked and it took all his self-control not to give in to the raging hunger he felt radiating from her body.

He wanted to make this special for her, after her surprising announcement. Even a woman only temporarily in love deserved to be treated like a wedding-night bride, so he reined in his own need while she stripped him bare, nipping him wherever she felt like. His belly, hip, thigh, even his pale, recently freed leg. The lady wasn't being all that delicate. She chomped on him as though she were starving!

Her speed and lack of finesse only made him more determined to hold back before they both combusted. It crossed his mind to take her right there, up against the wall with the moonlight fluttering over her body making her look like a provocative Greek statue. But there was nothing in the Parthenon that could hope to compete with flesh-and-blood woman.

He wanted her in bed, damn it, and in bed he would have her. Since she was acting half out of her mind with lust, he had to manhandle her a little which she didn't seem to mind at all.

At last they managed to stagger to the bed where, to his eternal delight, she tipped herself backward and fell onto the sheets. She didn't bother to burrow under the covers, as most women who'd shared this bed with him had been wont to do. Instead she lay sprawled and quivering, the scent of her arousal mixing with the fresh-laundry smell of clean linen.

She'd prepared candles and was obviously freshly showered. The thought she'd put into seducing him did the job as much as the preparations she'd intended for that purpose.

"My bed has never looked so good," he murmured, staring down at her.

"It's going to *feel* good if you ever get in it," she panted.

Good. His plan was to get her sounding like a marathon runner sprinting for the finish line. He had a quick image of her usual enthusiastic response to climax and revised his simile. His plan was to get her sounding like a banshee marathoner crossing the finish line, panting and screaming at the same time.

And from the way her hips were twitching restlessly, the panting and screaming weren't all that far off. And he couldn't wait.

Leaning over her, resting his weight on his knees, he pushed her already parted legs farther apart and pressed his lips to the silky smooth length of each inner thigh.

She threw an arm over her mouth and he knew she was

getting ready to bite her own wrist to muffle her cries of release. She reminded him of somebody having an operation with no anesthesia, the way they'd bite on a strip of leather.

He loved her with his mouth, taking her up, so she hovered at the peak, then reaching up to pull her wrist out of her mouth. He loved her lusty cries of release, and he wanted to hear them echoing around his bedroom.

She didn't disappoint him, yelling lustily as he pushed her over the edge with his tongue.

She hadn't even stopped crying out and she was grabbing for him urgently, her whole body pantomiming that she wanted him inside her. He couldn't wait to comply, almost diving on top of her in his haste. He buried himself deep and hard inside her and this time they dove over the edge together.

SHE'D LEFT ELLSWORTH'S files for last.

She felt ridiculous and disloyal to the man even studying his files, but as much as anything, it kept her mind occupied. She didn't want to think about the horrible fact that she'd finally fallen in love, and her lover didn't return the sentiment.

When she and Blake had made love in his bed, when she'd slept beside him all night and when he'd woken her this morning with his tongue, it had felt like he loved her.

Maybe, in time, she could convince him. *If there was time,* clamored a nagging voice inside her head.

Blake wasn't safe.

She had no idea where the feeling was coming from. She'd never been one for visions or hunches. She was a practical woman.

She'd warned Blake. More she couldn't do. Besides, her

feeling wasn't based on fact or information of any kind, but on pure, blind gut intuition.

The worst of it was he wouldn't tell her where the meeting would be held, and when she'd asked to go along he'd outright laughed. Jerk.

She was starting to get a headache from nerves and staring at the computer screen too long. No wonder Ellsworth won awards. Here was a wire from a company in London for five million dollars. Another from a New York firm for two million. Both were numbered companies. Many of his high net worth clients operated numbered companies, but, if she were to be as diligent as Blake, she ought to at least check out a couple.

She put a trace on the company that had wired the five million, hoping she'd never have to explain to Ellsworth that she'd done it. And why.

A couple of hours later, she was feeling a bit unnerved. The London company didn't appear to exist. Hmm. She tried the New York firm this time. Again, nothing.

Ellsworth?

She stared at the evidence in front of her of two companies that didn't seem to exist. It simply didn't make sense. But she couldn't pretend there wasn't something odd about two companies disappearing off the face of the earth after wiring her colleague huge sums of money. She tapped her fingernails on her desktop then jerked to her feet. Blake needed to know what she'd found.

But when she got to his office, there was no one there. She checked her watch. Damn it, almost five. He'd be getting ready for the meeting.

A thought so awful hit her that she slumped into Blake's chair.

What if Ellsworth was the one buying the new identity? As crazy as it sounded, it made a weird kind of sense.

Once Phil had tried to blackmail him, everything had changed. Now, a man had been murdered, Sophie'd almost been killed and he must realize his options were limited. If he was getting large bribes to take drug money, then he could afford a new identity.

And if he got to that meeting and saw Blake there, then all her intuition would be proven correct.

Blake would be in terrible danger.

She picked up his office phone with unsteady hands and punched in his cell phone. Damn it, he'd turned it off. She got voice mail. "Blake. I think I've found something. Please, please call me as soon as you can. It's really important."

With rising panic, she tried to marshall her wits. How else could she get hold of Blake? Of course, John. She'd get out of the bank and call him.

Rising jerkily, she headed out of the cubicle and bumped straight into Ellsworth.

She squeaked with alarm and took a step back.

He smiled at her, his usual friendly smile. "Did I scare you? Just looking for Blake."

"Oh. Blake." She felt herself beginning to tremble, but knew she had to maintain her cool. "I was looking for him, too. I think he must have left."

"It wasn't important. I'll see him in the morning." He looked at her closely. "Are you all right?"

"Yes." Her fingers trembled, knowing she looked anything but fine. She grabbed the first explanation for her odd behavior she could find. "Blake and I had a fight."

Ellsworth patted her shoulder. "Never go to bed angry, that's how Lillian and I have remained happily married. In fact, I'm leaving early to take her for an anniversary dinner. Good night, Sophie."

"Good night." She almost fainted with relief. What an

idiot she'd been to suspect Ellsworth of all people. Love was making her batty. A little more digging into Ellsworth's accounts and there would be some perfectly simple explanation for why those companies were hard to find.

She gathered her things and left for the day.

She said good-night to the security guard and headed down to the garage, wishing Blake's meeting was over. Wishing this whole awful mess was over.

Halfway to her car, she heard a cheery, "Ah, Sophie. I'm glad I caught you."

Ellsworth. Maybe she was foolish and rude, but her instinct was to run. "Can't stop, I'm late," she called back, and broke into a run.

He ran after her.

No. No! Her mind yelled as she raced for her car. She had the keys out, pushed the button to automatically unlock her doors, when she was grabbed by a second man.

She struggled and fought, but he was two hundred pounds of solid muscle in a dark suit. By this time, Ellsworth had arrived, flushed and panting. He opened the door to a dark sedan parked only a few spaces away from her car—that must be where the other man had been hidden.

There was a gun in his hand. And it was pointing at her.

Muscle man shoved her in the back seat then got into the driver's seat while Ellsworth slid in beside her.

A million thoughts jumbled through her brain, most as trite as, you'll never get away with it. But the one that emerged uppermost, that she said aloud, was, "Why?" She gestured helplessly to his expensive suit and briefcase.

He looked genuinely sad. "I'm so sorry, Sophie. I never meant for anything like this to happen." He looked as though he might cry. "I've got a gambling problem. I got in debt to some people." He motioned with his head toward the driver. "They let me pay off my debt by accepting investment money without asking questions."

"But that was drug money, Ellsworth. You must have known that."

"I didn't ask. I didn't want to know. I planned to stop, of course, but once I'd started, they didn't make it easy for me to stop. I not only made my commissions, but I always had money on my tab to gamble with. Always. Then, somehow, Phil found out." He squeezed his eyes shut.

"And you had him killed." Her throat felt like it was full of sawdust.

"I didn't know what to do. I had to tell them he was blackmailing me. I thought they'd simply warn him off. How could I know they'd…"

She refused to let him turn away from the truth. "Kill him? And what do you think they'll do to me?"

His eyes did look misty now. He was sorry she was going to die, she could tell. But behind his sadness, she knew he was a weak man who wouldn't stop her death. She was on her own.

"Why are you doing this, Ellsworth? I thought we were friends."

"You never should have got involved."

"What are you talking about?" It was awfully late, but finally she was getting the answers to the questions that had plagued her.

"Phil told my friends—" once more he gestured to the driver "—that he had an accomplice, that he wasn't working alone. I'm not sure they believed him at the time, but they told me to keep my eyes open. Next morning, you drove to Phil's apartment."

Her jaw dropped. "But, I only went there to see if he

was all right. He was late for work…'' She realized how absurd that sounded and petered off.

Ellsworth said, "How often do you visit employees' homes when they're late?"

She said nothing. Explaining that she'd overheard the blackmail threat would do her no good.

"My friends don't like coincidence. But I told them I trusted you. I thought I could just watch you for a few weeks and see if anything happened. I never thought they'd try and kill you, too. I tried to get you to stay away from work for a few days. Remember?"

She nodded. She also remembered how sick and shaken he'd been after both attempts on her life.

She tried to look more scared than she really was so he'd be lulled into complacency and she could surprise him when it came time to escape. But the truth was she'd never been this scared in her life and doubted she could look more scared if she tried.

"Now, you're…involved with Phil's replacement. I had to assume you were still planning to blackmail me."

"Ellsworth, how could you believe I would blackmail you? I thought we were friends?" She almost giggled at her own inanity. Friends or not, he was willing to let her be murdered. At least it didn't seem to have occurred to Ellsworth or his "friends" that Phil's replacement was an undercover cop.

The world outside seemed strangely detached as the blue car glided through thinning rush hour traffic. Couples strolled along the sidewalks, enjoying a crisp fall evening. Office workers hurried to car parks, bus stops and Skytrain stations.

Her heart beat painfully fast as she tried to marshall her wits and think of a plan of escape.

"Where are we going?"

"I'm buying a new passport and a new identity. This time tomorrow your friend Ellsworth will no longer exist. My friends will decide about you."

It was as she'd feared. Blake would be there, not knowing he'd be recognized immediately by Ellsworth.

And if Blake saw her, he was likely to perform some foolishly heroic act, sacrificing himself to save her.

He wouldn't do it for love, but out of duty.

But for her, it was love. And she wouldn't let him get himself killed. Somehow, she had to get away from Ellsworth and the sinister, silent driver on her own, try to get hold of him somehow and warn him.

Ellsworth had laid the gun on his lap, its muzzle facing her like a staring eye. Every time they hit a bump in the road she braced herself.

"What about all the clients and employees who trusted you?"

"The world is full of victims."

"You think running away to some…some primitive island in the middle of nowhere, some tax haven for criminals is strong? I call it cowardly."

His face twisted, and she saw him glance at the driver, as though to see his reaction to her taunt.

They'd entered Chinatown now. The signs in the windows were bilingual—fish markets, silk shops, Chinese herbalists. And everywhere, the restaurants. Normally she loved this area. Dim sum on a weekend, wandering the markets buying fresh vegetables and spices to try a new recipe.

If she could get that gun away from Ellsworth and make the driver stop the car, there was help out there among the tourists, the businesspeople, the shopkeepers.

Ellsworth knew about her panic attacks, and would have no trouble believing she was having one now—she was close enough to the edge, she'd believe it herself. She started with a theatrical wheeze, then began noisily dragging in air and put a hand to her chest.

"Are you all right?"

She shook her head. "Can't breathe." She dragged in another noisy breath. "Paper bag."

He was still holding the gun, but in a carelessly loose grip. She dropped her head into her hands, groaning, letting him think she was really losing it, while she peered through her fingers at the gun.

She made sobbing noises and let her shoulders shake, though she had to keep it in check, it would be all too easy to give in to real despair.

He had her purse at his feet. She pointed to it. "Paper bag."

"Of course. Hang on." He bent for her bag.

This was her chance.

She lunged at Ellsworth, grabbing for his weapon. Just as she reached it, his fingers tightened and they wrestled frantically. Her head was almost in his lap as they struggled, him tugging and cursing and her panting and holding on for dear life.

She turned her head and bit his thigh, sinking her teeth into him as hard as she could.

He uttered a strangled yelp and with another yank, she was the one holding the gun. Her chest heaving, she jerked back, spitting gabardine fibers from her tongue.

"You bit me!" he shouted at her, his hand clasping his thigh.

Flush with triumph, she turned her attention forward to tell the driver to let her out, only to find herself staring into the dark metal mouth of a gun that made Ellsworth's look like a toddler's plastic water pistol.

"I will take your weapon, please," the driver said with

the British-accented English she'd come to associate with
recent Hong Kong immigrants.

Defeat pricked at her like tears. She handed over Ellsworth's gun to the driver, who didn't give it back to her
former colleague, she noted, and slumped back into her
corner, staring hopelessly out of the tinted window.

Ellsworth muttered and rubbed his thigh, but she ignored him.

Within minutes, they'd pulled into a parking lot with
bumpy pavement, the odd tuft of tired grass struggling
through. They pulled up close to a squat, dingy building's
back entrance and Sophie's nerves tightened another notch.

Was Blake here somewhere? No doubt he was inside,
pretending to be a patron, but waiting for the deal his in-
formant had told him was about to take place so he could
catch the criminals red-handed.

Except he didn't know that Ellsworth was the one out
to purchase a new identity. He'd recognize Blake immediately, putting him in terrible danger.

The driver got out of the car and moved to open her
door. Ellsworth crowded her from the other side, so she'd
have no chance to escape. Even though Ellsworth had lost
his gun, the other guy had two that she'd seen. And he
didn't look as if he'd bother too much about using them.

"Make no noise," he warned her simply.

Her legs weren't entirely steady she found, as she
walked sandwiched between her two escorts, toward the
heavy metal door spray painted with graffiti, some faded
and some fresh. A quick glance round the parking lot
showed there was no point even trying to yell for help. An
assortment of cars, a couple of vans and a motorcycle. Not
a living soul in sight.

The driver opened the door and held it for them to enter.
Ellsworth grabbed her arm and pulled her inside.

The interior was dim and smelled of dust, cigarette smoke and the pungent aroma of frying sesame oil. When her eyes adjusted, she found herself in a back hallway of some kind of club or restaurant. Empty crates and boxes were piled on cracked linoleum.

As Ellsworth yanked her forward, she heard the rattle of dishes from a kitchen out of view, and the staccato chatter of the kitchen staff. She could break away and run into the kitchen, but somehow, she was certain, even if they spoke English, she wouldn't find help from that quarter.

They passed bathrooms and then came to a metal door. She heard voices and laughter and the clatter of dishes from the front of the restaurant, but this was obviously some kind of private room. She tried to brace herself for whatever was behind that door.

Ellsworth's hand tightened uncomfortably on her arm and she smelled fresh sweat coming off him. He was scared, her mind registered—at least as nervous as she.

Their thick-set escort knocked. The door opened a crack and then wider. Ellsworth pulled her into the room and her stomach dropped.

Ellsworth turned her until they were both facing a crowded table in the darkest corner of the room. A partially finished bottle of Johnnie Walker Red Label sat in the middle, and the individuals crowding the table made a cold shiver run over her spine.

She suspected that even without the dragon tattoo on the bare forearms of a couple of the men, she'd have guessed these frightening-looking hoods were part of a gang.

A movement toward the back of the table caught her eye and her eyes widened. A smoothly groomed man in a leather jacket raised his shot glass. An enormous emerald ring glinted. But the sight that had Sophie's heart pounding

in unfeigned panic was the woman sitting next to him—
the woman who'd stolen her car.

The woman Blake had tried to arrest.

The man spoke to Ellsworth. He spoke back. But all she
heard was the roar of her own blood pounding in her ears.

Oh, Lord. Not now. Not when she needed her wits about
her. She needed a point to focus on, a paper bag to breathe
into. Her vision was blurring and she felt light-headed with
dizziness.

She was down to two choices—stick her head between
her legs, or faint.

The woman whispered in her boyfriend's ear and
pointed at Sophie.

19

BLAKE CURSED.

Not for the first time this evening.

He'd radio'd the Emergency Response Team to be on ready alert the minute he'd seen the dark blue sedan cruise into the parking lot. From his vantage point inside the dirt-encrusted econo-van at the edge of the parking lot, he'd waited to see what sleazebag would emerge.

When he saw Sophie he'd damn near stopped breathing. So had she from the wide-eyed stunned expression on her face.

Then Ellsworth emerged behind her and grabbed her arm, and he'd had to quell an urge to march over there and take the slick loser apart.

How had Sophie managed to get herself in the middle of a takedown?

He had to stay calm and push his emotions out of the way if he wanted to keep everything safe and easy. He should have known it would blow up in his face when everything had gone so smoothly. Everything from the snitch's info checking out to the ease with which they'd been able to get into place without raising the alarm.

His radio crackled. "Isn't that the woman who—"

"Yeah." He cut John off before any more details emerged. "Sophie Morton. Possible hostage." He waited a beat, but the cop couldn't compete with the man. "Sophie's my...my..." He didn't know what to say. *Friend* didn't come close, though he realized how much she had become his friend in the time they'd spent together. Girlfriend was way too high school. If there was a word for what Sophie was to him, he didn't know it. So he simply said, "Sophie's mine. I don't care what you have to do or not do, her safety comes first. Everybody read?"

Detectives Chui and Ling were inside the restaurant, posing as customers. But Li and his bunch were in a back room behind two reinforced doors and now Sophie was being led inside. Sixteen ERT guys were standing by for his signal and he knew the time had come. He wasn't a religious man, but he prayed silently for Sophie's safety.

"Go," he said into his headset, and jumped out the back of the van.

Four went, as prearranged, to evacuate the restaurant. The remaining men moved like dark shadows in their black jumpsuits, bulky with bulletproof vests, headed for the back door. They got through that one easily enough, but had to set explosives to blow out the second door.

As soon as it blew, they charged in, MP5 submachine guns at the ready. He heard a woman's scream. "Everybody down on the floor!" somebody yelled.

Blake ran in with them, his own weapon drawn. Sophie, he had to get to Sophie.

At first all he saw was confusion. Gang members forced to the floor and handcuffed, dust and smoke from the explosion. A gun went off.

"Sophie, get down!" he yelled, though he couldn't even see her.

He called her name, and again, trying to be heard above the noise and confusion. To his left a woman was weeping, men were shouting and arguing, the police were yelling.

Someone called his name but he couldn't answer.

Sophie. What if he'd lost her? But he couldn't have. He

hadn't had a chance to tell her he loved her. Hadn't known until tonight.

Fate couldn't be so cruel as to give him love and then take it away in the same evening.

"Sophie," he yelled again as he caught sight at last of her blond curls.

"Blake." She raised her head and his relief that she was alive turned to deadly fear. Her blouse was covered in blood.

He felt the tears and didn't do a damn thing to stop them. Didn't care. If he could show her how much he cared maybe he could keep her with him.

He dropped to his knees, grabbing her to him. "Hang on, baby. We'll get an ambulance. I love you. It's going to be okay. I love you."

"Oh, Blake. I love you, too."

"Shh," he said, when she wiped at a tear on his cheek. "Don't talk. We'll get help."

She smiled through her own tears. "I'm not hurt."

"That's good," he soothed her, recognizing the signs of shock.

He turned and yelled, "Need a paramedic here!"

He turned back to Sophie, still smiling at him mistily. "Where did the knife hit? Do you know?"

"His neck." She gestured behind her and only then did he see Ellsworth lying on the floor, bleeding from his neck. She went back to pressing her hands against Ellsworth's wound to stanch the blood.

A paramedic arrived and Blake and Sophie stood and moved away to make room for him.

While she hovered over the wounded man, Blake took a moment to get back to his responsibilities. A quick scan of the room showed it was all under control. Li stared up at him from the ground, hatred gleaming from his eyes and he swore viciously when he recognized Blake.

"That's Li," Blake said to John, pointing to the gang leader. "Anybody get away?"

"No."

"Anybody hurt?"

"Just Sophie's friend over there."

Blake blew out a breath of relief.

Tomorrow they would need him. Tonight, his partner had stepped seamlessly into command. Already, order was being restored.

Stepping back to Sophie's side, he heard her ask the paramedic who was bandaging Ellsworth neck, "Will he be all right?"

"I think so. You probably saved his life."

A second paramedic handed her a disinfectant cloth and she wiped her hands, looking bemused. This wasn't her scene. She'd been amazing, but he needed to get her out of here.

"Come on," he said softly, putting an arm around her and walking over to John. "I'm taking Sophie home. Can you take it from here?"

A slow smile lit John's face and he stuck out his hand. "Looks like we did it."

Blake shook his partner's hand with feeling. "Damn right, we did it. I'll see you tomorrow."

John let his gaze flick back and forth between them. "Don't be in too early."

"I've got a vehicle a few blocks away," Blake told her as they emerged into the comparatively quiet street. "Can you make it?"

She glanced down at her blood-soaked blouse and shivered. "Yes. I can make it."

"Come on." He led her to the van and knocked on the back door, identifying himself.

"Wow!" she said when he'd helped her inside. She glanced at the telescope and camera equipment and the two guys in there, one watching the parking lot, the other on the radio.

Blake found her a spare VPD sweatshirt, and they turned their backs while she changed. He pushed her stained blouse into an evidence bag and they were on their way, walking hand in hand through the darkening streets.

They didn't speak at first. He didn't know what to say and the moment felt so perfect he didn't want to break it.

"Did you mean it when you said you love me?" she asked softly.

"Yeah."

"You cried." It embarrassed the hell out of him that he'd blubbered like a baby in public, but her sigh was so blissful, he assumed she liked sensitive crying types. Figured.

"I don't make a habit of it," he warned her. "And I'd appreciate it if it didn't get around."

She chuckled and reached up to touch his cheek. Somehow, he couldn't look at her glowing face, read the promises of love and the future there, and not kiss her.

And somehow, it went from a light kiss to a deep, soul-stirring one. He raised his head and panted, "I've got to get you home and in my bed. Come on." He grabbed her hand and they ran the rest of the way to the car.

He pulled away from the curb, suddenly not wanting to waste a minute of their future. "How do you feel about marriage?"

"In general or specific terms?"

He glared. "In you and me terms."

"I think I could be convinced."

"I promise to make you as happy as I know how," he said, using all his willpower not to give in to the urge to floor the gas pedal. The need to make love to Sophie, his wife-to-be, was pounding in his blood.

"I think you took a wrong turn." Her voice broke into his fantasy of exactly what he was going to do to her once he had her naked in his bed.

"Hmm?" He pulled his mind out of his Jockeys and realized she was right.

Then his jaw dropped and he turned to see a mirroring expression of amazement on her face. "I thought you couldn't tell left from right."

She threw back her head and laughed, blond curls bouncing like giggles. "I must have a pretty good sense of direction. It led me straight to you."

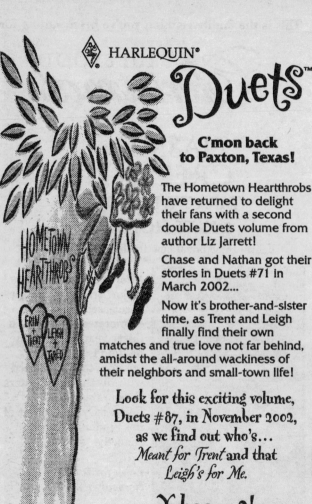

The holidays have descended on

COOPER'S CORNER

providing a touch of seasonal magic!

Coming in November 2002...
MY CHRISTMAS COWBOY
by Kate Hoffmann

Check-in: Bah humbug! That's what single mom
Grace Penrose felt about Christmas this year. All her plans
for the Cooper's Corner Christmas Festival are going wrong—
and now she finds out she has an unexpected houseguest!

Checkout: But sexy cowboy Tucker McCabe is no ordinary
houseguest, and Grace feels her spirits start to lift. Suddenly
she has the craziest urge to stand under the mistletoe...forever!

If you enjoyed what you just read,
then we've got an offer you can't resist!

Take 2 bestselling
love stories FREE!

Plus get a FREE surprise gift!

$\mathscr{F}$ALL IN $\mathscr{L}$OVE
THIS WINTER
WITH
HARLEQUIN BOOKS!

In October 2002 look for these special volumes
led by *USA TODAY* bestselling authors,
and receive MOULIN ROUGE on video*!

*Retail value of $14.98 U.S. Mail-in offer. Two proofs of purchase required.
Limited time offer. Offer expires 3/31/03.

See inside these books for details.

Own MOULIN ROUGE on video!

***This exciting promotion
is available at your
favorite retail outlet.***

Only from

HARLEQUIN®
Makes any time special ®